Praise for *I'm*

"Gurtler's writing unfurls with the exquisite grace ... will cheer Tess' triumphant awakening as she blooms in the shade of insecurity, family tragedy, and sibling rivalry to discover a strength and beauty all her own."

—Sarah Ockler, bestselling author of
Fixing Delilah and *Twenty Boy Summer*

"Powerful...A gripping read, Gurtler allows real life to prevail, avoiding the all-too-easy, 'after-school special' ending many writers might have chosen. Major characters are well-developed, and even adults are portrayed in a realistic, although not always positive, light."

—*VOYA*

"Just right for fans of Sarah Dessen and Jodi Picoult, this is a strong debut that attempts to answer the question, What does it really mean to live?"

—*Booklist*

"Gurtler balances humor and tragedy beautifully and the plot moves along quickly, yet smoothly. Cute and quirky, with sentimentality reminiscent of Judy Blume, this is a book for the keeper shelf—one that readers will devour again and again!"

—*RT Book Reviews*, 4.5 stars

"Subtle, believable, and satisfying."

—*School Library Journal*

"Completely honest and realistic. The writing is crisp and the dialogue is authentic. The relationships are heartbreakingly truthful. This is a must read for teens and those of us who want to understand them."

—*Sacramento Book Review*

Praise for *If I Tell*

"Gurtler handles complex issues of race, identity, friendship and fidelity with laugh-out-loud humor and engaging frankness...once you're in you won't regret it."

—*RT Book Reviews*

"Gurtler unabashedly tackles several sensitive topics without sacrificing the story line and constructs a beautiful paradox."

—*Booklist*

"A touch of conflict stirred into a simmering romance."

—*Kirkus*

"The characters are believable, as is the small town setting. Recommended."
—*Library Media Connection*

"This character driven teen drama is a terrific tale..."
—*Midwest Book Review*

Praise for *Who I Kissed*

"A powerful look at the place where guilt and innocence collide into one confusing, heartbreaking, and life-changing moment that will leave you thinking about intent, assumptions, love, and the importance of hanging on...as well as letting go."

—Jennifer Brown, author of *Hate List* and *Bitter End*

"Without excess heavy-handedness, Gurtler weaves a tale of collective responsibility as several teens reflect on their actions that one fateful night. A well-crafted story about a student's fight to feel normal again when a community of peers turns on her."

—*Booklist*

"Gurtler demonstrates sensitivity toward her characters and insight into their emotional responses...the characters breathe with life."

—*Kirkus*

how i lost you

janet gurtler

sourcebooks
fire

Copyright © 2013 by Janet Gurtler
Cover and internal design © 2013 by Sourcebooks, Inc.
Cover design by J. Marison
Cover image © Laura Doss/Corbis

Sourcebooks and the colophon are registered trademarks of Sourcebooks, Inc.

Published by Sourcebooks Fire, an imprint of Sourcebooks, Inc.
P.O. Box 4410, Naperville, Illinois 60567-4410
(630) 961-3900
Fax: (630) 961-2168
teenfire.sourcebooks.com

Library of Congress Cataloging-in-Publication data is on file with the publisher.

Printed and bound in the United States of America.
VP 10 9 8 7 6 5 4 3 2 1

For Linda Duddridge, who was there from start to finish.
And who also rocks her purple hair hard.

chapter one

The boys were watching us, trying to get us to make mistakes. I knew from the swear words they were flinging around that they'd underestimated us. Inexperienced players shouted a lot. Kya and I didn't.

A surge of excitement blasted though me, and I grinned behind my paintball mask. Playing paintball made me feel alive, like licking a lollipop of adrenaline and wanting to explode with the rush. With my best friend, Kya, at my side, I sensed what it might be like to be invincible. Our goal was simple: shoot them before they shot us. Especially since the game was being streamed on a webcast. The people watching could change our lives.

But we had work to do. They had three players left. So did we.

At first, the other team wanted to kick our butts because of the girl thing, but now they knew we were good. Actually, if I were inclined to brag, I'd have to say the two of us were pretty great. I don't. Brag, that is. But Kya's a different story. And based on the way they were shooting right now, the other team not only wanted to hit us, they wanted to make it hurt.

It's easier to rock at paintball when you know someone has your back. I had Kya's and she had mine. No question asked. It made us somewhat unstoppable. She lifted her hand and pointed. I nodded, understanding.

Kya gave me the thumbs up, so I took a deep breath, stood, and then ran as fast as my legs could move in my gear. She shot crossfire, and a flurry of paintballs popped around me. One ball whizzed past my head, but with her diversion, I managed to dive behind a bunker without getting splattered.

Another flurry of swear words ripped through the air and then Kya yelled to me.

"Grace, you're a PAINTBALL PRINCESS."

"Kya, you da QUEEN!" I yelled back. It was our version of trash talk. We knew to speak naturally and stay calm in the midst of huge adrenaline rushes. We only yelled to rattle. Paintball wasn't really life or death. It only felt like it sometimes.

I couldn't see Kya's grin under her paintball mask, but I imagined it. When she smiled, it lit up her already beautiful face. She didn't smile a lot—she'd seen bad, bad things at a young age. Too young.

"Would you two quit glorifying and tell me what to do," yelled James. He was the only other player left on our team—Kya's best friend since second grade, mine since Dad moved us to Tadita the summer before seventh grade.

"Don't get shot," Kya called to him.

James was crouched behind a bunker. Paintball doesn't flow naturally through James's veins the way it does for Kya and me. He tended to panic a little, even though we look after him. He'd only agreed to join our team because one of our players didn't show up and the Lady Grinders scout had requested footage from the game. The Lady Grinders was a National College Paintball Association team out of Seattle University, the college team Kya and I would give up unborn children to play on. A college with an all-female paintball team. It couldn't get much better. But first we had to prove ourselves.

I glanced around, checking out the other players' positions, strategizing how we could lure them into the open.

Kya looked at me and tapped the side of her mask. My heart thumped in my chest as I nodded back. I was in a bad position. There was another set of loud pops, and James raised his hand in the air, then walked out from behind his bunker.

"I'm hit!" he yelled. "Sorry, Grace," he added before he started toward the deadbox. He'd given himself away when he'd shouted to us. I didn't blame him for it. He tolerated the game; he didn't live and breathe it.

I waved to him, but a paintball whizzed by my arm, missing me by inches. A tall boy had stepped too far from his bunker and shot too fast. Kya took advantage and popped him, and then I caught his teammate running toward another bunker.

Two down. One to go.

Kya and I locked eyes and she tilted her head to the right. I blinked quickly and frowned, understanding her meaning but not wanting her to make the sacrifice for me. She ignored my signal. She flew out like Superman and ran hard to give me a chance to move to a better position.

Whack!

She took a hit in the shoulder, but as intended, she'd drawn out the last guy. I lifted my gun, aimed, and pulled the trigger.

Thwap!

I hit him right in the back of the head and the webcam caught it all. The Lady Grinders would be impressed. Kya had set me up to look like the hero.

Kya whooped and ran toward me. When she got close, she jumped at me for a midair bump. I jumped to meet her and we smashed bellies. Then she grabbed my hand and held it in the air as if I were a boxer declared winner of the round.

"And that, my friends, is how it is done," she yelled at the top of her lungs.

We put a hand around each other's hips and kicked our legs up like Vegas showgirls. Our version of the victory dance. My heart burst with love for my BFF. We ignored the angry callouts from the guys we'd beaten and let the game outcome speak for itself.

"I could not have made that shot without you," I said for the benefit of the webcam as well as my best friend. Plus, it was true. I would not be the player I was without her.

She pulled off the headband outside her mask, and shut off the webcam attached to it.

"That was freaking awesome!" I yelled, still pumped up by the high of the win. I pulled off my mask and scrunched up my face in a faux dirty look. "But you totally sacrificed yourself to make me look good."

She flipped her mask up and shrugged. "You're worth it. I know how much you want to make the Grinders."

"Yeah. And you do too." I punched her lightly on the shoulder and put my gun up on my shoulder as we walked toward the exit of the speedball arena.

"Consider it an early birthday gift," she said.

"My birthday isn't for a month," I reminded her.

"That's why I said early." She rolled her eyes at me.

"We have to make that team," I said for the millionth time that week. "I wish we could have gotten tickets for the Paintball Manifesto," I whined, also for the millionth time. "That party would have secured our spots for next year." VIP tickets for the first giant Paintball Tradeshow in Seattle sold out, and without them we had no way to get into the VIP Players Party. The Lady Grinders would be there. A perfect chance to get on their good side.

"I know, Skanklet," she said.

"Good game, girls," Dad called. He stood on the top bench of the bleachers, outside the ropes, waving down at us. I hadn't known he'd been watching the game, but it didn't surprise me.

Years back when he found out what happened to Kya, Dad drove both of us to Splatterfest, the paintball place he'd bought after retiring from the police force, and made us suit up. He didn't tell anyone to go easy on us. He said he wanted to toughen us up and build our confidence. He said we needed to learn to excel in a male-dominated world like paintball. That it would help us in "real life."

I think how much we both loved paintball surprised him. We were both playing in tournaments by our second season. He said he'd thought it would be a good place for Kya to feel like she was taking back control. It made me sad that she needed to. But she did. There was nothing we could do to change what happened. Except be her friend.

I loved her before I found out what happened. I loved her more fiercely after. I would do anything to protect her.

"Solid footage. They won't be able to turn either of you down, even without going to the VIP party." He took a lot of pride in our paintball skills. He'd obviously heard about the webcast we were making for the Grinders, even though I hadn't told him.

I waved at him, and Kya raised her hand and then turned back to me.

"Don't worry, my Skanklet. I have ways of making things happen."

"But—" I started to say.

"Butt," she interrupted, turned, and shook her butt at me as we headed out of the playing area.

I laughed. Kya grinned back and then placed her free hand on her belly. "God. I'm so bloated. I have a monster case of PMS." She shook her butt some more and someone wolf whistled. We both automatically lifted our middle fingers without even looking over. Dad yelled something at the boys as he clomped noisily to his office in the back.

"You too, right?" Kya said with a grin. "PMS?"

Yes. We were so close, even our cycles were in harmony.

"You mean, Pass My Shotgun?" I asked, unable to resist, and lifted my paintball gun in the air.

She giggled. "No. Pass Me Sugar. Or Psychotic Mood Shifts." She scrunched up her mouth and made a face. Then she giggle-snorted again. Kya had a ridiculous and contagious laugh that always made me lose it.

Another laugh spurted out of me and I covered my mouth. "Oh no." A giggle fest started building, the contagious laughter tickling and threatening to erupt. We'd played this round of acronyms before with scream-laughter developing.

"Perpetual Munching Spree." Kya blew up her cheeks again so they were puffy and round.

"Provide Me with Snacks," I answered with a snort.

"Pimples May Surface," she said, grinning and pointing at my forehead.

My amusement died. Panicking, I reached up to feel my skin. Kya broke out into another peal of wacky laughter.

"What?" I demanded, suddenly immune to her laugh.

She pointed at me. "You searching for zits. You're such a worrier, Grace. You're fine." She laughed aloud. "Look at your face... Priceless Mood Shift."

"Please Shut Mouth," I said, and stuck my tongue out at her.

"Seriously?" James said when we stepped out of the roped-off area. He was already at the back counter cleaning out the rental gun he'd borrowed from my dad's supply. Dad ran the most organized indoor paintball place in the world and the neatest one too. Since James, Kya, and I were all his employees as well as players, we took good care of his equipment.

There was a blast of sound from Dad's office. Deaf in one ear from an on-the-job accident years before, he did everything a little too loudly. It sounded like he was testing the new speakers Mom bought him for his birthday last week.

"You really have to talk about female reproductive issues here?" James gestured around him to the boys in paintball gear and the counter filled with ammo and guns. "Voices carry, you know."

"Like we care," Kya said. "And trust me. Periods have nothing to do with reproduction at this point in our lives."

"You better hope so," he mumbled.

"You guys." I glared at both of them.

Usually they didn't take their bad moods out on each other. I wanted them to quit fighting and make up already. James turned his back to put away the paintball gun he'd borrowed.

Kya's secret was lodged right in the middle of our three-way friendship. I wished she'd let me tell him. But she wouldn't. And because he didn't know, he was harder on her. He saw me taking her side. Sometimes he didn't understand my need to protect her from the world.

Dad says I'm a human sponge for anyone with a sad story. Me? I think everyone has a sad story if you look hard enough. Dad agrees, I know he does, but his years as a police officer hard-boiled him a little. Not all the way; he's still a tiny bit soft on the inside.

But he looks out for Kya. My mom too. They're the only other people who know what happened to her.

We guard her secret feverishly. And we guard Kya too.

chapter two

The next night, Kya was late for work. I should probably have been mad at her, but instead, worst-case scenarios ran through my mind. My dad tells me she needs the same standards as everyone else, but I worry about her.

Pop!

There was a burst from the back office as Dad cleaned guns blocked by chopped paintballs. That loud noise didn't bother me, but when something soft brushed against my shoulder, I jumped and whirled around with a scream.

Kya stood behind me, her finger poised in the air from tapping my shoulder.

"You scared the crap out of me," I said with my hands covering my heart.

"I see that. Need to change your pants?"

Before I could say anything, she held up her other hand. A gift bag dangled on her finger.

"For you." She thrust it at me. "Early birthday present."

I hesitated, then reached for it. The pink bag sprouted yellow tissue, blooming out like spring flowers. Not something I'd normally associate with Kya and kind of out of place at Splatterfest. But call me a gift slut, because it improved my mood.

"I texted you." She perched her butt on a stool behind the counter. "You didn't answer."

"Dad confiscated my phone."

"Again?" She nodded toward the bag. "Open it."

I glanced at the computer screen but pulled the paper from the bag and peeked inside. My heart thudded.

Tickets lay on the bottom.

I held my breath. Stuck my hand inside. Pulled them out and read.

"How? How? How?" I squealed.

She grinned the smile that made boys stumble over their feet or offer pretty much whatever she asked. "You don't want to know."

No. For once, I didn't. "My parents will never let us go," I moaned, kissing the tickets.

"Don't worry. I already cleared it with your mom," she said. "She's coming to Seattle with us. She's going to come to the tradeshow, but you and I are solo for the party!"

"No way!" I squealed and hugged the tickets to my chest, then tucked them back in the bag and busted into a dance step.

"In like skin," she said. The shine in her eyes gave away how pleased she was.

I stopped dancing midstep. "But wait. Aren't you supposed to go camping that weekend?"

Kya lifted her hand and made a symbol. Two fingers entwined. Me and her. Best friends. Sisters before misters. Buds before studs.

"I canceled. You're more important than a boy."

I jumped up and down again and then grabbed her by the shoulders and pulled her in close for a giant hug. She allowed a longer squeeze than usual before wiggling out of my grasp.

"James will be pissed." She flipped her long dark hair over her shoulder. "He's on a mission to find you the best gift ever so you'll fall madly in love with him. But I win!" She raised her hands in the air and jogged in place to break an invisible victory ribbon.

Now wasn't the time for another lecture about being nicer to James. "James is not in love with me," I told her.

She scowled toward the back of the warehouse where James was working.

"And birthday presents aren't a competition," I added gently.

"I'll tell James to get you a gift card for clothes," she said. "Then we can go shopping and get new outfits for the party."

"Fat chance of that." For a boy, James oddly prided himself on his gift-giving skills. "And the show is before my birthday."

"Well. We have to go shopping. We need killer outfits for the party."

That would be painful. Her idea of an appropriate outfit and my idea of an outfit were two entirely different things. We had to deal with crap from boys in paintball already. We didn't need to dress like girls from beer commercials.

She gestured her head toward the bag. "I did good, right?"

I clapped my hands. "Best. Present. Ever. We are going to rock that party." I reached for Kya again, wrapping my arms around her, not caring about overdoing her hug quotient for the day.

"Seriously? Hot lesbians?" said a deep voice from the other side of the counter. "This place is better than I thought."

We'd been so absorbed in our conversation, we hadn't noticed a couple of boys approach the other side of the counter.

I glared at them over Kya's shoulder and let her go. The one who spoke was big. As in linebacker-sized, kind of built like my brother, Indie, with the same man-swagger. I imagined it must cost his parents a lot to feed him. Mom complained about feeding Indie all the time.

I had an urge to give the boy the finger but decided against it. I could almost hear Dad's lecture about the proper way to conduct myself with difficult customers. Secretly he might be pleased if I stood up to the Neanderthals, but I took my job responsibilities seriously. I didn't flip off customers, even if they asked for it with a cherry on top.

"Can I help you?" I coated my voice with ice, picked up the gift bag, and slid it on a shelf under the counter.

The boy leered as if we were wrapped around a stripper pole and not wearing oversized Splatterfest T-shirts. His eyes fixed on Kya, but that was to be expected. Her weird combination of sharp features somehow worked together to make most guys her personal slaves. Long, thin nose. Pointy chin. Big eyes that seemed to look right inside people's souls. She even had vampish incisors that were wicked when she smiled. She could have been one of those high-fashion models who wore alien-like clothes and still made people want them.

"We're here for the two o'clock league. Glad we're early. That was smokin' hot."

"For real? How hot can a hug be?" Kya placed both hands on

the counter and leaned forward. "And, FYI, her dad owns this place." Kya looked him slowly up and down. "He's also an ex-cop who doesn't like it when customers say inappropriate things to his daughter. He's been known to aim paintballs at private parts."

He didn't look away. I saw her notice that too.

"Have you filled out your liability form?" I asked sweetly.

"Grace could totally kick your butt out there." Kya nodded toward the arena.

"But she's so little. And cute," said the boy behind him. I'd almost forgotten he was there, the way he quietly took up space.

I glared at him. "Seriously?" I hated the cute label. Like a bunny rabbit. Or a baby chick. Especially in comparison to Kya's exotic looks. Everyone said we made odd BFFs.

"So is a honey badger, but don't let it fool you," Kya said. But she didn't take her eyes off the linebacker. He kept his eyes on her, not the least apologetic or intimidated. He had cojones, I'd give him that.

I straightened my back and stood taller. "I'm not that little," I told the taller boy. "And definitely not cute."

He grinned. "Sorry. I didn't mean it as an insult." His looks improved when he smiled.

"Hmmph." I handed him a waiver form to sign and pretended to see something urgent appear on the computer screen.

"Some paintballs hurt more than others," Kya was saying to the linebacker. "Especially if you know where to aim. I don't suppose you thought to wear a cup?"

She was testing him. She never worried about saying proper

things to customers or the wrath of my dad. I glanced at the guy, and the look on his face was perfect. His hands moved down.

"Her dad has nothing to worry about." He winked at Kya. "I'm harmless. I've never played paintball before. I'll probably suck. Levi's the one who plays." He gestured at the taller boy.

"Only outdoor. Woodsball," he said to me and slid his waiver across the counter. I glanced at the signature. Levi Lewis.

"I've never run into female ballers. Especially cute ones."

I narrowed my eyes again, but he smiled and winked.

"Good luck, Romeo," Kya interrupted. "Gracie doesn't let guys get close on or off the field."

My face warmed. He'd been talking about paintball, not dating me.

He tilted his head. "You're a force to be reckoned with?" he asked and crawled under my skin a little more.

"Careful of our Levi," his friend said. "You don't want to piss him off."

Levi lifted his middle finger. My heart skipped a beat. I wasn't sure if it was fear or intrigue.

I made a mental note to shoot him first if I played against him.

James walked out from the back room holding the cordless mike he used to talk to players in the arena. He almost tripped over something on the floor and made an oomph sound as he righted himself. He tended to move like a puppy with oversized paws and was the polar opposite of agile. His forte was brains, not brawn. I lifted my hand, and he grinned and pushed his glasses up his freckled nose.

James trotted closer. "Hey, Grace." He put the mike down on the counter.

"What's the matter, James, I don't get a hello?" Kya said without taking her eyes off the linebacker. James glanced at him and then Kya.

"She writing a book on how to flirt using only her eyeballs?" he asked me.

Kya lifted her middle finger but didn't look at him. The linebacker seemed confused but the word flirt noticeably lit up his eyes.

I clicked Levi's name into the computer. "You can go get your coveralls over there." I pointed to the locker room and glanced up as he walked off, pretending not to notice the perfection of his butt.

James pulled something out of his pocket and threw it at me, distracting me from perverted thoughts. I caught the box out of reflex. "Nerds!" I cried a little more enthusiastically than necessary.

"That's not a nice thing to call James," Kya said without looking.

James snarled his upper lip. I wished they would make up already. I shook the box to hear the magical clacking Nerds before shaking a pile of colorful candies into my mouth, crunching into an explosion of tangy flavors, and smooching my nose up at the sensation.

"My name is Lucas Lewis," the linebacker said to Kya, turning his back on James and me.

"His parents have awesome alliteration skills," James said under his breath. "Loathsome Loser. Hey, look! I can do it too."

Luckily, Lucas wasn't paying attention to us. His eyes were on Kya and I think, even through her oversized T-shirt, he sensed the new push-up bra she'd invested in. It made me uncomfortable the way he practically devoured her with his eyes, but she didn't seem to mind.

James held his palm out and I filled it with Nerds. He threw a handful in his mouth as we watched Lucas and Kya flirt.

"You're on the Lasers," Kya told him. She slid a waiver form his way.

"Hallelujah. Another L word. His parents will be loopy. Lucas Lewis on the Lasers," James mumbled.

I bit into my Nerds and threw James a warning look. His mouth sometimes burbled out thoughts he should keep inside his brain.

"You two brothers?" Kya nodded at where Levi had been standing.

"Cousins. He got sent to live with us because his parents think he's a badass."

"Badass?" I asked, but the two of them didn't even look at me. They exchanged low words I couldn't hear.

"There're coveralls in the room over there," I called to Lucas. He glanced at me and I pointed to the room Levi disappeared in. "You'll need a mask too," I said, raising my voice. "Put the coveralls over your clothes and then go to the training room and wait for the rest of the players." I poured more Nerds directly into my mouth. "Go get suited up." I nodded my head at James. "He'll take you."

James gave me a dirty look but walked away and Lucas followed. When they were out of hearing range, I turned to Kya. "What the hell?"

"I want to play that guy," Kya said.

"You might get the chance. Dad said he might need us. Some of the guys can't make it tonight." I pretended to shoot an imaginary paintball at her. "He's hardly a match for you." I glanced over to where he'd disappeared. "Newb."

"I didn't mean in paintball."

"Gross," I said. even though I'd known what she meant.

"He was hot." She nibbled at her thumbnail.

"Hot? What about Brady? Your adoring boyfriend? Remember him?" Kya's boyfriends had short shelf lives but still…

"Brady is a boy," Kya said.

"I think that's kind of the point," I said.

"Well, unlike best friends, boys are replaceable." She waggled her eyebrows. "Lucas is hotter than Brady, don't you think?"

Her current boyfriend was on the chopping block. My turn to raise my eyebrows and make a face. We could totally communicate through facial expressions, but she ended our discussion by turning away. Then she bumped my hip with hers. "So how about those tickets?"

My exasperation with her dwindled. "You're the best."

We were already on the Lady Grinders' radar. Going to the VIP party in Seattle would give us a chance to firm up a spot on the team by impressing them in person. We could show them how much we wanted it and how dedicated we were to the sport. The party could literally change our lives.

I couldn't wait for the chance for the two of us to shine. I wanted it so badly my hands shook with excitement.

chapter three

The front bell on the door of the Splatterfest entrance rang, and a group of boys strutted inside. A gaggle of girls followed behind them, chattering loudly.

"You grab waiver forms and I'll sign these guys in," Kya called as the boys walked toward the counter.

I opened the drawer Dad had neatly labeled in his perfect printing. Nothing was misfiled or lost at Splatterfest. The boys lined up to sign in and I handed out forms. Their groupie girls huddled behind them. I recognized a couple girls from school, but they were younger and I didn't know their names. After a circle whisper-fest, one of the girls stepped forward. "Aren't you Kya Kessler?" she asked.

Kya glanced up and smiled. "That's what they tell me."

The girl beamed with reverence. "I thought so! You're a senior next year, right?"

"Mmm-hmm." Kya went back to writing but nodded.

"Cool." The girl beamed happily. "I mean. I've seen you around. We're going to be sophomores."

Kya smiled. She was used to girl crushes from younger girls. I loved that she treated them nicely.

"We were hoping you'd be here. I mean. Playing. We heard you worked at Splatterfest. It's so cool that you play paintball, but you're still so pretty and stuff."

"Thanks," Kya said. "You're pretty too."

I thought the girl was going to pass out from happiness.

"You should try playing instead of spectating. You might love it, you know. " She gestured at me. "Grace plays too. And we rock."

The girl aimed some of her Kya worship at me. "I know. You're Grace Black. It's so cool."

Famous by association. Story of my life. "Sign up," Kya told her. I nodded agreement.

One of the guys put an arm around her shoulder. I recognized him. Steve Blender. Tourney player. Jerk.

"Nah. Stay in the bleachers, babe," he said. "You look sexier in that outfit than you will in that one." He pointed to a couple of guys going to the training room in their rental gear. He winked at her and then went off in the same direction.

I pretended to gag. "Cool story, bro," I called.

"That guy is a perfect example of why you should learn to play paintball," Kya said. "You can shoot him."

"Grace, Kya!" James peeked his head out from the training room. "Your dad said you'll need to gear up."

Grace and I high-fived each other. The girls clapped and I heard squeals of "Awesome. They're going to play."

"He said not to mow down any newbs," James called.

"A couple girls?" Kya said with a laugh. Kya's fans giggled happily and set off for the viewing bleachers outside the roped arena.

"Use rental gear, not your own. Rental markers too." Markers was the term for guns. James gave the giggly girls a pained look and disappeared.

Kya and I changed and then went to the back counter and got out rental markers, pods, and paint for the players and spent a few minutes matching boys with guns and paint and answering questions.

James's voice boomed out over the speaker system in the arena, explaining the rules for the first teams, while he roamed outside the netted playing area. I smiled at the Darth-Vaderish imitation. A while later, Dad called for Kya and me. When James started the countdown in his Darth Vader voice, I tucked my head down.

Dad grabbed me by the arm. "Take it easy on the new guys," he said.

On "one," I wiggled away from him and ran. The popping of guns from eager amateurs had already started. Dad roamed into the middle of the arena with a bright orange vest on, acting as referee. He yelled at a player who accidentally shot him, and I laughed even as I ducked behind a bunker. The cheap rental masks were stale and my breath vibrated against the plastic. The visor was beat-up and scratched, and it was hard to see where Kya had gone.

I spotted her heading into a sniper position to back me. For her, sniper was painful because of the waiting and calculating. She preferred to move. I knew she'd signal me for a run-through when she was in position. My heartbeat sped up. A run-through was basically a suicide mission to take out other players and meant almost certain elimination.

She nodded and I darted out into the open.

Shots pelted out. Kya shot suppressive fire and I made it behind the bunker. I peeked around the corner and Kya gave me thumbs-up from her position.

Barely a second later, a guy on our team shouted, "I'm hit," and stood, his hands in the air to show the other players he was out. First out on our side; both teams had four players left.

As he started walking toward the deadbox, Kya called, "Grace. Run-through. Go. Go. Go!"

I hesitated but went out, firing shots. I recognized Levi behind his mask and grinned because he was my first hit. I hit another player as I tore down the field line. Then a sting blasted me on the shoulder.

"I'm hit!" I yelled, ignoring the pain and lifting my hand in the air, shaking off the taste of defeat. I didn't like getting hit early in the game, but at least I'd taken out a couple of guys, including Levi. I started moving toward the deadbox when another sharp pang hit my leg.

I gritted my teeth and forced myself not to respond. There was a shout of laughter.

"Bonus ball lovin'," called out a male voice over pops of fire. It was impossible not to recognize the pompous, grating voice. Dirty to hit a dead player, but typical of Steve Blender.

I held in a yelp as another ball stung me in the fleshy part of my thigh and the pain was harsh. Then there was a snap of gunfire.

"Eat that!" From her sniper position, Kya jumped out and snapped Steve again with a decent hit to the head.

I couldn't help grinning under my mask. How could I not? But I knew she'd be getting an earful from my dad.

"Don't mess with my bestie," Kya yelled.

There was another flurry of pops from the other team and then a splat hit her. "Can't handle some bonus balls then get out of the game," Steve shouted at her. Or me. Not sure.

"I heard the girls called you trigger-happy, Steve, but I thought they were talking about the trigger in your pants," Kya called.

The girls in the bleachers laughed.

"Okay. That's enough. You're going to seriously piss him off," I told her.

Steve lifted his middle finger at her and headed to the deadbox.

The other team quickly took down our other new guy and then our last player was pinched and hit and we were done. Game over.

Dad stomped over. "You threw the game," he yelled at Kya.

"Steve Blender hit Grace with bonus balls," she said.

"Grace can handle it." He waved his hand in the air toward the guys moving off the field. "We're not teaching them the game properly if you're acting like a hothead."

"Steve does stuff like that to us all the time. He asked for it." Kya flipped up her mask, jutted out her bottom lip. She shook her temper off and changed her expression, opening her eyes wide, sticking out her bottom lip, and flopping down on one knee. "Can you forgive me, Mr. B?"

Dad spun around and stormed off to give Steve a blast too.

I put out my hand to help her up, but Kya ignored it and stood on her own. I swatted her lightly on the back of her head. "You gotta admit that wasn't the smartest move."

"Well, I did it for you. It pissed me off the way Steve disrespected you." She threw her gun over her shoulder and started walking.

"Male pride," I said as I fell in step beside her.

"Male asshole."

"Not all guys are like that," I reminded her gently, understanding her sentiments.

"That's true," said a deep voice behind us.

We both turned. Levi. He'd lifted his mask and trained his dark eyes on me.

"He pulls crap like that and we're supposed to put up with it?" Kya asked.

He glanced at Kya. "Hey. Give him some credit. The way I see it, he'd do the same thing to most of the guys too," he said.

I silently agreed.

"It pisses us off, guys who play dirtier because we're girls," Kya said.

"Try doing what Grace does," a voice called from outside the netting. We all stopped walking and turned. Lola Deane sat on the bleachers, watching us. Lola managed the outdoor paintball place. Dad and the owner were friends and helped each other out with leagues and sponsors. More importantly, Lola was also good friends with Betty Baller, the captain of the Grinders. I hadn't even known she was there, hidden behind the groupie girls who watched the exchange with interest.

"Grace keeps her head down and stays professional. Even when someone ball-bounces her," she said. "You get respect by earning it. Not by reacting to jerks."

"Excuse me for sticking up for my friend," Kya called, and then stomped off the field.

Shoot. Not smart. I watched her go, knowing it was best to let her cool off before I said anything.

"How's it going, Lola?" I turned my attention back to the bleachers and pulled off my belt, checking my pods and seeing I still had paintballs left, thank goodness. They were too expensive to waste. Dad gave me a discount, but I had to pay for my own stuff. It would be awesome to reach the point where sponsorship would help pay for equipment. Making the Grinders would do that.

Lola got up and stretched long arms in the air. "Good. I stopped by on my way to work to check out your dad's new league. Nice run-through, Grace. Glad to see you're working on it."

Lola glanced to where Kya had disappeared. "You two still a package deal?" she asked.

"Of course," I said, tweaked by a tiny worry that Kya's behavior might reflect badly on me. "Kya's having a bad day."

Lola nodded but didn't look convinced. "You want to come to our place Sunday?" she asked. "Practice with Thrasher?"

My heart pumped. Her semi-pro team.

"Both of us?" I asked.

"If both of you are looking to improve," she called, and trotted down the bleacher steps and jumped onto the ground. "I have to get to work. See ya later! BYOP."

Bring your own paintballs. She walked past the viewing area, and when she was out of sight, I pumped my fist in the air.

"Who was that?" Levi asked. I'd forgotten he was behind me.

I turned, beaming. "Lola. She knows everyone in paintball."

"Awesome." Levi walked with me to the back counter. "That

was nice you made sure your friend was invited too." He stepped aside to let me move ahead of him to put my gear down on the back counter.

"We're a team," I told him.

"Yeah?" He put down his marker. "She lose her temper a lot?"

"No. She had my back. You know?" Part of me wished she hadn't, but I wouldn't admit that. I glared at him, remembering what his cousin said. That he was a badass with a temper of his own. "Steve thinks girls should be on the sidelines strutting in bikinis instead of playing on the field. He's a jerk."

"I've had the dubious pleasure of meeting him. I concur."

He sounded like James. My anger evaporated and I smiled. Maybe not so badass.

Dad walked over, reached for my rental marker, and nodded at Levi. "Kya has steam coming out of her ears," he said. "Can you make sure she's okay and then change and cover the front counter for a few minutes until James gets back? He had to get some medicine to his mom."

I nodded. Dad took the guns and hung them up. "I hear you're going to the tradeshow after all? Kya got tickets to the VIP party?"

I grinned and he smiled back.

"You better behave."

I laughed and waved at Levi and then hurried to the change room. The girls' room was buried in the back by Dad's office. It had a couple of lockers and benches, a bathroom, and a shower. The boys' locker room was bigger and closer to the entrance but didn't have a shower.

I pushed through the door. Kya was already changed and sitting on a bench. She pulled out her earbuds as soon as she spotted me. "Can you hurry? I want to get out of here."

"Chill out, cranky pants." I smiled though, and she stuck her tongue out. "I have to stick around for a few minutes. Until James gets back. He's working late but had to leave to get something for his mom."

I pulled my gym bag from a locker while she groaned. Then she lay flat on the bench, chewing her thumbnail, holding her phone, and staring up at the ceiling.

"Where do you have to go in such a hurry?" I asked her.

"Nowhere." She fiddled with her phone.

"Kya? You okay?" I wondered if she was upset that Lola had seen her blow the game.

"Fine. Stupid Steve Blender." She closed her eyes. "Whatever. I'm over it. Those guys sucked anyhow."

I yanked off my Splatterfest coverall and tossed it into the laundry basket near the lockers.

"What about you. Did you see something you liked earlier?" she asked. "Rhymes with Devi."

"Devi is not even a word," I told her.

"It is now."

I kind of wanted to talk about Levi, ask her opinion of him, but she wasn't into dissecting boys, wondering why they looked at her a certain way or what something might mean. If she liked a boy, she went for it. I suppose her blindness to the possibility of rejection made her immune to it.

"You grounded tonight?" she asked.

I nodded.

"As usual. What degree?"

"Minor. Phone privileges for the day and I have to stay in for the night."

She never said so aloud, but I think in many ways Kya was almost jealous when I was grounded for my frequent infractions. She rarely got in trouble for anything. It was like her parents still felt too guilty over what had happened to ever punish her.

"Your parents going out tonight?" she asked.

"Dancing."

"Your parents are so weird." She said it with a smile though. "I'll come over later and bring a movie," she told me. "Your mom and dad won't mind."

Even when I was grounded, she could charm her way past the door. Unless it was a serious offense, but those were few and far between. Dad expected us to obey his rules. But funny enough, so did I.

Kya stood and picked up her gear bag, tossing it over her shoulder. "If you have to stick around, I'm going to see if I can catch a ride with those girls," she said. "I want to get home."

I hid my annoyance that she was ditching me and waved as she pranced out the door, her bad mood apparently dissipating. When I finished changing, I headed back to the front counter and picked up a magazine, hoping James wouldn't take too long.

A few minutes later, the door dinged and James walked back inside.

"Graceling," he said. He walked behind the counter. "You grounded tonight?"

Was I really that predictable? I nodded, jumping off the stool and picking up my bag. "Kya's coming over with a movie. You should stop by."

"I'll probably be too late." He rolled his eyes. "And not so much into breathing the same air as Kya these days." He took over my spot on the stool.

"What'd you do to piss her off?" I asked.

He glared at me. "Why do you always take her side?"

I glared back. "Because you can never seem to resist teasing her."

He picked up the magazine I'd been looking at and flipped it open. "Maybe we've merely outgrown each other."

"Oh please, James. Get over it," I said. "You love us, you know you do."

"She's turned into someone I don't know," he said, softly flipping to a new page and not looking up. "Maybe I never really did."

I stared at him, but he put down the magazine and then searched through a drawer, pretending to look for something.

"It'll be quiet in here tonight. No games scheduled. Guess I'll be stuck cleaning."

I ignored his attempts to change the topic. "Kya needs people to look out for her."

"She's doesn't need me," James said and jumped off the stool.

"She does. She needs your help believing in herself. What she can be. Not what other people expect her to be."

"What makes her so special?" he asked softly, almost sadly, as he knelt down and opened the cupboard where Dad kept cleaning supplies.

"James," I replied equally softly. "She's our friend. We're the Three Musketeers."

I wished we could talk about the real reasons she struggled.

"I love both of you," I said.

"Whatever you say." He pulled out a bottle of toilet cleaner and made a face.

I sighed. "What'd she say to piss you off this time?"

"Nothing." He glanced up and smiled but it looked kind of sad. "And now I literally have to go and clean shit up."

Neither of them would tell me what they'd argued about. I knew James had a strong sense of right and wrong. He didn't understand that sometimes circumstances could sprout up a lot of gray. Bad things sometimes tarnished people's souls. Kya had stains. There were some things she couldn't get over. It wasn't always black and white.

chapter four

Kya pointed at Brady. She'd brought him over along with her DVD of *The Virgin Suicides*. We were at her favorite scene in the movie, where the boys take the Lisbon sisters to a school dance. Brady was almost fast asleep on the sofa beside her. She wrinkled up her nose, lifted her hand to her forehead, and made a capital L sign with her fingers.

"Loser," she mouthed to me and glared at Brady.

Apparently, his number was up. I faked a smile, kind of sorry for Brady. He certainly didn't know he'd failed a major test. One should never show boredom during a viewing of *The Virgin Suicides*.

Boyfriends were disposable to Kya. She'd treat boys like crap and they'd fall at her feet, trying to win her over. Usually they'd turn to me for help. I got to play the friend role. Over and over again.

Brady reached up to grab her hand and mumbled something I couldn't hear, but she pushed him away and jumped up from the couch. Distracted from the movie, which was much more her favorite than mine, my insides squished with unease for Brady who didn't even know he was past his expiration date.

"You want a soda, Grace?" she said, walking toward the stairs.

"Hey, what about me?" Brady called.

She ignored him and his face drooped, betraying his disappointment. Once she made up her mind, there was really nothing to stop it.

"Sure. I'd love a soda. Oh, and make yourself at home," I called, well versed in the art of sarcasm, thanks to my mom.

Kya turned back to stick her tongue out and then smiled, disappearing down the stairs toward the kitchen. I heard the fridge door open and her voice and my brother's. Indie treated her better than he did me most of the time.

"Kya says you're into paintball and stuff," Brady said to me.

I looked at him. Eloquent, Brady. Especially since we've been in the same school for three years and you're only now bringing this up.

"Yup," I turned my attention back to the screen. No use trying to bond with him at this point. Ex-boyfriend-to-be. Soon it would be my job to ignore his existence; he just didn't know it yet.

Kya returned up the stairs, holding three cans of soda. She tossed one to Brady. At him really. It almost smacked him in the head. Then she walked over to the couch where I sat and scootched in, snuggling up beside me, handing me a can, and then resting her head on my shoulder. She plopped up her feet up on the coffee table in front of us.

"Oh, I almost forgot," she said, and reached into her hoodie pocket and pulled out a box. She tossed it in the air. "Nerds for my nerd."

I grabbed it. "Yay!" I ripped open the box with my teeth, poured some in my hand, and held out the box but she shook her head.

"So. There a party tonight?" she called to Brady.

"I thought you wanted to stay in? Watch a movie. At your bestie's." He imitated her voice on the last sentence and frowned at me as if it was my fault Kya could make him do whatever she wanted. Including hanging out at my place on a Friday night. It really was something, how much boys liked her despite the way she treated them.

I ignored him, less and less sorry for his impending heartbreak. I poured Nerds into my mouth and swirled them around my cheeks with my tongue.

"I told you, Grace is grounded," she said to him. "Again," she growled at me and shoved her elbow in my side. "On Friday night."

Brady spoke slowly, as if thinking carefully about his next words. "Danny is having some people stop by. His parents are home. But we could go there if you want."

"Nah. I don't want to leave Gracie alone." Kya sipped her soda loudly. "But you should go. You like parties."

Brady protested but Kya interrupted. "No, really. It's okay, Brady." I glanced over. She smiled the smile that melted hearts. "I can tell you're not into this movie. Not everyone is. You should go and have fun with your friends. I'll stay and keep Grace company."

She untangled herself and jumped up from my couch. My shoulder cooled from the sudden loss of her body heat. She walked to Brady, grabbed him by the hand, and pulled him to his feet. He slid his arm around her waist but she wiggled away. His mouth turned into a pout.

"Go have fun with your friends," she said. She pulled him out of the family room.

"How about tomorrow night?" I heard him ask. "Can we hang out then? Just the two of us?"

I stared at the TV and tossed some more candies into my mouth.

"Grace and I are working," Kya told him as she walked him down the stairs. I heard a buzz of noise, and then the front door slammed and she returned a few minutes later without him.

"We aren't working tomorrow night," I told her. "You are so mean to boys."

"Only the ones who let me." She laughed. "Which is why I'll always love you better." She snuggled up beside me and we stared at the TV screen together, so many things unsaid.

I tried to think of something comforting to say. To let her know I understood her reluctance to get emotionally close to a boy. "Buds before studs," I said instead.

"Sisters before misters." She rested her head on my shoulder and sighed. "You're so much easier than a boyfriend."

"Watch who you're calling easy," I joked.

She laughed and it reminded me of the first time we met.

I was alone in my new bedroom, feeling sorry for myself when I heard a noise. Our house was on the corner of a cul-de-sac, and my bedroom window faced the right side of our yard. I peeked out the window and there they were on the trampoline. James and Kya. Having a blast. A noisy one.

A minute later, Kya looked right into my window. Busted and embarrassed, I shrank down on my bed. My face burning. Hiding. When I peeked out the window again, she grinned and motioned to me. Waved her arms in the air as she bounced.

"Hey, new girl. We can see you. Are you going to watch all day, or are you going to come over and jump?" she yelled. I looked around my room. As if she might be talking to someone else. But I was the only new girl peeking out her bedroom window.

My heart pounding with nerves and excitement, I slipped downstairs and slid open the sliding doors in the kitchen that led to the deck and the backyard. I walked to the middle of the grass and then stopped, looking around. I hadn't thought it through very well, given the fence closing in our yard. It gave an illusion of privacy in the suburban wastelands.

"Climb over," Kya called from her yard.

I sized up the fence. It wasn't designed for climbing. I shook my head. "I'll come around to the front on the street."

"Come on. Climb over. You're already out here. It's not hard. We'll catch you," Kya shouted.

It was a test. One she didn't necessarily want me to pass. I found out later how much Kya liked to test people.

"Come on, new girl. Try," Kya called.

I could hear James protesting, trying to stick up for me.

But the challenge trickled over the fence. And right there, I fell for her hard. Actually, I fell right on top of her. I climbed the fence and when I swung my leg over the top of it, my pant leg caught on a branch of lavender. I hung there until Kya grabbed my leg and yanked. Hard to say which was louder, the rip of my jeans or my shriek, and then I landed on top of Kya. Fortunately, she laughed. The crazy snort laugh didn't suit her stunning looks but it was contagious. I started to laugh too and then James joined in. Lavender flowers came down with me and tickled at my skin, and when I pulled them out of my pant leg, the smell filled my nose, mingling with our laughter. We'd ended up sniggering so hard we had to go into her house to use the bathroom. Lavender would forever remind me of that day.

When we got back to the trampoline, I found out Kya always wanted to jump higher. Do more flips. She reeked of excitement, along with a twinge of danger. We were meant for each other. Two pieces of a puzzle that fit together. And James fit in too.

"You want to go to hot yoga with me tomorrow?" I asked after a moment.

"Can't."

"Why not?"

"I have plans."

I waited, but she didn't say more. I knew better than to pry. Sometimes she liked to have secrets from me. I guess because I knew more about her than anyone else.

"Hmm. Well. What about coming over for breakfast? Saturday morning. Dad's cooking. You know how that goes. There will be monkey pancakes. James is coming. *Monkey pancakes are so great…*" I sang.

"Your family is so weird." She smiled though. She had a standing invitation to join us. Mom and Dad thought filling her belly with monkey pancakes might somehow help.

"Anyhow, James won't want me there." She lifted her thumb to her mouth and chewed.

"Give me a break. Besides, you and James have to make up," I said. "Why not over monkey pancakes?"

She shook her head and reached for the remote. "Want to start the movie from the beginning?" she asked.

I didn't. It was not my favorite. It was hers. And I'd seen it so many times already.

"Sure," I said. "If you do."

"You're the best." She blinked quickly and held her arm next to mine. "We have to get back to the beach soon. I am totally losing my tan and summer is fading fast."

She was many, many shades darker than I was. My paleness required copious amounts of sunscreen and sun-shirts. I wasn't as crazy about the sun or beaches. Her skin soaked up rays and turned a deep brown. Mine turned pink and then back to white.

I glanced at her. She seemed distant. Sad. She smiled at me but it faded fast.

"You okay?" I asked.

Something was bugging her. I knew the way you know things about your best friend. I also knew Kya well enough to know that, if she didn't want to talk about it, there was no use trying to force her. It was hard, staying quiet about something that mattered so much. I wanted to help her, but most of the time I didn't even know how.

chapter five

While it rained outside, Indie and Dad cooked. James and I sat on the floor in the living room, playing Mom's original version of Super Mario Brothers on the old Nintendo system. She'd pulled it out of the basement for a garage sale a few weeks before, but James refused to let her sell it. We'd become obsessed.

From the kitchen, the scent of bacon wafted out, with puffs of smoke filling the living room. Fat sizzled on the griddle. Saturday morning breakfasts were feasts and, unlike most meals at our house, healthy wasn't an option. Every Saturday, Dad's manager opened Splatterfest and ran it on his own all day. Mom and Dad firmly believed in countering working out and healthy eating with a weekly morning of overindulgence. Attendance and gluttony were mandatory. Friends were encouraged.

James used his controller to race Mario through the Mushroom Kingdom on screen. "Damn!"

I glanced at the TV. He'd lost another life.

"I hear you're going to the Seattle show." He glanced at me, taking his attention from the game for a second. "Shoot!" he shouted when he glanced back. He'd accidentally entered Minus World on the game and would stay there until he ran out of lives.

"You should come with us! We don't have an extra ticket for the party, but we could try to get one. And you could come to the tradeshow for sure."

"Not my scene, Jelly Bean. Plus me sharing a hotel room with you and your mom and Kya." He shuddered. "Too much estrogen."

His battle with the video game went on until Mom's voice interrupted. She walked down the stairs toward the living room and burst into a spontaneous song. Loudly. She walked to James and me, incorporating us into her song. "Stop playing games and come eat," she sang, and stepped over top of us, singing on about monkey pancakes.

Neither one of us even flinched. She'd been abusing hits from the radio, making up her own words, and singing at the top of her lungs for as long as I could remember. I don't know how many verses I'd listened to about the horrors of menopause or about starting a paintball business in your retirement years. Mom turned everything into a wacky song.

She wore her favorite new T-shirt. Black with tiny white writing. *Sarcasm is a service I offer for free.* She'd ordered it for herself from eBay. No wonder I'd craved affection as a kid. I turned the game off. James and I stood and followed Mom to the kitchen.

At the stove, Dad wore his Saturday morning apron with a picture of a woman's body in a bikini. Indie stood at the table, placing down a plate piled high with bacon. In a glass jar in the middle of the table, an arrangement of lavender celebrated our cheery ritual.

Mom slid up beside Dad and patted him on the rear. He wiggled his butt at her and she moved to the cupboard to get coffee cups. We all put aside any differences on Saturday mornings. It was family time and we all got along, whether we wanted to or not. "Coffee? Indie? James?" She didn't ask me since she knew I couldn't stand the taste. I went to the fridge to pull out orange juice and then grabbed some glasses and set them down on the table that Indie had already set. Saturday was man-day in the kitchen.

"Not a lot of kids showed up for the new paintball league," Dad said to all of us from the griddle, where he was pouring batter into his coveted monkey-pancake pan. Around the pancakes, he was scrambling up a huge pile of eggs. Indie scooted past me to grab toast that popped up from the toaster and spread butter across the top.

"I'm sure there're more pseudo-criminals needing to rehearse for future years of delinquency." James slid into a chair at the kitchen table. "No offense, Mr. Black."

"Oh my God, James. Could you be any funnier?" I bumped my elbow into his arm as I sat down in the chair beside him. "Oh. Yes. You could."

Dad chuckled. "What would we do without James's healthy doses of cynicism?"

"What can I say? My blood type is B negative."

Dad smiled at James and flipped over a monkey pancake. "So your dad is gone for a few more weeks?" he asked.

James nodded. "Yeah. Maybe longer. He wasn't sure last time we Skyped."

"And how's your mom? We need to get her over here for dinner soon." Dad scooped up a pile of eggs on his spatula, walked to James's plate, and plopped them down.

"She's not very mobile this week. But she's doing okay." He glanced at my mom. "Mrs. B keeps us well fed," James said. "I keep telling her to stop sending so many lasagnas and casseroles but they keep coming. I'm pretty sure my mom wants to make out with your entire family."

"Sign me up," Dad said. He scooped a pile of eggs on my plate and winked at me.

Mom threw a towel at him and they laughed.

I smiled. James's mom's condition sometimes left her tired and unable to do much on the physical side of things, so when his dad was away on duty, which was about half the year, the bulk of the household duties were left to James. He'd learned to cook pretty young and had always had a lot of extra chores. A nurse came in to look after his mom's physical needs, and once a week there was a house cleaner over, but as the only child, he was left in charge of keeping the house running smoothly. It was a lot of responsibility looking after a mom with MS, but he handled it without complaining. He even made his own spending money working at Splatterfest whenever he could. Dad was flexible with his hours. Mom helped by sending over food. Indie used to shovel the walks and his driveway in the winter and mow the lawn in the summer time. Now James did that.

"How come Kya's not here?" Mom asked as she dug her fork into some eggs. Indie dished her a couple of slices of buttered Texas toast.

I shrugged, pretending not to be worried. "She said she had plans."

"Probably with that boy who was over last night." Indie shoved an entire piece of bacon in his mouth.

I glared at him. "Just to watch a movie. And she kicked him out early, before the movie even ended." I glanced at Dad, but he flipped another pancake and didn't say anything.

"That girl has had way too many boyfriends." Indie tossed me a piece of toast but completely missed my plate.

"She doesn't take them seriously." I grabbed the toast from the table and put it next to my eggs. "Besides, aren't you the guy who majors in changing girlfriends?" He'd had a serious girlfriend for a couple of years, Shari, but since they broke up, there'd been a revolving door of girls. Even though Indie was five years older than I was and had finished college, he lived at home and worked at Splatterfest while working toward becoming a cop.

Mom did his laundry, bought his underwear, and let him bring girls home for free dinner dates. There was no debating that what she lacked in parental warm fuzzies, she made up for in physical nurturing.

"Kya never takes anything seriously," James mumbled. "Except perhaps a single-minded pursuit of average." He shoved back an entire mouthful of eggs and made a face as I grabbed the bottle of ketchup and squeezed an inch-thick layer on top of my eggs. "What's not average is the amount of ketchup your family consumes in a month," he said.

"What can we say? We like to support tomato farmers. Anyhow, stop talking about Kya when she's not here to defend herself," I said.

"How about you?" Indie slid behind a chair, grabbed the ketchup bottle from me, and squirted a high pile on his plate. "We've never seen you with a boy unless you have a gun in your hand. Other than James. And he doesn't count. Maybe you need lessons on how to be less revolting to the opposite sex. First step, stop shooting them all the time."

James squinted at him as he finished chewing. "I count. And unlike you, I can count without using my fingers. You should try it sometime. Thinking, I mean."

"James, you seriously need to get laid," Indie said, and shoved a huge mouthful of food in his yap.

James's ears and face turned a shade to match the contents of our Heinz bottle.

"Indie. He's seventeen years old. He does not need to get laid," my mom interrupted. "Good lord, how did I raise such foul-mouthed children?" She took the ketchup bottle to layer her own eggs in a sea of red.

"Um, by being a foul-mouthed parent?" Indie shot back.

"Child. Not children. I do not have a potty mouth." I mouthed a swear word at him as Dad approached the table with a plateful of finished pancakes and he saw.

"The boy speaks the truth," Dad said as he flipped a monkey.

Mom directed her dirty look at him.

"Don't worry, Mom. We love you, despite your potty mouth." Indie grinned at her.

"You sow what you create," Dad said to Mom as he placed pancakes in the middle of the table.

"Asshole," she said back.

"Family time. No fighting," I reminded them.

"I just felt your grandmother shudder in heaven," Dad said. "But..."

"She never understood our family." We all finished the sentence with him. Even James. He'd hung around my family enough to hear that a million times. My grandma had been an ultra-conservative woman who believed soap in the mouth was the way to clean out bad words. My mom would have gone through a bar a week. Mom and Grandma were total opposites, and while in many ways I'd craved a more affectionate and cuddly mom—one more like my grandma—I knew my mom had my back.

I stuck my fork in the ear of a monkey pancake and Indie and James smothered theirs in syrup and sang the traditional Saturday morning "Monkey Pancake" song to the tune of "Twinkle Twinkle Little Star."

Monkey pancakes are so great,
Pile some pancakes on my plate.

"Okay, James, Indie," I said. They sang louder.

Up above the pancake pile,
Pour some syrup, make me smile.
Monkey pancakes are so great,
Pile some pancakes on my plate.

"I made up that song when I was five," I said. "We should really let it go."

"Songstress just like your mama," Mom said, batting her eyelashes and then biting into a slice of crispy bacon.

"The problem with this table is too many freaks and not enough circuses," I said.

"But there are flying monkeys." James tossed a monkey pancake in the air and it landed on my plate.

Dad joined us and soon we were busy mixing and sopping up syrup and ketchup and buttery toast in a giant feeding frenzy. After the carb load and some groaning and stomach patting, we all helped clean up the messy kitchen. Soon Mom and Dad were off to another Latin dance class.

"You going out?" Mom called, her hand on the front door.

"Hot yoga later."

"All right. Your dad and I will probably go out with the Simpsons for dinner. You can fix yourself something? Don't wait up." She laughed as she closed the door behind her, but the truth was they usually stayed out later than me.

"You working this afternoon?" I asked James.

"Nope." He headed back toward the living room for the Nintendo. "Robert is. He's hot, right?"

James liked to check in sometimes on other guys' hotness quotients. Trying to figure out what girls liked, maybe. Robert was a semi-pro baller and he ran Splatterfest most weekends.

"Very hot. But he's too old to go out with you."

"Wow, Grace. That was as low as your brother's IQ."

"I heard that, James," Indie called from the kitchen.

"You were supposed to." James sat on the floor, crossing his legs like a kindergartener. "You want to go first?"

"Go ahead."

He turned on the game and waited.

"You want to come to hot yoga with me later?" I asked, and plunked down on the floor beside him, bopping my head along to the catchy Super Mario theme song.

"What? Running around playing speedball isn't enough of a work-out for you?" He glanced at me as if I were crazy.

"Yoga relaxes me," I said.

He picked up the controller as the game started up, not answering my original question.

"I take it that means no."

"Thanks for asking, but when have I ever expressed a desire to go to hot yoga?"

"Think of all the ladies there, James," Indie called as he bounded up the stairs. "Maybe not taking advantage of situations is one of the reasons you haven't gotten laid."

We both ignored him as he cackled away to himself on his way to his room.

The Super Mario game dinged as James ate up some coins. I stretched my feet out and lay back on the floor beside him, holding my bloated stomach. "Have you talked to Kya today?"

"Not since work."

"I wish you two would make up already."

"Dream big, Graceling. Dream big."

I sat up and hit him on the arm.

"Hey, watch it," he growled. "You almost made me lose a life."

"I'll make you lose a life all right. You two will make up. You're my best friends. If she puts up walls, James, it's only because she wants you to break them down."

"Curse you, Mario," he yelled. "Stupid game glitch." He'd lost his final life. "Will I ever beat you at this video game?"

"I doubt it."

In an abrupt whoosh, he put down the controller, switched off the game system, and got to his feet. "You know, maybe I'm not big on breaking down walls, Grace. I've got to get going. Check in on my mom, see if she needs anything."

Surprised by his quick departure, I pushed myself up and chased after him as he bolted to the front door. When he turned, I reached to swoosh up his hair but he ducked and straightened his glasses. "Kya said she wants to go to the beach soon," I said. "I know you can't resist glowing with whiteness in the sand with me."

"We'll see," he said. "Until we meet again," he said the same way he always did when he left.

"See ya, James."

The door closed behind him. My belly churned as if something were about to go wrong. Very wrong. Dad always told me never to ignore my feelings. Gut instinct, he called it. You'd make a good cop, he'd say. But Indie was going to be a cop. One child was enough for our family.

Something bad was brewing.

I could feel it.

chapter six

Sweat beaded down my back and over my shoulders. I pressed my hands and feet into the yoga mat, my butt in the air in the downward dog position, contemplating my belly button, trying to stay focused instead of being hyperaware of the guy at the back of the class who kept sneaking looks at me. I was irrationally mad at him. His presence was interrupting the quiet that should have been in my head. I pretended it was him, not Kya, who had me upset.

Tina, the instructor, flowed into a plank and I glanced in the mirror at the boy's reflection. His dark eyes met mine and he smiled, but I quickly looked away and swooped down into plank.

I dripped bacon-smelling sweat on my mat, but instead of enjoying the grease cleanse and being in the moment in yoga, my mind and body weren't connected. When the class finally ended, I still had the little ball of anxiety in my belly. I rolled my yoga mat in record time, grabbed my towel and water bottle, and rushed out.

After a long cool shower, I wrapped my wet hair up in a bun, dressed, and left the change room. I slowed down when I spotted the boy leaning against the counter in the reception area, chatting with the owner. A warm smile lit up his face when he spotted me. I lowered my eyes.

"Hi, Grace." He spoke in a low tone, slightly above a whisper. Part of yoga etiquette. Speak in low voices. "I played paintball with you and your sister yesterday."

"I remember." Levi. The boy with the temper. The badass. "She's my best friend. Not my sister." I matched his low tone but smiled because he thought we were sisters. I'd always wanted a sister. Besides the obvious allure of sharing clothes, maybe a sister could help analyze the foreign minds of boys. Maybe share chores. Something other than Saturday morning breakfast. I always got to be the one to do the "womanly" stuff around the house. I'd never seen my brother scrubbing a toilet.

"Oh. I thought you were related." As if he should know anything about me at all. He paused. "My cousin has a crush on her."

Of course he did. That's probably what this conversation was about. To get information for his cousin.

"Tell him to get in line," I said, but smiled to soften the message.

"He's already butting his way to the front. Trust me."

I took a deep breath, appropriate given the wonderful smells that filled the reception area and the slogans about inner peace painted on the walls.

"So, you're into hot yoga as well as paintball?" he asked, changing the subject. Seems we both liked to challenge stereotypes.

"Grace has been coming faithfully since we opened," Carly, the owner, told him, sparing me the need to say anything. Carly glanced at me. "Levi told me he was a regular at hot yoga in Canada. He moved here from Vancouver." There was a slight buzz of excitement in her voice. "He's going to be going to your high school."

I groaned. "Ugh. Don't remind me about school." It started up in a couple of weeks.

"I know," Levi said. "Summer goes by fast."

I stared at him. Maybe he wasn't movie star good-looking, but there was definitely an appeal to him. Height. Confidence? "Did you like Splatterfest?" I moved past him to sit on the bench across from the shoe rack and slipped on my shoes.

"Yeah. Even though I sucked."

"I've never tried woodsball. Speedball is faster." I stood up.

"Grace is one of the best female paintball players in Washington state," Carly said.

Actually, Carly had never seen me play, but it didn't stop her from trying to pimp me out.

"Well, since it's my dad's place, I'm kind of obligated to be good at it, Carly. But I'm hardly the best." I pulled my yoga mat strap over my arm and hiked up my bag.

"Not true. She's amazing," Carly said.

I rolled my eyes. "Kya's better." I gave Carly a look, but she grinned and subtly lifted her eyebrow higher. I looked from her to Levi.

She followed my gaze and gave Levi an even bigger smile, as if we were an interesting TV channel she was watching.

Levi was focused on me though, and he shifted on his feet. "So, um, I was wondering if you were busy right now?"

"Uh." I couldn't think of anything to say.

"I told him you weren't seeing anyone," Carly said, as if she was being helpful announcing this fact to both of us.

"Carly!" My face burned and I ducked my head down and stared at my sandals.

"Oh man," Levi said. "Awkward."

I glanced up, and he was grinning but his cheeks were red. It made me feel less like hiding in my room with my covers pulled over my head.

"You want to grab a coffee?" He pointed out the door to the coffee shop across the street. "Over there?"

Carly giggled but we both ignored her. The front door opened, and I watched an older woman walk in, pink yoga mat in her hand. She slid off her shoes and went to the reception desk to scan her tag.

"Uh." I was used to my role as sidekick girl. The one boys talked to when they wanted more info about Kya. Hazard of having a gorgeous best friend but comfortable. Easy.

"You should go, Grace," Carly said, breaking into my stupor after she'd scanned the woman's tag. The woman glanced at Levi and me with a tiny smile on her face and slipped past Levi toward the change room.

"Levi doesn't know a lot of people in town. It would be nice for him to know someone when he starts school." Carly grinned, her happiness to be playing a part in the coffee date scribbled into her features. I remembered her telling me she used to own a dating service before Breathe Hot Yoga. I kind of wanted to strangle her. Never mind *namaste*.

I also wanted to point out that a guy who asked a stranger out for coffee and made friends with the owner of a yoga place on his first visit probably didn't need much help getting to know people. "Um, sure," I said. "For a little while. I have to get to Splatterfest soon."

"You working?" he asked.

I wasn't. I needed to pick up my sweater and I wanted to see if Kya had been by, but he didn't need to know that. Levi held the door open. I slipped by him. He smelled good. Clean. Freshly showered. His dark hair was still wet on the ends.

"See ya, Carly," he called.

She completely ignored my narrowed eyes.

Levi and I stopped at our cars to put away our yoga gear and then walked on to the coffee shop. Levi carried the conversation while I gave dorky one-word answers. When we got to the coffee shop, he insisted on buying, took my order, and suggested I find a table. I headed to an open spot, threw my zebra purse underneath, and sat. Music filtered through speakers in the ceiling but I heard Levi and the barista chatting as she got the order ready. Soon Levi joined me and placed my usual lavender tea in front of me. Then he plunked down a mug of hot chocolate with whipped cream and chocolate drizzles opposite me. It smelled heavenly and I wished that I'd gone with the same thing. I always forgot about other choices and went with the familiar.

"You want to switch drinks?" he asked, nodding at my drink as he sat. My face must have given me away.

I shook my head quickly. "No. That's okay."

"You sure?"

I nodded.

"You're worried about calories?" he asked.

My face warmed. He laughed aloud and put up his hands in defense. "No. I did NOT mean it that way. Obviously, you don't have to. Arrgh." He slid his hot chocolate in front of me. "I need to take some lessons in talking to girls."

My cheeks cooled to pink. "You don't have to give me your drink."

"It's the least I can do. I can't believe I said that." He took my lavender tea, sipped at it, and his nose squished up as if he'd swallowed medicine. "Mmm," he said.

I smiled. "Lavender tea one of your favorites?"

He coughed but grinned even as he choked. He pointed to the drink he'd slid in front of me on the table. "At least drink the hot chocolate. I didn't mean to be a jerk."

I took a sip. Foam tickled my lip and I wiped it away self-consciously. It tasted delicious. When I glanced up, he was staring at me, a half smile turning up his lip. "I have a confession to make," he said.

My brows pressed together, expecting something horrible.

"I heard you were going to hot yoga today. I mean, I honestly did go to hot yoga in Vancouver. It helps with stress and with breathing, for running." He paused, took another sip of tea, and grimaced. "But today, I was hoping to see you."

I stared into the whipped cream, at a loss as to how to respond. "You run?" It's not what I wanted to say.

Do you like me? Do you think I'm pretty? Is that stress related to the temper your cousin mentioned?

"Actually, I play soccer." He looked kind of mortified. "Do I sound like a stalker?"

"Yes," I answered with a straight face. He looked horrified and I laughed. "I'm kidding. But how'd you hear about yoga?"

"Kya said something."

"She did?" I took a sip of hot chocolate and stared into it. "You know, usually guys want to meet her. Not me."

"Really? I mean she's pretty and stuff. But she's more my cousin's type. Not that you're not. Pretty, I mean. Not Lucas's type, but, oh God, I need to stop talking."

I laughed and shook my head, wanting to ask what his type was. Me? There was a pause in our conversation as my brain stopped functioning. Jazzy music played in the background.

"So. Tell me about paintball," he said when it must have become glaringly apparent my ability to converse without prompting no longer existed.

I took another sip of hot chocolate to buy myself time. "Why I play? I love it."

"Yeah. You're good. But how'd you get into it? It's kind of different. For a girl, I mean. No offense. I think it's hot." He grinned and then tried another tiny sip of tea.

My stomach swooped. Hot? "My dad owns the place." I smiled. "He got me and Kya into it." For a very particular reason, but Levi didn't need to know about that.

A swarm of moms buzzed noisily into the coffee shop, each pushing a stroller the size of a shopping cart, talking among one another as they lined up to order drinks. The babies were quieter.

I turned back to Levi. "Kya and I might play college paintball next year."

His expression suggested he had no idea what I was talking about. "NCPA. National College Paintball Association."

"Seriously?" he asked.

"Yup. There's a team at Seattle University. The Lady Grinders. All female. They're amazing. We're going to a party in a week to meet the players."

"That's cool." He tapped the side of his head with his finger. "You're already thinking ahead. Your future."

I smiled. "Not really. I have no idea what I want to do with my life. But since I'm expected to go to college, I might as well play paintball while I'm there, right? My parents are pretty good, but they don't want me to become a contract killer."

One of the babies in a stroller chose that moment to wake up with a curdling scream, and we both jumped and then laughed.

"Contract killer?" Levi asked, turning back to me.

"Pro baller. Contract killer. Not exactly like being a cop, right? Or a lawyer, like my mom used to be. But if I get on with the Grinders, I figure I can give it a whirl and worry about the rest of it later." As soon as I said that, I wanted to pluck my words from the air. I'd never admitted to anyone that I might want to go pro. Not even Kya.

A mom with a long brown ponytail expertly whipped her crying baby out of the stroller and jiggled it around. The crying stopped immediately. She didn't even break her conversation with her friend.

Levi nodded and rubbed his chin. He looked intrigued by my confession, not disgusted or even bored. "What about you?" I asked to switch the spotlight off my lame ambitions.

"Ironically, I'm thinking of taking a gap year after graduating. Traveling. My parents aren't impressed."

"Why ironically?" I glanced at his face, and when our eyes met, my stomach swooped again.

"My parents moved to China. They wanted me to go with them but I didn't want to."

The chatter of moms got louder. I glanced at them and then back at Levi.

"They'll be working eighteen-hour days and would have left me to make my own way in a country where I don't even speak the language. I want to travel on my own terms."

"That's why you're in Tadita?"

He glanced over at the moms. "Mostly, yup. It's weird, not being with them, but they still control my life as much as possible. They make me Skype every couple of days." He took a tiny sip of tea, made a face, and caught me watching. We didn't take our eyes off each other. My face warmed and I cursed my fair skin. Blushing was impossible to hide.

I imagined my parents moving to China and leaving me alone with relatives, but it didn't compute. Another baby screech broke up our staring contest. I watched a mom pluck a baby out of the stroller and rock it in her arms. I sent a silent thanks to the baby for the distraction. "Are you and Lucas close?"

He laughed. "Not so much," he confirmed. "Lucas and I are different."

Thank God, I wanted to say, but resisted.

"How?" I asked, aware of my nosiness.

He shrugged but didn't elaborate.

"Well," I said. "It's not so bad in Tadita. I mean besides having to do your senior year at a new school. That probably sucks for you. I'll show you around if you like." My cheeks heated again, imagining how stupid I sounded. Did I really offer to be his school buddy like we were in fifth grade? I cleared my throat and coughed.

"That," he said, "would be awesome."

My cough died and I hid my smile. "So, um, how come you joined the league at Splatterfest?" I asked.

"My aunt thought it would be a good idea. She's trying to encourage a relationship between Lucas and me. And since I have no friends." He leaned back in his chair. Based on his expression, he didn't seem too bothered by it.

Again, I sensed making friends wouldn't be an issue for this guy.

"Lucas's friends are..." He stopped and tapped his finger on the rim of his cup.

"What?"

"Well. They're kind of idiots."

I laughed out loud. A mom looked over and grinned at me.

My cell phone rang, interrupting us. My heart skipped. I grabbed for my purse and dug my hand inside, searching for my phone. I pulled it out and glanced down at call display. Kya's name.

Thank God. Worry had lingered under my skin all day. My senses were buzzing expectantly. Waiting for something. Dreading.

"I have to take this," I said. I clicked the phone on and put it to my ear. "Kya?" I asked.

A squeaky noise filled my ear. I frowned. It sounded like crying.

I swiveled on my seat and turned away from Levi. "Kya? What? What's wrong?"

She hiccupped into the phone.

"Kya?" I said, my voice louder. I could hear the urgency in my own voice. "What's wrong?" I repeated.

"Gracie?" She sounded like a scared little girl. "He did it again." She sniffled. "He did it again."

I held my breath. Terrified.

chapter seven

M y body froze. Goosebumps ran up my arms. I turned further
away from Levi.

"Are you okay?" I whispered. I wanted to reach through the
phone and hug her close to me. Protect her from his darkness. Evil.

Kya didn't answer. Over the phone, the background noise
changed. Someone was knocking on a door.

"Kya," I said sharply. "Where are you? I'll come and get you."

She covered the phone. I heard muffled sounds. She called to
someone. A door opened and the noise got louder. I heard bottles
clink. She giggled but it was a messy half laugh, half sob.

"Kya!" I called.

"Hold on. Give me a sec," she said in a slow over-enunciated
voice. "I'm talking to Grace."

Over the phone, the door closed. It got quieter. Kya breathed
loudly into the earpiece. "I hate..." She didn't finish her sentence
but breathed heavily into the receiver. The words hung in my ear.
Asking to be completed.

"Kya," I said in a louder voice. "I'm coming to get you. Right
now. Where are you?"

A boy called her name. The phone rustled around again. I heard
faint giggling and then the phone was hung up.

I pulled it away from my ear. Hit redial.

"Kya?" Levi mouthed softly. I nodded as it rang. Someone picked up, but before I said a word, it clicked off again.

"What the hell?" I dialed again and it rang and rang and rang. "Shit." The phone was heavy in my hand and my heart hammered. From the corner of my eye, I saw a girl about my age piggybacking a guy into the coffee shop. They were laughing and happy. Envy filtered through me for a moment and then it was gone.

"Is she okay?" Levi asked, bringing me back to the moment.

I wondered what he had gotten from my end of the conversation.

"No." I pushed on the table to move my chair back and threw the phone back in my purse. "I'm sorry. I need to go. I have to find her."

He frowned and reached across the table, grabbing my hand. "What's wrong with her?"

His hand gripped mine. Too tight. I pulled hard to get away from him. The look on his face scared me. I remembered the warning. His temper. His eyebrows pressed together and his lips were one tight line. As if he was irritated. What could he possibly have against Kya?

He leaned across the table, his eyebrows squished together in a thick unibrow. I frowned, my stomach twisting.

"I have to find her," I repeated, bothered by the intensity in his face. All flirty coffee banter had vanished. "I have to go."

His entire demeanor changed. Anger. He was angry.

Disappointment bubbled under my skin and I longed to go back to the conversation before Kya's call, but I didn't have time to deal with his issues or even my reaction to them.

He let me go and sat back. "I think I know where she is." I stared at him. "She was with my cousin earlier." He gazed into his tea and then back at me. "She probably still is," he said in a softer voice.

"What?" I glared at him with anger of my own rising to the surface.

"She came over this afternoon. My aunt and uncle are in Seattle for the weekend. Lucas and I are alone. He had a few guys over. And Kya." He pushed back on his chair and stood. "Come on. I'll take you there."

"What do you mean?" I demanded as I stood. His words were perfectly clear. I didn't want to believe them.

"Kya was in the basement when I left. With a couple of Lucas's buddies." He glanced at the giggly happy couple picking up their coffee drinks. "They were drinking."

I snatched the unfinished cup of hot chocolate from the table to throw in the garbage on the way out, gripping the cup so tightly, some of it spilled on the floor. "Why didn't you tell me?"

Levi picked up the almost-full tea and put his free hand on my back to let me move ahead of him. "I'm sorry, Grace. If I'd known you were looking for her, I would have told you right away." His voice was gentle again, the anger gone.

We hurried through the coffee shop, ignoring the curious stares from the barista and the moms, and dumped our drinks in the trash. He held the exit door for me. I slipped by him and my skin touched his bare arm. Dark and warm. I shivered. Outside, I hurried toward my car and he easily matched my pace. "I didn't know you were worried." He paused. "And she seems like a partier. I thought it was normal for her."

"You don't know her," I snapped.

"I know enough." I glared at him and picked up my pace.

"Sorry." He reached for my arm. "I know she's your friend."

I jerked away from his apologetic touch. "It's complicated. She's complicated." I wanted to tell him he was wrong about Kya. Sometimes she was a party girl. But he didn't know why. And I couldn't tell him. We reached his car and he stopped.

"I'm right here. Why don't I drive you?" he said. "It'll be easier. We can come back and pick up your car later."

"Fine." I nodded, focused on getting to Kya quickly.

He opened the passenger door of a shiny blue hatchback. "We're not far. It won't take long." He reached across me to brush fast-food wrappers off the passenger seat. "Sorry. I'm kind of a car slob." He straightened and his cheeks had blotches of red on them. "I have to clean it before my aunt gets home."

At any other time, the embarrassment would be kind of endearing, but I climbed inside, snapped on my seat belt, and said nothing. "How did she even end up at your place?" I mumbled when he got in the driver seat.

"Lucas got her number yesterday. Before the paintball game." He started the car. "He was bragging about it."

I cringed on Kya's behalf, imagining the less than poetic way Lucas probably put it. Another Neanderthal to add to her list.

"I guess they arranged to hang out today."

So these were her plans. Brady was definitely over.

"What time did she get there?" I asked as he backed out of the parking spot and drove through the lot, headed for the main street.

He kept his gaze focused out the front window. "About four? They started drinking right away."

I stared at Levi's profile and for a second wished neither of us was involved in this. We'd been having a good time. He'd been sweet. And so cute. I had an urge to leave Kya to figure this out on her own for once. But I glanced out the window and shook off the thought. She needed me.

And thank God Levi was involved. If it weren't for him, I'd have no idea where she was.

He came to a halt at a four-way stop. He flicked on the right turn signal and glanced over. "I hope I didn't screw things up by not telling you about Kya earlier."

A ticklish feeling wiggled inside my belly. I bit my lip to hold back an entirely inappropriate smile but couldn't stop a swoop of pleasure that washed away some of the bad feelings.

"Let's go and get her, okay?" I said softly. "I need to know that she's all right."

Trouble was, I didn't know if she would be. Not for a very long time.

chapter eight

L evi drove down a quiet suburban street in a newer area of Tadita, with earth-toned matchy-match houses and well-maintained lawns. The whole street reeked of lavender and the less subtle scent of successful young couples and perfect but invisible children. There was no activity anywhere. Quiet, unused trampolines sunbathed in backyards with no sign of life.

"This is where you live?" I asked when Levi pulled into a driveway with a triple-car garage. Huge planters filled with colorful flowers lined the sidewalk all the way to the front door.

Levi turned off the car and nodded. "Temporarily."

"It's nice."

"Appearances can be deceiving. Come on."

We hopped out of the car, and I followed him up the driveway and waited while he punched numbers into the code-locked door. I crept into the house behind him but stopped on an area rug in the front hallway. He walked further without taking off his sneakers.

The front entrance was large and dim with dark hardwood running down the hallway into a kitchen visible around the corner. A large, mirrored closet behind me reflected a table with a vase filled with bright sunflowers. They looked fake, but I couldn't be sure.

"They're definitely not here," Levi called. "Too quiet. They were whooping it up in the basement when I left." His footsteps clomped downstairs and then a door opened. A minute later, he returned to the front hall, shaking his head.

"Damn," I said. "What the hell is she doing?" I pulled my phone from my purse and speed dialed James's number.

He answered on the second ring and I heard the groan of a vacuum cleaner shutting down in the background.

"James?"

"That's what my parents called me," he answered.

"Have you talked to Kya?"

"I'm swellsville, Grace. Thanks for your interest in my well-being. But negatory. I have not had contact with our dear Kya this entire day."

"Shoot." I sensed Levi watching but didn't look at him.

"What's up?" James asked. "What's she done now?" He didn't bother to disguise the edge of impatience in his voice.

I swiveled slightly on my heels. "I'm worried about her. I need to find her." I heard footsteps and turned to see Levi going to the kitchen.

James sighed. "Well. You know Kya. If she's on a mission of self-destruction, she'll go dark if she doesn't want to be found," James said. "I wouldn't worry about her."

In the kitchen, water whooshed out of a tap.

"James, this is different." He was right, of course. Kya did disappear sometimes and ignored phone or text messages. She'd emerge when she was done being dark and depressed or whatever she did when she hid out. But something had happened. "I need to find her."

"People who have nothing to hide hide nothing," he said.

I sighed. If only it was that easy. Levi popped his head around the corner and held up an empty glass to see if I wanted water. I shook my head. On the other end of the phone, James mirrored my sigh.

"Do you want help looking for her?"

"It's okay. You're busy." I glanced toward the kitchen.

"It's stupid housework. I can do it tomorrow. Mom had a rough afternoon. She's medicated and out for the night. She's been in a lot of pain so we upped her meds. She won't notice if I vacuum tomorrow."

The clanking in the kitchen stopped. Levi walked around the corner and stopped by the table and vase, pressing his hip against the wall.

"Is your mom going to be okay?" I asked James.

"The six-million dollar question. She's sleeping now, not in pain. That's as good as it gets some days."

I nodded, my heart going out to him. "Don't worry about Kya, okay? I have help. I'll find her. I thought you might know something."

"Nada."

In the mirror, I caught the reflection of Levi's flat stomach. A section of smooth tanned skin showed where his shirt caught on the wall. I quickly looked away.

"Thanks, James. I hope your mom feels better. Talk to you tomorrow?"

"Yeah. Tomorrow."

I clicked off the phone before he asked questions about who was helping me. I tucked it back in my purse. Levi raised his eyebrows.

"James. My other best friend," I told him. "And Kya's."

"The guy from Splatterfest? The one who did the announcing. Glasses? Black hair?"

I nodded. My mind was busy trying not to think of his bare skin while also trying to think where Kya could be.

Levi pushed off the wall. "I think I know where they might have gone." He straightened and his shirt slid down. Disappointment and relief fogged my brain. I blinked to windshield-wipe away the perverted thoughts.

"Steve Blender's," Levi said. "He was here. He has a pool, and since it finally stopped raining, I bet they went there. Lucas took me when I first moved here."

"Steve Blender's? Are you serious? He doesn't even like us." I shifted from foot to foot and caught sight of myself in the mirror. Pieces of hair had escaped from my bun and pointed all over the place. Zero makeup, a plain white T-shirt, and black yoga shorts. The only color on my body was a yellow stripe outlining my zebra-print purse. I looked like a flat-chested and boring preteen.

"Well. Based on what I've seen and heard, he doesn't base his opinion of girls on their personalities. But so you know, they seemed to be getting along fine."

"I can't believe she'd go there."

"Only one way to find out." He held his hand out for me to walk out the door ahead of him.

"Do you know where his house is?"

"I have his address." He lifted his phone from his pocket. "Lucas texted it the day I went there. I haven't been invited back."

"I'll take that as a good character reference." I twisted my hand around the doorknob and pushed. "Can you take me?"

"Of course." He shadowed me outside and hurried ahead to open the passenger door on his car. He drove a few blocks to another part of the suburb. The houses looked like they'd been fed growth hormones. Even the lots were triple the size.

He slowed down in front of a house with a long, wide driveway. Levi pulled behind a couple of SUVs. "This is it." He killed the ignition and pointed to the right. "You can see the pool in the backyard."

A fence wrapped around the yard. Through the slats, pool water shimmered in the sunlight. It was hard to associate Steve Blender with this place.

"That's my uncle's car." Levi pointed to a Mustang in front of the driveway, boxed in by the SUVs. "Dumbass is driving it when he's been drinking," he muttered.

We hopped out at the same time and hurried up the driveway. Whoops and hollers floated over the fence from the backyard. Obnoxious music polluted the air but it wasn't overly loud. Noise bylaws, I guessed.

I heard a high-pitched giggle and walked faster. Levi reached the gate first, slipped his hand inside, and opened it. We hurried along the side of the house. I stopped, taking in the scene.

Out by the pool, three boys sat on lawn chairs facing Kya. She was standing on top of a lawn chair wearing her favorite pink bikini top with black boy-short bottoms. She knew she gave good butt in them and to prove it, she was dancing on the chair and shaking it. The boys were holding beer bottles and staring at Kya with pervy expressions. One of them held up a phone as Kya danced.

Her fingers slid up behind her back, reaching for the knot in her bathing suit strap, a drunken impression of a stripper. She stumbled as she tried moving seductively to the bass pulsing out of invisible speakers.

"Show us your tits," the boy with the phone yelled to Kya.

"Kya!" I yelled louder.

Lucas glanced over and spotted Levi and I, and his eyes narrowed. The boy with the phone spotted me and grinned. It was malicious and he winked. A chill slithered up my back.

"Levi brought more talent," he called.

Levi swore.

I rushed toward Kya who recognized me despite the glazy eyes. She stumbled a little and giggled. "Skanklet. My best friend in the whole world!" she cried.

"This is private property," Steve said, waving his beer at me. "No one invited you. Get off it."

"Kya!" I yelled.

She'd pulled on the strings too hard and was holding her bikini top in her hand, giving the boys a free show.

"Whoa," Lucas called as if he was as shocked as I was.

"Turn that off," Levi yelled to the guy with the phone. His voice sounded deeper and his words were soaked with rage.

"Woo hoo," cried the guy with the phone, ignoring him and standing up to get a better view. "Bare boobies. Skin for the win."

Levi turned, his face almost unrecognizable. He charged him and grabbed for the phone. When the guy held it out and away, Levi punched him in the face. The phone dropped to the pavement and the boy howled and reached for his eye.

I gasped and my hand flew to my mouth.

Lucas jumped up and in a flash was on Levi, holding him back by the shoulders. "Chill out," Lucas growled. "Chill the hell out."

I ran and grabbed the towel by Kya's chair, helped her step down, and wrapped the towel around her at the same time. She giggled softly but almost manically then made an ooomph sound and stumbled into a planter. I steadied her and nothing got broken.

"Dude!" The guy with the phone yelled, holding his eye. "You punched me." Fortunately, instead of attacking back and starting a brawl, he mumbled and complained as he bent to pick up his phone.

Lucas was holding Levi, talking to him in a low voice. The phone guy plunked down in his chair, seemingly more concerned with his phone than his eye.

Steve Blender jumped up from his chair, still holding a beer bottle. "You should leave before I call the cops," Steve said, staring at Levi. "You want to press charges, Cameron?" Steve asked.

I glanced at Cameron, the boy Levi punched. He'd taken his hand off his eye and was inspecting the phone, mumbling about his mom. He shook his head.

Kya giggled and I pulled her in close, trying to shield her from the arguing as if she were a child.

"Lucky for you." Steve walked toward Levi and Levi struggled, but Lucas held him back. "I hear you don't need more trouble with cops."

Levi stared Steve down, his eyes slits of anger. His lips were a thin line of rage. Steve grinned. I sensed the danger beneath Levi's surface and shivered.

Lucas didn't take his hands off Levi's shoulder. "Hey guys, chill out. We're not going to call the cops." He glared at Steve and then back at Levi. "You don't need more trouble," Lucas said softly and something else. It sounded like "probation."

Steve stepped toward me and I moved in front of Kya, shielding her even as he looked down his nose at me. "This is a private party," he said. "And unless you're going to show us your tits, you're not invited. Do you want me to call the cops?" He tilted back his beer but didn't take his eyes off me as he drank it.

"Like you'll call the cops." I stood toe to toe with him until Kya wobbled and stepped back. I fought to keep her upright.

"Oh wait." Steve dragged his gaze up and down my body. "Come to think of it, you don't have anything worth viewing. Leave."

I lifted my chin, but warmth lit up my cheeks. I died a little inside.

Levi pushed Lucas away and stomped over, putting himself between Steve and me.

"Take your little girlfriend and go," Steve said. He smirked at Kya and I moved closer to her, trying to shield her from his eyes. "Kya can stay."

"She is not staying," I growled.

Steve strolled back to his lawn chair, took a long pull from his beer, and then sat. "See ya, losers. Leave the *cute* girl behind."

"Kya is coming with us." I tucked my arm through hers and tried to get her to start walking.

Lucas walked closer to me. "Kya's a grown girl," he said. "She can stay."

I glared at him, every ounce of anger burning through my eyes. "She's leaving."

"She came with me. I'll take care of her." Lucas tried to put his arm around her but I elbowed him in the gut.

"Ow," he said with an oof.

"Cause you're doing such a great job of that already." I pulled harder on her arm. "You've made sure she's in no condition to be left alone with you guys. You redneck with shit for brains."

Kya teetered on her feet, confused, looking back and forth between Lucas and me. "Skanklet. It's okay!" she slurred, wiggling away from me. The towel slipped off again as she staggered. Her bones were liquefied and she wiggled, giggling and slithering. The boy with the phone whooped. I flipped him the finger and reached for the towel and her bathing suit top.

"Party pooper," she said with another giggle.

"Kya," I snapped. "Put your friggin' top back on."

I helped her do up her bathing suit top and Levi held the towel up to block her from the phone perv. Kya giggled. "You're my best friend in the whole world." She kissed me on the cheek and then dirty danced on my leg.

"What did you give her?" I snapped at Lucas. She seemed more than drunk.

Levi pushed him away.

"Beer," Lucas said.

"And a few pills," Steve added from his chair, obviously amused.

"You should try a few, Grace. Might loosen you up a little. You're no fun outside the paintball arena. At least there I can bounce you."

"Shut up, man." Levi took a step toward him but Lucas intercepted him, grabbed his arm, and pulled him back.

"Take your friend and go," Lucas said. "You don't need extra trouble."

Kya started to cry. I put my arm around her shoulder. She smelled horrible. Boozy and cheap.

"Grace. Take me home," she said in a little-girl voice that sounded scared and very un-Kya-like.

I glared at the boys. "You're disgusting," I spit out, eyeing them one by one.

Levi hurried back and put his arm under Kya's. She whimpered and shrank away and he glanced at me for guidance. I shook my head and he let her go.

"Grace. I'm scared," Kya said, wrapping her arms around me. A raunchy song in the background added a sinister feeling to her voice.

"It's okay, sweetie, I'm taking you home." I turned to Lucas. "Asshole," I said through gritted teeth. "You are an asshole."

He blinked, his eyes open wide, contrite.

"I'm sorry." He hurried closer and picked up the towel as it slipped off her shoulders again. He put his arm around her. "Hey, Kya. Don't cry. Why're you crying?" He adjusted the towel over her shoulder and said something in Kya's ear but she only sobbed louder.

"She's not very big, but I didn't know she couldn't handle her liquor," he said to me.

"Not such a tough girl now, is she?" Steve called from his lawn chair.

"I will hose you down the next time I see you," I promised Steve through gritted teeth. As if spraying him down with paint in a game of paintball could somehow help Kya now.

"I'm scared," he said in a taunting tone.

I shot him a look meant to freeze his dark soul, but he merely grinned. Lucas patted Kya's arm but Levi moved in, and this time she let him and he started to walk her away.

"Is she okay?" Lucas asked me.

I glared at him. "Does she look okay to you?"

She looked like a TV with no reception. Broken. I turned my shoulder, cutting him off with my body.

"You should take her home," he said in a low voice. "I didn't know they gave her pills."

"Gee, thanks for the advice. And for taking such good care of her." My mama-bear instincts flared.

"Where're her clothes and stuff?" I demanded. Lucas scooped up her fake Gucci purse and a pair of shorts and T-shirt from the grass and brought them to me, and I joined Levi to walk her slowly toward the gate.

"Where're we going?" she asked. Her shoulders hunched over and her eyes were hooded and glossy with tears. My heart broke for her a little more.

"Tell her I'll call her," Lucas called as we left him behind us.

"Yeah, why don't you not do that," I growled over my shoulder, trying to help steady Kya and walk her to Levi's car.

Between Levi and me, we managed to shove her in the backseat. I leaned down and strapped her into the seatbelt. "I should sit back there with her," I told Levi. "To make sure she's okay." I crawled over Kya and sat on top of the middle seat, tucking myself in beside Kya and fastening my own seatbelt.

She moaned and grunted. "Do you hate me, Gracie? Please don't hate me."

"I don't hate you," I said and she snuggled up beside me, her bare skin hot and her smell rank. She leaned her head back against the seat and closed her eyes. She slurred a few words, but in a matter of seconds, her face went slack and she seemed out.

Levi jumped into the driver seat. "Where to?" he asked, turning his head back. "She going to be okay?" He pulled out of the driveway and drove away from the house.

"I think so. She needs to sleep it off. God, I can't take her home like this," I said. "My parents would have a complete fit. And her parents can't deal with it."

Our eyes met in the rearview mirror. "She can come to my place," Levi said. "There's no one home. We could put her to bed for a while, let her sleep most of it off. She have a curfew?"

A motorcycle roared past and I glanced out the window. "Not really. But she is expected to come home." I thought about his offer and shook my head. "What about when Lucas gets back? I don't want her waking up there. It would be awkward. And no offense, but I don't trust him with her in this condition."

Levi pulled up to a red light and stopped, turning back to look at us. "I'd like to kill him," he said, "for his part in this. But I don't think he would do anything to a girl who was passed out. That's sick."

I nodded as the light turned green and he turned his attention back to the road.

"One thing I've learned is that there's a lot of sick in our world," I said.

We drove in silence for a couple of seconds. "I'm sorry you had to learn that," he said.

I didn't respond, even though it sounded a little like a question. "Can you unroll the windows back here? She stinks."

He pressed a button and opened both windows in the back a smidge and fresh air filtered in.

"She get like this often?" he asked. I heard judgment in his voice.

A spark of defensiveness flared up for my friend. "No. Not like this. Whatever they gave her knocked her out."

Kya snorted a piggish snore as if to agree. Silent conviction floated to the backseat.

"She's a good person," I felt compelled to say, and then a sudden flare of anger sparked up. "And what about you?" I snapped, irrationally angry and directing it at him. "Why're you worried about cops?"

"None of your business," he snapped back.

He took a deep breath then and let it out slowly. "Sorry," he said softly. "I made a mistake. I had some trouble with the cops. I'll tell you about it another time if you want. But this isn't the time or place. This isn't about me." Behind us, a car honked and Levi lifted his middle finger at the driver. "I'm going the friggin' speed limit," he snarled, even though no one could hear him but me.

Remorse washed away my misplaced anger. "I'm sorry. You're

right." I glanced down at my sad-looking best friend. I reached over and pushed back her hair from her eyes. She didn't even flinch. "She's been through a lot. I mean, I know it's not really an excuse. I'd never get this way." I wanted to protect her, but a selfish part of me also wanted to let him know it wasn't something I'd ever do.

"It's okay." But his reflection in the rearview mirror kind of told a different story.

My heart raced. I also wanted him to like me. My mind bounced back and forth. Self-interest. Protection of my friend. Levi. "She was raped," I blurted out.

Then my eyes opened wide and my hand flew up to cover my mouth. My pulse pounded and guilt mixed with blood whooshing to my head. An instant headache blasted me. I stared down at the unresponsive lump who was my best friend, waiting for her to suddenly come to life and crucify me for betraying her.

I'd never told anyone before.

What had I done?

chapter nine

My heart thumped and guilt swirled heavily through my body. My head pounded even harder. The radio DJ chirped at a low volume in the background.

"For real?" Levi asked.

"Unfortunately. Very real." I kept my gaze on Kya but she didn't move. "I never told anyone that before," I said quietly. "I shouldn't have said anything."

My parents knew, but only because they found me a crying mess in my room after the trial. I'd never told another soul. Yet, with this boy I barely knew, the secret spilled out.

My face burned. I pressed my lips tight, placing my hand protectively on Kya's arm, though she was completely unaware. Her head tilted back, her lips were open with drool coming out one side of her month.

It wasn't the image of the girl I loved. But. It also was. I swallowed an incredibly powerful urge to cry.

"Man." Levi swore under his breath. "I'm sorry."

An overwhelming need to talk brought tears to my eyes. "It happened before we met." I stopped. Waited for something bad to happen. I half expected Kya to open her eyes and scream at me. But there was nothing. No repercussions.

"It's okay," Levi said softly. "If you want to talk."

I took a deep breath. Maybe it was because we weren't facing each other, or maybe I trusted him. I did. I wanted to talk.

"When we were fifteen, she asked me to come with her to the rape trial. She'd only been thirteen when it happened. I'd had no idea." I took a deep breath. "She didn't cry. She pretended it was no big deal. She said she'd never told anyone else. Not James. None of her friends. Just me."

I paused, closing my eyes to keep tears inside. Flashes from streetlights danced like tiny fireworks under my eyelids.

"I'd do anything to protect her."

He nodded his head. "I get that, Grace. I do."

I took another deep breath and continued, "It was awful, the trial, but at the same time, I was so proud of her for taking him to court. She tried to keep it from happening again. It took a lot of bravery to do that."

"It must be hard," he said. "Keeping her secret."

"No. It's not. I'm her best friend."

Silence.

"I can't believe I told you," I finally said softly. "Please, don't say anything. Especially to Lucas. No one knows. Not even James."

He looked at me in the rearview mirror. "You have no idea how good I am at keeping secrets."

Something about his attitude, something in his voice, made me want to cry again and my breathing came out in short panicky hiccups.

"Seriously, Grace. Trust me."

"Okay." And for whatever reason, I did.

Silence hung thick in the air.

"It makes more sense now, why she kind of went off the rails today," he finally said.

"Yeah." I glanced out the window as we passed by a mostly abandoned strip mall. Real estate signs littered weedy grass in front of it. "The worst of it is that the guy got off light." I looked back to Kya. Sprawled out, looking half-dead in her bikini. She was a mess. But how could I blame her? "He wasn't convicted. He was put on probation, but only for statutory rape."

Levi shook his head slowly back and forth.

"She'd had a fight with her dad on the way to their cottage."

Kya made a noise and rolled her head to the side. I touched her shoulder. She groaned but didn't wake up.

"Anyhow, she'd demanded to be let out. To walk the last mile. So her dad pulled over and let her out. It was cold and she had on a thin hoodie. He'd wanted to teach her a lesson."

Levi didn't say anything but whistled between his teeth.

"It wasn't the lesson he intended. I mean, even now he can't deal with it. Her dad sold the cottage. Her whole family is a mess. Her mom hardly talks and she gained, like, a hundred pounds. Her sister moved out. Her dad is angry all the time and never without a beer in his hand. Kya pretty much does whatever she wants and they don't say a thing about it."

I caught sight of a big white house on a corner. We were close to my street. "Would you mind driving around for a while? To see if she comes around?"

"Sure," he said. "Of course." He made a sudden turn to a street leading in the opposite direction and Kya's head rolled again. I moved it so her neck wasn't at such an odd angle.

Levi slowed the car down, someone honked, and he swerved to the right.

"Jerk! Sorry. You guys okay?" The passing lights lit up his profile. He had beautifully shaped lips and an interesting nose. Kind of bumpy, but it suited him. Embarrassed by my thoughts, I glanced down at Kya.

"Yeah. Fine."

Kya and I never talked about the rape. Or the trial. The only time she brought it up afterward was to tell me that he got off. I reached for her hand, but it was limp and she didn't move or respond to my touch.

"At the trial, he told the judge he turned to religion," I told Levi softly. "He talked about all these great things he'd done in the name of God since the 'incident' two years before. As if that made a difference."

Kya's head flopped to an uncomfortable angle again and hair caught in her mouth. I fixed her. She reminded me of a sleeping little girl, a hurt little kid acting out. I blinked back new tears. I understood. The innocence she'd lost.

"Did she ever get help? Like a psychologist or something?" Levi asked.

I looked up, surprised by his question. "A couple of times. But her dad comes more from the 'suck it up' school of philosophy. She says she's fine, but of course she isn't."

We drove in silence for a while and I saw the old rundown house that James was convinced was haunted when we were kids. I think he still believed. One could never be sure with James. I patted Kya's bare knee at the thought of our friend and it gave me an idea. "Hey, can you throw my purse back to me?" I asked Levi.

"Sure." He reached across the passenger seat, grabbed my purse from the front floor, and tossed it over his shoulder. I pulled out my phone and pressed two on speed dial.

"Do you know where Cowrie Road is?" I said to Levi, waiting for James to pick up the call.

"Turn right on MacLeod to 194th and down past Reesor Park?" Levi asked.

"Yeah. And then turn left at the first stop sign past Reesor Park."

"Hello?" answered James on the other end of my phone.

"James?" I repeated.

"Who you know and love," he answered.

Levi pulled a U-turn at the four-way stop.

"Is your mom sleeping?" I asked, leaning into Kya with the rapid turn.

"Out like an overloaded circuit," James answered.

"Good."

"Good? When did you begin to harbor such dark thoughts about my mom, Graceling?"

"No. I didn't mean it like that. It's…well…Kya."

There was a pause. Then he groaned. "What'd she do now?"

I glanced down at her. "Not sure exactly. Beer for sure, and some pills. She's passed out. We need to take her somewhere where she can sleep it off."

"Good lord, the dereliction is tragically on schedule. Boozy stage. Check. Just what we need…an alcoholic Kya."

"She's hardly an alcoholic." I avoided Levi's eyes watching me through the rearview mirror.

"Give it time. Did you inform her it's not even ten o'clock yet?"

"I said she was passed out, James. So it's not like we're having in-depth conversations about time. It's a long story. Anyhow. Can I bring her to your place tonight? Your mom won't hear anything, right? I thought she could crash there? Sleep it off. If I take her to my place, there will be hell to pay from Mr. George Black." I glanced at the street sign we passed. We were getting close to home.

"How're you going to explain her absence to her parents? I think even they'll notice if she doesn't show up at home." There was an edge in his voice. More than anger.

If anything, it might do her whole family good if I dumped her off at home in her current condition. Make them face the mess. But Kya would kill me. And it wouldn't change anything.

"I'll use her phone and text her mom. Pretend I'm her and say I'm sleeping at Lola's. They won't check."

"And therein lies the key to the problem," James said with a sigh. "Parental neglect."

"I know. But, James. She needs our help."

"She needs psychiatric help."

He didn't know the half of it.

He sighed. "Fine. Bring her over here. But you both owe me."

"You're the best."

"Tell that to my karmic advisor."

I hung up and put my phone away. "We can take her to James's. He lives next door to me. If you don't mind, you can leave me there and I'll pick my car up tomorrow."

I glanced out the window. We were heading toward our street.

"Sure. If that's what you want to do."

I told him where to turn and he pulled up to the front of the house when I pointed at it. "Remember, James doesn't know. About...Kya."

Levi glanced at me in the rearview mirror. I patted Kya's shoulder. "She doesn't want anyone to know."

Except now Levi did.

If he couldn't keep a secret, I was in big trouble.

chapter ten

I banged my fist against James's door while Levi held half-naked and fully passed out Kya across his arms like a little kid asleep from a long car ride.

James opened the door, smiled, and then it faded when he saw Levi holding Kya behind me.

"Seriously?" he said. "She passed out in her bikini?"

"I know. The NCPA would love this."

"Forget your college paintball aspirations, what about my mom?" James said. "Can you put a pair of sweats and a shirt on her? I can come up with a story for her crashing here but not in her friggin' bikini." He shook his head. "She is going to owe me for this. Huge."

He stared at Levi as he spoke.

"Oh, sorry. James, this is Levi," I said.

"One of the merrymakers at Kya's get-loaded fest?" James asked.

"Hardly," Levi said.

"No," I added. "Levi had nothing to do with it. I got a call from her when we were having coffee. Levi was at hot yoga with me. He just moved here." I played with my hair and glanced around the front porch, avoiding James's gaze.

Levi shifted Kya in his arms. "I'd love to do the whole introduction thing, but she's kind of heavy," he said.

"Sorry." I stepped aside and Levi walked past, carrying her inside the house. "James? Where should we put her? Your room?" I followed behind him.

James blew out a puff of air, made a face at Kya, and flicked his hand in the air for Levi to follow him. "God, who cares about the sanctity of my bedroom? I'll have to fumigate it later. This means I get to sleep on the couch. I swear to God, if she pukes in my bed, she is cleaning it up herself."

"Good call," Levi said, and followed James to his room. I trailed behind them, watching as he plopped her on the bed. Kya groaned and then curled over on her side in the fetal position. Her bare butt was practically exposed and I pulled a blanket over her.

James shook his head. "You're aware that most friends don't involve you in their illegal acts. You know that, Grace, right?"

I ignored him and stood looking down at her. "Can you give me a pair of your sweats and a shirt? I'll put them on her," I said without glancing his way.

James pulled some clothes out of his dresser and handed them to me. I looked over at Levi, who was leaning against the wall. James followed my gaze and winced. Levi had slightly wrinkled the Pokémon poster that had been on his wall for as long as I'd known him.

"I'm going to put some clothes on her," I told them.

"Oh." They shuffled out of the room together. She made a couple of whimpering sounds but stayed heavy and limp. I managed to pull pants on her and got a shirt over her head and arms, then tucked her back under the blankets and checked her breathing, wrinkling my nose at the odors coming off her.

I said a silent and quick prayer to God for her in my head. I'm not overly religious. My family goes to church for weddings and funerals, sometimes on Easter or Christmas, depending on the year, but I still had silent conversations with God sometimes. And I figured Kya could use some extra help.

When I walked out to the living room, Levi and James were sitting across from each other on the couches looking uncomfortable. They looked almost little on the oversized leather couch James's dad loved so much. The whole room had sort of a country-western video feel to it. Very much his dad, very little James. In the corner of the room, a dog bed overflowed with colorful flannel blankets.

"Where's Brian?" I asked. Brian was a cute little mutt James adopted in ninth grade, and the love of his life.

"He's in bed with my mom. If she's in bed, he doesn't move from it."

Levi stood when I walked into the room. "I should get going. Among other things, I have a cousin to go home and torture," he said.

"Please do," I told him. James looked back and forth at us.

"Levi lives with his cousin, Lucas," I explained. "The guy Kya was out with."

"You were in the new paintball league yesterday, weren't you?" James said, still sitting rigidly on the couch.

Levi nodded.

"You got your ass kicked," James commented dryly.

Levi nodded again.

"I approve," James said.

Levi glanced down at the dark hardwood under his feet but I detected a smile.

"Levi is a good guy, James. He can't help who he's related to. He helped me find her and get her out of there. She was at Steve Blender's. A mess."

"Kya is becoming very adept at messy."

I gave him a dirty look and turned to Levi. "Come on. I'll walk you out."

"See ya around," he said. James nodded but didn't look up or get up from the couch.

Levi followed me to the hallway. I glanced back toward the living room but couldn't see James from where I was standing. Levi moved around me and opened the front door.

"I'll walk you to your car," I said as he headed outside. I followed, wrapping my arms around myself, shivering. The night air had dipped in temperature as it always did.

"Your friend doesn't like me," Levi said when we reached his car.

"He's pissed at Kya. Not you."

Levi shrugged and reached in his pocket for his keys.

"Anyhow, thanks," I told him. "For helping me get her out of there." I hugged myself tighter. "Try not to judge her too harshly, okay? She had a shitty day."

He reached for the car door and opened it, keeping his piercing gaze on me.

"Please don't say anything," I added quietly. "About what I told you."

"I won't, Grace. I said you can trust me." He leaned on the door and smiled at me.

God. I had to. Trust him.

"You okay?" he asked.

"Fine."

His key chain tinkled in the quiet, cool night air. So tranquil. Innocent darkness that almost softened the harsh realities of what had happened earlier in the night.

"So I programmed my number into your cell phone. I hope you don't mind."

"When did you do that?"

"In the car. I am stealth. Like a ninja."

In spite of everything, I laughed.

"You want me to come by and get you tomorrow, to pick up your car from the yoga place?"

"No, that's okay. My brother can drive me. He owes me for some late-night pick-ups when he had too much to drink."

He smiled, his bright white teeth sparkled, and my heart pitter-pattered. I dropped my glance to my feet.

"Well, let me know next time you go to hot yoga."

I glanced up then and nodded, biting my lip to keep an overeager smile from taking over my face.

"Okay," he said as he slid his long legs inside the car. "I should go." He started up the ignition.

"Thanks again," I said, stepping back and giving him room to drive away. "For helping with Kya."

"You're welcome, Grace," he said softly. He smiled again and then shut the door. I liked the way my name sounded from his mouth. He didn't emphasize the G like most people, but lingered and gave the S sound a long, soft finish. He said it like it was important and rounded out the vowel.

I watched as he drove away, and then, with a sigh, turned and went back into James's house. He was still in the living room plunked down on the couch. It almost appeared to be eating his body. He stared at me when I walked in. "You love him, don't you?"

I frowned, narrowed my eyes, and sat on the opposite couch. There was still a slight warm spot from where Levi had been sitting. "No. I don't love him. I barely know him." I wrapped my arms around my knees and pulled my legs up to my chest.

"Well, you have that look. Kya's look. I've never seen you with it. On you, it's a little scarier." He stood. "You want something? A soda?"

I shook my head, waiting while he stormed out of the living room to the kitchen, but since the entire bottom level of his house was open, I watched him as he went to the fridge. He opened the door and stood in front of it, staring for a moment, and then reached in, taking out a can.

"He probably has a really inferior IQ. With muscles like that," he said when he came back in the living room, popping the lid with the pssst sound.

"You mean Levi? You were checking out his muscles?" I joked.

"No. But he did carry Kya all the way upstairs without even getting out of breath." He walked over and sat beside me. He took a sip from his Mountain Dew. Our favorite.

"And what self-respecting male does hot yoga?" James asked and held up the can to offer me a sip. I took one and handed his drink back. He leaned against the sofa and put his feet up on the coffee table.

"Lots, James. I always invite you to come. And you always say no." I swatted at his legs on his mom's behalf and he dropped both feet to the ground with a loud thump.

"I guess I'm not into public humiliation for my non-flexibility or my physical shortcomings." He brought the soda can to his lips and tilted back his head.

"You're perfect the way you are," I said softly and stood. "I should go home. Be nice to Kya in the morning, okay, James?"

He noisily slurped at his drink. "What if that thought makes me feel queasy?"

"Suck it up, James." I turned back to stare down at him, trying to drill some sense of obligation into him with my eyeballs.

"Why do you always do that?" he asked softly. "Stick up for her? Even when she makes a complete mess of things. Which she is showing exceptional talent for more and more lately."

"She's our friend," I said, hoping he'd take that simple concept and think it over. "Friends are there for each other," I continued, in case he didn't. "Even when they screw up."

"Yeah? I don't know, Grace. I don't know if she even is my friend anymore." He leaned forward and took a coaster from a square stack on the coffee table, placed it down, and put his drink on top. "We don't even talk. The only thing we have in common lately is you."

"You have history. Tell her what you told me. Best friends can call each other on crap, so if she's giving you attitude, tell her. She looks up to you." I smiled but he didn't smile back, so I put my hands on my hips and tapped my toe for effect.

"The only reason she looks up to me is because I am vertically superior."

I took a few steps over to punch him on the arm. Hard. "James. You aren't going to lose her friendship, no matter how hard you try. I won't let you."

"Ow." He rubbed at his arm and made a face at me. "For a little person, you have a big punch."

I made my hand into a fist and held it up. "Don't make me do it again."

"You know what? If you hadn't moved here, I don't know if we would have stayed friends. She'd probably have gotten bored. When we were little, she hung out with me because it made her feel important. You know? She'd fight anyone who said anything. But you came along and kind of insisted we all stay friends." He glanced up at me with a sad half smile on his lips.

"You and Kya would totally still be friends," I said.

He reached for his soda again, avoiding my eyes, and took a long sip.

"It's been the three of us for so long," I said.

"Yeah?" he said with a wry smile at his can of Mountain Dew. "What about buds before studs?"

"But you're not a stud, James," I teased. "So that's okay."

He looked up then with a flash of anger in his eyes. He blinked and it was gone. "Thanks a lot."

I shifted my stance and adjusted my purse. "You know what I mean. You're our guy. "

He rolled his eyes.

I forced out a giggle. "Come on. You want to be a stud? How about we fix you up with Angie Harrison? She's been in love with you since seventh grade."

"Angie Harrison smells like cat litter."

I giggled for real. "Well. They do have a lot of cats at their house."

"Four," he said. "Her little brother told me. And one of the cats is pregnant."

"Hmm. That does seem a little excessive. And kind of sad that a cat is getting more action than we are. Okay. What about Denise Puzey?"

He made a face and we joked around for a minute about possible dates for James. He didn't tease me about anyone I might date.

"I should go," I finally told him. "You'll be okay with Kya?"

"She can stay in the bedroom. I'm not going anywhere near her." He stared down at the floor.

"You want me to walk you home?" he asked.

I smiled. "James. It's like fifty feet away."

"Give or take. Never mind. It's dark out, thought I'd ask." He searched the can of Mountain Dew again as if it held answers to mysterious questions.

"I think I can handle it, but thanks. Dark doesn't scare me. That's Kya's phobia, not mine."

"Wish she was afraid of more useful things. Like alcoholic beverages."

He glanced up then and we smiled at each other, understanding each other without words. I lifted my hand and walked toward the front door. He stood up from his chair and followed me. "Until next time, Grace," he said softly.

I wished again that he understood Kya. It would make life easier for all of us. Fresh guilt hit me about telling Levi. I wanted to tell James, but Kya would sense it on us like a drug dog sniffing out some weed. James wasn't known for his poker face. Me either, for that matter.

The door clicked as he locked it behind me.

chapter eleven

Something pressed on my feet. I opened my eyes to see Kya at the end of my bed, sitting on my toes. Her eyes were wide but dull, as if someone sucked out the sparkly part of her soul. The hair sticking out in every direction highlighted the abnormal paleness of her face. Purple shadows puffed her eyes into slits. Not even Kya could pull off that look. I glanced at my clock on the dresser. Crap. I was supposed to be at Lola's paintball place in forty-five minutes. I'd overslept by almost an hour, probably because I'd tossed and turned most of the night worrying about Kya and distracted by thoughts of Levi. I never usually needed an alarm clock to get up, so I hadn't bothered to set one.

"I woke up at James's," she said, dipping her head and picking at my comforter.

"I know." I pulled my feet out from under her and sat up slowly. "His mom was out. I would have brought you here, but his place seemed smarter. Less trouble for you."

"So it was you who took me there?" she asked in a hoarse and throaty voice. "I wasn't sure. I don't remember any of it." She coughed and it came out like a sob. "Grace, I'm scared."

"Oh, Kya." I leaned forward, trying to hug her, but she turned so I ended up patting her shoulder instead.

"I keep screwing up," Kya was saying. "I don't mean to, Grace. I don't want to. But I keep doing it. I screw up everything."

"You don't," I told her. "You were upset. You drank too much. You'll get past this."

She kept her head down and chewed her bottom lip. "Sometimes I want to feel better, you know. Forget everything." She sighed heavily and dragged her hand over her hair. "I'm so messed up."

I reached for her hand, squeezed it, and glanced at the pictures on my dresser. Framed photos of James and Kya and me. My favorite was a recent snap of Kya and me in our paintball gear, our faces shiny with sweat. She was holding my arm up in victory. We'd won a tournament together.

I put my hand under her chin. "You're going to be fine. I get it, but seriously, from now on, less drinking and more yoga or something, okay?" I smiled and she attempted a smile back, but her lip shook. She gave up, moved her head away from me, and stuck her nail back in her mouth.

I swung my feet over the side of the bed. "Did you talk to James before you left?" I asked. I stood and walked over to my dresser and peered into the mirror above it. I hadn't taken off my makeup, and it smeared underneath my eyes.

"No. He was still asleep on the couch. It was completely silent, nothing from his dog even. His mom must have been in her room. I snuck out and came here. I figured you'd know what happened."

I grabbed a Kleenex, dabbed some lotion on it, and wiped away old makeup. "You could have asked James." I slid an elastic off my wrist and pulled up my hair, wrapping the elastic around it and securing it on top of my head.

She stood up and walked over beside me, glancing in the mirror and sticking out her tongue. "I didn't want to wake him." She went back to the bed and sat on the edge facing me. "James hates me. I don't blame him."

"He doesn't hate you." We both paused as a thump of footsteps walked up the stairs. Kya glanced at my reflection in the mirror and I held my finger to my lips. Since it was Sunday, Mom was probably out running with her training partners, and no way Indie was even close to a conscious state yet. The footsteps walked to the outside of my closed bedroom door and stopped.

"Did my dad answer the door?" I whispered to her.

She nodded.

"What'd you tell him?" I whispered.

She shook her head. "Nothing. I asked if I could go up and see you," she whispered back.

"You girls okay in there?" Dad called from the other side of the door.

Kya and I stared at each other. I heard the other things he wasn't saying. Why had Kya shown up at our door this morning looking like hell? What was going on? Did we need him to help?

"We're fine, Dad," I called.

"I'm okay, Mr. B," Kya called out, and the forced bravado and fight for normalcy in her voice broke my heart a little.

"You're sure?"

"Kya had a fight with her dad," I called to my dad, blatantly lying. "She's all right."

I could almost hear his brain working on the other side of the door. No way had he missed that Kya reeked of old booze. He didn't move away. "Can I do something to help?"

"We're fine, Dad." I knew he didn't believe me. He may have retired from the police force, but he still had his instincts. He usually knew when I was lying. It used to be always, but as I got older, I was better at it. It wasn't something that made me particularly proud.

He cleared his throat. "Aren't you supposed to play with Lola at the Outdoor Palace today?" he asked. He was right, but if I didn't leave in the next few minutes, I'd miss the practice. What I wanted and what Kya needed tore at me.

I paused, avoiding Kya's gaze. "It's okay, Dad. They've got enough players for two teams. And it's a practice, not a game."

He was silent for a moment and his self-restraint drifted under the door. "You're not messing things up for them?" he finally asked.

"No, Lola's running drills today. She can play if she has to," I called.

"She'll be pissed off," he muttered.

Kya and I stared at each other until his footsteps walked away from my door.

"Shoot," I said. "She is going to be pissed."

Kya's eyes filled with tears. "I'm sorry, I'll go."

"No, no, it's okay." I said, reaching to hug her. Kya needed me more.

She wiped under her eyes. "My mouth tastes like I've been licking clay, and my head pounds worse than Indie on his old drum
set." Fortunately for all of us, Indie's rock-and-roll wannabe stage
had ended a few years ago.

"More reasons not to drink."

The remorse in her eyes made me feel like I was flaunting my
moral standards at her, which would be okay except she was in kind
of a vulnerable state. In my heart, I'd already forgiven her for messing up, but I sighed. I'd definitely be missing Lola's practice today.

I went to grab my purse from the wicker chair in the corner and
pulled out my phone. "I'm going to text Lola and let her know
we're not going to make it."

She blinked and concentrated on nail chomping. "You sure? You
could go. Your dad's right. Lola will be pissed. I don't care, but I
know you do."

"It's okay." I turned the phone on, staring at the screen saver, a
picture of Kya, James, and me, our heads mushed together, goofy
wide grins on our faces, our arms wrapped around each other.

I hesitated. Lola would be pissed at me for jamming last minute.
She'd wanted to coach me on my snake-side crawls today. She had
plans to round me out so I could play the whole paintball field. At
one time, Lola had focused more on Kya, but she'd switched more
to me.

I was an honest player, like Lola. We wouldn't slide or dive to
wipe off a paintball hit if we could get away with it. Kya would,
given the opportunity. Lola and I both played to win, and we
played tough, but we played clean.

"I can tell by your face you want to go. It's okay. I'm fine," Kya stood up but her voice was low, her eyes on the floor.

"Sit down. You're not fine." I punched out a quick text to Lola and then put my phone away. I walked over and sat on the bed beside Kya.

"What happened?" I asked softly.

She didn't say anything for a minute.

"It's okay," I whispered. "It's me."

"He did it again." Her voice was robotic.

"What do you mean?" I asked slowly.

She sniffled. "Another girl. Someone else. A girl called my house," she said in an exaggerated whisper. "He goes to the same church as her. Mr. Born Again. But he raped her. Her lawyer dug up my name. He wasn't supposed to do that, Gracie. But he did. People do bad shit all the time, but lawyers? The girl tracked down my number." Her voice was slow.

"Oh, sweetie," I said. "I'm sorry."

Sorry that the girl called. Sorry he did it again. Sorry he existed.

I remembered his face clearly. The way his voice squeaked at the end of his sentences when he was in the witness stand. His phoniness when he praised God. As if that would change what he did to my best friend.

Kya sighed and wiped under her eyes, sniffling and trying to get herself under control. She shook her head back and forth. "God." She dipped her chin to her chest. "What did I do, Skanklet? Last night? How did I end up at James's?"

She closed her eyes and rolled her neck to one side. And

then to the other. I waited. She seemed to be talking to herself. Not me.

"I remember calling you from Lucas's," she continued. "Then the last thing I remember is leaving with him and his friends." She made a face. And then nothing. "Ugh. Steve Blender was there. And I was being nice to him."

I nodded. "I know. We came and picked you up. You were at Steve's house."

She coughed. "I was at Steve's? I don't remember. I don't even remember you picking me up."

"Not surprising. You were out of it. You passed out on the way home."

She groaned and covered her face with her hands.

"In your bikini," I added.

She groaned again. "James must be so pissed at me."

I stood up again, went to my dresser, pulled open a drawer, and perused my sock choices for the day. "He's okay. I mean, he wasn't happy, but I called him at home and his mom was on her meds and out, so he said it was okay." I pulled out a pair of pink Angry Bunny socks, a gift from James.

Every year at Christmas, my family and I tried to outdo each other with outrageous socks. Another weird Black family tradition. James joined in the year after I bought him skeleton bone socks. Kya had rolled her eyes and stayed out of it.

"I didn't want to bring you here." I glanced toward my door. "You were out of it. Would have caused problems for both of us. Anyhow." I sat down beside her again and pulled my socks all the way up to my knees. "James was totally there for you." I punched her gently on the arm and she flinched. "Even though you were a sloppy mess."

She closed her eyes, breathed heavily, and then opened them.

"So you and James picked me up? How'd you find me?"

"Uh." I swallowed and pretended to be interested in the stubby length of my nails. "James didn't pick you up. I was with Levi."

"Lucas's cousin, Levi?" She nibbled her thumbnail and tilted her head, thinking it over. She squinted at me. "I remember seeing him at Lucas's house. He lives there, right?"

"Yeah. He's staying while his parents are in China."

"That's the we who picked me up?"

I nodded.

She pulled her thumb from her mouth. "Explain."

"He was at hot yoga at the same time as me." I didn't mention that he'd planned it. "We had coffee after and I was with him when you called. He told me he saw you, so we went to find you, but you weren't there. He guessed you were at Steve's and we drove over and found you." I glared at her. "A drunken mess."

She shook her head. "You were having coffee with Levi?"

"That is hardly the point. How on earth did you end up at Lucas's house in the first place?"

"I gave him my number yesterday. When you and James were stuffing yourself with Nerds. He invited me over. Bad timing." She paused. I thumped my foot against hers. "I mean, because I went over right after the call from that girl. I mean, it wasn't his fault that I got so wasted. After she called, I wanted to forget everything."

She sighed. "I guess I succeeded." She lifted her thumb back to her mouth and pretended to study the posters on my wall, even though she'd been in my room a million times and had given me half of them for birthday or Christmas presents. The Fat Lady Charms, the Femmes Fatales.

"You think?" I mumbled. "I covered for you with your parents by the way. Texted your mom with your phone, said I was you and that you were staying overnight at Lola's place."

She nodded and glanced at me with a tiny smile of thanks.

"You always do things big, you know that, right? Do me a favor and don't get that loaded again. Okay? You had me so worried." I stood up then and walked back to my dresser, pretending to look for something on top of it.

She laughed, but it morphed into an odd sound, closer to a sob. "I'm scared, Grace. I don't even remember leaving or anything."

I didn't tell her it was probably just as well. I wasn't going to overload her with images of what she'd been doing when I found her. Not right now anyhow. It could wait.

"One of those assholes gave you pills." I told her. I reached for my hairbrush and pulled it through my hair, watching her in the mirror.

"Really?" She scrunched up her nose. "What was it?"

"I have no idea. You're lucky you didn't end up in the hospital or something. Dead. And you know how much I hate wearing black." I plunked down the brush and spun around.

"Okay, Mom."

"I'm serious." I narrowed my eyes. "It washes me out."

She flopped down on her back, her arms out as if she were making an angel impression on my bed.

I walked over and stood looking down at her. "Steve has a huge freaking house with a pool. That's where we found you."

"Steve has a pool?" She sat up and held out her arms for a hug. I sat down and she collapsed against me, covering her face.

"That's not even close to the point." I tried not to inhale too deeply. She really was rank.

"I know. But it makes me hate him even more. Who has a pool in Tadita?"

"Still not the point. Don't go near there again, okay? He's a total pig. I plan on giving him a good hose-down next time we play paintball."

"I'll help."

"Yeah, you will." I gently pushed her back. One of the first times I'd ever broken a hug first. "No offense, Kya, but you stink."

"I know. I'm even kind of offending myself." She dropped her head to her chest again and sighed.

"You're lucky we found you when we did," I warned her. She glanced at me, a question burning in her eyes, but I looked away. "Steve and his friends are assholes."

"Lucas is a good guy, but Steve. Ugh." She got up from the bed, walked to my mirror, and stuck her nose up to it. "I look like hell."

"What makes Lucas such a good guy?" I asked. "He fed you too much alcohol and he was there when his friend gave you pills."

She picked at her skin. "He's okay, Gracie. He has good manners and stuff." She laughed but it died quickly. "He had no control over my drinking." She smiled but that failed too. "At least he's hot?" she tried.

I pressed my lips tight to keep my opinion to myself. At least with her track record, he wouldn't be around for long anyhow.

"What about you?" She licked her lips and attempted another smile. "You were having coffee with a real live boy? My Skanklet on a date." The grin didn't reach her eyes and she rubbed her temples with her fingers. "God, my head hurts."

I gave her a dirty look.

"No, no, it's good. He's cute. And your type? I mean"—she paused—"do you even have a type? He sucked at paintball."

"He was better than Lucas." I pretended to study the poster of Keely Watson, my favorite paintball player of all time.

"Oh my God, look at your face. You do like him!"

"I do not." I covered my warm cheeks with my hands but didn't even convince myself.

"I want to be happier for you, I do, but it's hard to process the fact that you had a date."

"Thanks," I said dryly.

"You know what I mean. You're the pickiest person in the world." She puckered her lips up and made kissy noises but it was half an effort. "Did he kiss you?"

"We had coffee." I glared at her. "And then we had to leave to go on an adventure to find you, remember? Not terribly romantic, rescuing your drunk friend."

Her face crumpled.

"Sorry," I said. "I mean, it's true. But I didn't mean to sound so bitchy about it." We both stared down at our feet. After a pause, I said. "He's a nice guy." I was throwing her a bone to ease the tension a little.

She smacked me on the arm, leaving an imprint of fingers. "Well, that's practically a declaration of love for you." Her voice reeked of forced cheer, both of us trying to act as if everything was fine.

"Hardly." My stomach swooped though, thinking of Levi.

"Well, it's weird, right? The whole cousin thing. Maybe we can double-date!" She grinned as I bounced up off the bed, not wanting to even go there in my head. Kya tilted her chin up, watching me. "Well, it's good. I mean kind of serendipitous. He led you to me, after all."

"God looks after drunks and fools," I said, repeating one of Dad's favorite quotes. He'd seen a lot of weird stuff while he was a cop.

"I guess I qualify for both."

I smiled and patted her shoulder. "Temporarily. I mean, at least you were being watched over."

She grabbed the neck of James's oversized T-shirt she wore and peered under it at her bathing suit. "I guess Levi doesn't have a great first impression of me." She winked but the sickly look on her face detracted from her attempt to joke. "Unless he likes drunken girls in bikinis."

"Who doesn't?" He'd seen more than her swimsuit. I leaned close to her, pressing my shoulder against her, ignoring the fumes wafting off her. She rubbed at her eyes.

"James, for one." She ran her fingers through her hair and shook her head. She plopped her butt down into the beanbag chair in the corner of my room by the dresser. "God. I don't even remember being at a pool. I'm lucky I didn't drown."

"I don't think you actually got around to swimming." An image of her on the chair dancing and taking off her top made me cringe. "What happened, Kya?" I said quietly.

She shook her head and pressed her eyes shut. "God, Grace. I don't want to talk about it."

"Kya? You need to deal with this. And not this way." I lifted my hand up and tilted my head back, pretending to chug a drink. "Talk to me." I said. "Please."

She sighed so deeply it seemed to come from the bottom of her toes. She closed her eyes and tipped her head back against the beanbag chair. She swallowed and blew out a breath of air.

"I knew he was going to do it again. Because he got away with it once. The girl was crying on the phone. But she sounded hopeful that she'd make him pay. You know?" She shook her head, but her eyes stayed closed.

I went to the beanbag chair and crouched down beside her, but she pulled away from me. I plunked my butt down on the floor across from her.

"I told her never to call me again. I can't help her. I don't know legal stuff, but I know what they said. That it was my fault. I was found guilty. Not him."

"It was not your fault!" My voice came out in a furious yelp. I swallowed and took a breath. "Kya, I'm sorry this is upsetting you. But it was NOT your fault."

She tucked her hands under her legs. "Honestly, I don't want to talk about it anymore." She shook her head, closing her eyes again.

I sighed. "Okay. But you know I'm here. Always, right?"

She nodded, chomping her bottom lip. Then she lifted her chin and opened her eyes. "I should probably get home." She looked down at herself. "You told my parents I was at Lola's?"

I nodded.

"Then I probably shouldn't go home wearing James's clothes. That would require an explanation and I am far too hungover for that. Can you lend me something to wear?"

"Sure." I went to my dresser to pull out some clean clothes. "You should probably shower too. Get rid of some of that stench."

I pulled out a pair of yoga shorts and a tank top.

"And you need to go over and thank James later." She shrugged and I gave her the evil eye as I thrust my clothes into her arms. "I want you two to make up."

She rolled her eyes. "I'm sick of his shit."

He said the same about her. A little more eloquently perhaps, but the same message.

"Yeah, well, he's sick of yours too. You forgive friends for their shit. That's what you do."

She cleared her throat. "I hate how he looks down on me. He gets his jollies making me feel stupid. I'm sick of it. I'm sick of him." She tugged at her hair and shifted back and forth on her feet.

I wasn't about to let her escape yet. "He doesn't look down on you. He loves you." I stared at her, trying to get her to look at me. She owed me her ear for a moment at least.

"Grace, he's frickin' pretentious and he's getting worse. All he does is try to talk over people's heads. Use his big words to make himself sound smart. He likes to put me in my place." The anger in her voice stirred up my own.

"Your place? You don't have a place. James doesn't think that way."

"Not about you. He thinks you're closer to being his intellectual equal."

"Kya." I squeezed my hands into fists and my voice came out deeper than usual.

"Forget it. I don't want to talk about James." She licked her lips and avoided looking into my eyes.

"He was there for you last night."

Her eyes flashed and she finally met my gaze. "Was he? Or was he there for you? I think he only let me stay so you would be happy."

I threw my hands up in the air. Given her current mood, it wasn't the time to argue James's insecurities versus hers. "Go get in the shower before Indie gets up." I pointed at my door.

She shuffled out of my room, clutching the clothes in her hands as if they were a security blanket. She looked like a little kid, trying very hard to be brave.

I grabbed my laptop, flipped it open, and logged on to the Internet. Levi's name may have been typed into the search engine.

When Kya came back to the room, I slapped the cover down. She looked slightly better, with some color back in her cheeks. Wet hair made her look less shriveled and dehydrated. She tossed her bikini and James's clothes on the floor and sat on the edge of my bed.

"Gross. Put that in my laundry basket."

"You throw your clothes on the floor all the time."

"Yeah, but they're my clothes. Aren't you the neat freak in this relationship?"

Kya picked up the clothes and tossed them into my laundry bin. "You're right. I'm not myself."

She sat on my bed with her legs crisscrossed and stared at me. "Do you think your dad would let you get a tattoo?"

I stared back. "Out of the blue much?"

She didn't glance down or look away from me.

"That's what you were contemplating in the shower?" I asked. "Not regret or thankfulness at how lucky you are to have me looking out for you?"

"Trust me. I have enough regret for both of us." Then she grinned. "You know I love you. That's why I was thinking we should get tattoos. Because we're always there for each other. Thick and thin." She raised her eyebrows. "So? Do you think you'd be allowed?"

I smirked. "Have you met my mom? Or my brother?"

She squished up her nose and nodded. A sleeve of tattoos covered Indie's arm. Mom had small tattoos on her shoulder and wrist. Surprisingly enough, it was my dad who was overly conservative about tattoo ink.

"I know. But would they let YOU get one? You know your dad. Different rules for you and Indie."

She was right, but at the reminder, I snarled. "I can totally get one."

"Yeah?" Her grin reached her eyes for the first time that morning. "What if we do it this summer? To mark our last year before college." She pointed at her wrist and then grabbed my wrist and held it up. "Right here. Matching ones."

I gently pulled my hand back. "I'm not sure about self-inflicted pain and all that."

"Come on, Skanklet. You take paintball hits like they're nothing. You could handle a few needle pokes. We'd get something meaningful. Best friends. Buds before studs." She grinned even wider and it looked like my friend was back, a thousand percent better than when she'd walked in my room this morning. "BBS. In a fancy font. I'm totally making an appointment."

I smiled, but it was forced. There was desperation behind her giddiness, as if she needed me to prove I'd be there for her. Even when she screwed up, I had her back. I didn't necessarily need ink to remind me.

"I'll think about it," I told her.

She squeed, because with her track record, she'd pretty much proved she could talk me into anything. "You'll be eighteen soon, so asking your dad is formality. I'll book at the Inkpot and get Wouter. He's the best."

I shrugged. "Why don't you go home and get some more sleep before booking tattoo appointments?"

She rolled her eyes but pushed off the bed with a lighter step. She danced to the door and glanced back over her shoulder. "Buds before studs. Right, Grace?"

I lifted my fingers, twisted them together, and held them in the air until she breezed out the door. The empty space still smelled like shampoo. I stared at the void and a surge of protectiveness filled my chest. The pain from a few needles poking permanent ink in my body wouldn't hurt as much as what she had to deal with every day of her life.

She pretended to be tough. What happened to her was more permanent than a tattoo. She could never have the memory of the rape removed from her body.

A few minutes later, Dad knocked and stuck his head inside my room without waiting for an answer. He stared at me for a long moment and I barely resisted confessing everything I'd done wrong since I was ten years old. He was that good at the stare.

He nodded once though, releasing me from his gaze, and glanced down at his watch on his thick and hairy wrist. "You missed time with Lola."

"I know." I sat up and swung my legs over the end of the bed. "It wasn't a game. Just a practice."

"Just? I have a feeling you wouldn't have missed if it wasn't for our friend Kya. Did you call Lola at least? Let her know you wouldn't be making it?"

"I texted her." I stared at him, hoping he'd take the hint and leave.

He pressed his lips tight, and then he lifted his eyebrows to make me baste in my own sweat. Fortunately, dealing with parental guilt was old news for me. Practice makes perfect. Cliché. True.

"Is everything okay with Kya?"

Lying or making up a story wasn't how our relationship worked, but he also didn't need to know all the details. I pressed my back against the bed. "She's okay." Honesty was the best policy. He'd forgive a lot more with the truth. "She had too much to drink last night so she stayed over at James's. She felt terrible when she got up and wanted to talk. So you know. Lesson learned and all that."

Dad gave out lectures about the perils of being lured into drugs and drinking the way other dads gave out weekly allowance. Years of seeing too much as a cop.

He pushed the door open wider and leaned his hip against it. "I hope so." He sighed. "I worry about that girl."

Me too, I thought. "She'll be okay, Dad."

He pressed his lips tight. "Did she black out?"

I cringed and wondered for a second about the bliss of having a parent who lived in denial and believed if you didn't talk about things, then they weren't happening. That might be nice at times.

"She got some upsetting news and went a little overboard. That's all."

"You let her off too easy, Grace. She kept you from making a commitment. I know how much you want to play with the Grinders. You don't want to miss opportunities because of your friend." He paused and I could tell he was holding back his investigative skills and need to dive in with a lot more questions.

"She wants to play too. But, well, the guy who raped her. He raped another girl." I caved before he cracked me on his own.

He inhaled sharply and his ears turned pink. He rubbed at the stubbly grey hair he still wore in a military-style cut.

"The girl called Kya. She wanted her to talk to her lawyer. Kya said no."

He scratched more at his scalp. "Poor kid," he said. "I wasn't expecting that."

JANET GURTLER

I nodded. "Neither was she. So, you know. I kind of had to talk to her."

"I feel for her, I do, but you know you have to make decisions based on what you want from life too. There're better ways of handling things than getting drunk, right?"

Did I mention my parents hand out opinions like candy on Halloween? Free and in fistfuls.

"Preaching to the choir, Daddy-o."

He moved his fingers down and grazed at his chin. "I hope so, kiddo. You can be there for your friend, but don't let her, you know, steer you in the wrong direction."

"You know me, Dad. Nerd, through and through."

He pushed his hip off the door and reached for the door handle. "Nothing wrong with being a nerd. Except you're not. You're too beautiful to be a nerd."

I smiled. "Thanks, Dad." He was kind of non-objective, considering his role in creating me and all, but still. It was nice to be called beautiful. Even if it was from my dad. He closed the door softly behind him.

I glanced at my alarm clock and then grabbed my purse. I reached inside. I wiped my sweaty palms on my pj bottoms and took a deep breath.

My heart pounded at the thought of what I needed to do.

chapter twelve

The phone looked innocent. We were on pretty good terms as far as inanimate objects went. It couldn't hurt me.

There were other choices of course. I could text Levi. Reaching him that way would be easy too but would also leave physical evidence. I didn't want my words intercepted by someone else. At least, that was my story, and I was sticking with it.

I took a deep breath and picked up the phone, noticing fingerprints on the screen. I contemplated searching for Windex as my stomach fluttered with nerves, excitement, and dread.

Hello, I mouthed to myself. This is Grace. Grace Black. Arrgh. As if Levi knew a million Grace Blacks in Tadita. I took a deep breath, tapped my contact list, and scrolled to L. I tapped on his number. Waited.

He picked up on the third ring.

"Levi? Hi. It's Grace. Uh. Grace Black." Ugh. I rocked back and forth on my sit bones and called myself names in my head.

"Hey, Grace." His voice rumbled out, low and sexy, over the line. Sexy invited lusty.

I managed to make small talk for exactly two full sentences. Then there was an uncomfortable pause.

"I'm glad you called," he said into the uncomfortable lull, his voice sending shivers up my arms.

"You are?" *Do you like me? Do you want to kiss me? God. I want to kiss you.* "I mean, I'm glad. I, uh, wanted to call and talk to you to make sure, you know, that what we talked about last night…uh, stays private." My cheeks flushed from my efforts and I prayed he couldn't tell what I'd really been thinking.

"No worries, Grace. I got it. Like I said, you can trust me."

The warmth in his voice made me want to dance around the room. This wasn't supposed to be about me crushing hard on Levi. Or imagining us hooking up. This was a serious matter about my best girlfriend.

"Thanks. I just want to make sure. Kya was really out of it and not herself, and that's kind of why I said something. It's super private."

"It's okay."

"Good." I paused and then plunged on before it got awkward again. "She came to see me this morning. Straight from James's. She's okay. You know, hungover and stuff, but she'll live." I closed my eyes, wishing I'd stayed quiet.

"Good," he said. "Not the hangover. But that she'll live." I heard a smile in his voice.

"Yup," I said. And then my mind blanked. It turned off and there it was, another awkward pause. I wasn't used to calling boys. Kya said I was too picky, as if she didn't realize most of the boys wanted her, not me.

Why hadn't I texted? Dork. I was a dork.

"Hey, Grace?" Levi said.

"Yeah?" I managed.

"Do you want to go out sometime? With me? Like to a movie or something?"

I let out the breath I'd been holding. Even his Canadian accent—"oot"—was adorable.

"I love movies," I said solemnly.

"Me too." The smile in his voice unfroze my facial muscles. "Do you work tonight?" he asked.

"No." I had to work hard not to let the happy dance going on in my head show in my voice.

"Would it be weird if I asked you out tonight?" he asked.

"No. It wouldn't be." A giggle escaped. "Tonight would be great."

"Cool. What's playing that you want to see?" he asked.

We chatted about movies and then he arranged to pick me up. I hung up and threw my phone on the bed. Totally uncool and not sophisticated, I squealed like a four-year-old and then covered my mouth with both hands.

I was going to a movie with Levi?

My phone rang again. I looked at caller display and picked it up, grinning from ear to ear. "Skanklet Black's Hangover Cures," I said to Kya.

"Grace." Kya's voice was heavy and hoarse with emotion. "Can you come over? I need to see you." She sniffled. "Now."

chapter thirteen

The front door of Kya's house was unlocked. "Hello?" I called into the foyer, but no one answered. The clock in the front hallway ticked ominously.

I closed the front door behind me, slid off my flip-flops, and hurried down the hall. I knew the layout of her house as well as my own. I ran to the kitchen but she wasn't in there. "Kya?" I called.

Spotting a large piece of white paper stuck on the fridge under a cowboy hat magnet, I moved closer. A messy handwritten note was scrawled on the paper.

Dad and I have gone to Patty's. Home later.

The note burst with emotion and love. Not. Sighing, I went to the living room but she wasn't there so I dashed two by two up the stairs and hurried down the hallway to her room.

I knocked but there was no answer, so I pushed open the door. Instead of crazy chaos like mine, her room was pretty much spotless and it always kind of freaked me out. No paintball posters or notes taped to her walls. No clothes spilling out of the laundry basket. Her dresser was neat with only a couple of framed, black and white photos. The floor was spotless. In the middle of the room, Kya curled up on her king-sized bed in a fetal position. She lay perfectly still on top of her comforter. A tiny kid on a giant bed.

"Kya?" I hurried toward her, but she didn't respond. "Kya?" I reached over, grabbed her shoulder, and shook. She'd tucked her whole body into an unmovable ball, and her eyes were squeezed shut.

My heartbeat raced as I shook her again. "Kya?" She didn't move. "Kya. Did you take something?" I yelped, remembering the boy in tenth grade who swallowed a bottle of pills before Christmas. We'd heard he had his stomach pumped in emergency and then was shipped to a psychiatric hospital. We'd never seen him again.

"Kya!" I glanced around for her phone. I hadn't even brought mine.

Something puffed out of her mouth. Part laugh, part cry. "No," she mumbled. "Don't worry, I'm not brave enough to do that."

"That would *not* be brave." I sat on the bed and put my hand on her curled-up hip. "Don't even say that. Oh, sweetie. What's wrong?" I said. "What happened?"

"You mean other than blacking out last night?" She squeezed her eyes tighter.

I scooted closer and reached to smooth her hair, but she turned away and curled up into a tighter ball.

"I hate her. For calling me." Her voice stayed flat. Angry and hollow. "She's brought all this stuff back."

Kya liked to keep tight control. Most of the time. Until it became too much, like last night.

I patted her hip, trying to think of something to say. "You don't have to talk to her. Or do anything." I'd stand in front of an oncoming car to stop anyone from making her say anything she didn't want to. I couldn't hate the girl though. Somewhere, wherever she was, she probably had a best girlfriend who wanted to protect her as much as I wanted to protect Kya.

I hoped so.

"My parents weren't even here when I got home." She shoved her fists into her eyes. "They left. So they don't have to deal." Sniffling, she seemed to struggle to keep herself together. In the ball with her hair messed up, no makeup on, she looked about five years old. I stared down at her, feeling helpless to do anything to take away her pain.

"You're mad they left you alone?" I asked softly.

"It's pretty obvious, isn't it, Grace? They don't want to talk to me. I told my mom about the call and you know what she said? She said 'oh.' And then she said she was sorry and she started to cry and then she went to the kitchen to make a snack. That's when I left. To go to Lucas's. She didn't even ask where I was going."

I sighed.

"And now when I come home, they're not here. Not a word from either of them about the girl. Or asking me how I feel. And you know what? They're going to pretend it never happened. I guarantee they won't say a word about it."

A surge of anger swallowed my sadness. "You can talk to me," I said, even though I wasn't enough. I wasn't what she needed.

She rolled over to look at me. "They've always thought it was my fault."

"Oh, Kya." I reached for her hand and pretended to admire the fresh polish she'd recently painted on her nails. Kya didn't mind repeating the effort to make them look pretty. I kept mine plain and short.

"Your mom and dad feel guilty. They don't know what to do. Or say." We both knew they should be here for her. I wished they were home so I could give them some serious suggestions or physically shake some sense into both of them. I wanted them to tell Kya they didn't blame her. She needed to hear it and they should be smart enough to figure that out.

She picked at an invisible thread in her comforter. "She shouldn't have called. I want to forget."

"But, Kya," I said softly. "You can't make it go away." I squeezed her hand and another surge of anger filled my lungs. I blew out a long, noisy breath, trying to clear the negativity out.

"I never should have gotten out of the car. Or fought with my dad," she whispered.

"It was *not* your fault." My voice came out louder than I intended.

"I do bad things. I'm impulsive. Irresponsible. An accident waiting to happen."

"Kya, you're not. You're amazing. You take big chunks out of life. If I could be half as brave as you are. Half as outgoing…"

She shook her head.

I squeezed her hand harder. "Yes. You're special. Do you know how many people wish they could be like you?"

She snorted. "They don't know anything." She curled back into a ball, so I spooned beside her. I wrapped my arms around her as she shook with her effort not to cry. She let me hold her for a moment and then moved away, flipping onto her back. She stretched out her legs and put her hands behind her head, staring up at her ceiling.

I stretched on my back beside her, staring up at the glow-in-the-dark stickers she'd had for years. She loved stars. When we were young, we used to lie on her trampoline late at night to watch them. She'd point out constellations and James would correct her and tell us the right names. Our legs pressed side by side, hers so much darker and curvier than mine.

"What can I do to help?" I asked softly.

She turned and reached over, touching my hair, tucking it behind my ear. "You already are." We smiled at each other. I pointed up. "I haven't slept over in so long. I'd forgotten about your glow stickers."

"Yeah. Remember how we used to watch them while we told scary stories?"

I huffed. "You didn't tell scary stories. You taught me the facts of life. And ranked all the boys in school."

She laughed. "Yeah. Well. You thought that was scary."

"I still do."

We smiled at each other and stayed on our backs, saying nothing, and then her lips turned up.

"You want to do something tonight?" she asked softly.

I blinked and glanced away, hesitating too long. Thinking of Levi and his invitation to the movie. "Uh. Sure." I could call him. Put it off for another time.

Kya rolled on her side, leaning up on her elbow. "Wait a minute. Look at your face." She sat up. "You're all red! You're supposed to see that guy tonight, aren't you? Levi?"

I stared at the ceiling, not moving. "He asked me to go to a movie, but I can do it another time." I sat up, facing her. "It's no big deal. I'd rather hang out with you. I'll call him"

"No!" She slapped my arm. Hard. "Gracie, look at your face!" I rubbed at my arm and bent my head down, hiding behind my hair. "You're blushing. You like him! Don't you?"

I silently cursed my fair complexion and crossed my legs, running my fingers along my calf. They were prickly. I needed to shave.

"No way!" she shouted again. "You *do* like him."

I opened my mouth to deny it, but I wasn't exactly known for my poker face.

"This is a big friggin' deal," she declared, crossing her arms in front of her and grinning.

I glanced around, looking at anything except her. "It's not. And whatever. I can go out with him another time. I want to hang out with you."

"Nuh-uh." She uncrossed her arms and her body seemed to inflate with new life. "Forget it, Skanklet." In a quick motion, she swooped her legs over the end of the bed and stood. "Oh my God. You're finally going to live up to your nickname. Aren't you?" She clapped her hands gleefully. "And it was supposed to be ironic."

"It's still ironic. Trust me." I gave her a dirty look.

"You are *so* going on that date tonight. And I am going to pick out something fabulous for you to wear."

I protested, but she shook her head. The dead look in her eyes was gone. I decided maybe the distraction was good for her and shut my mouth.

"Lucas texted me earlier," she said. "He asked me to do something with him tonight, so don't feel bad. I'll hang out with him. Surprisingly, he's not mad at me for last night." She frowned for a second, then pivoted and danced toward her closet.

"Mad at you?" I asked. "Why would *he* be mad at *you*?"

"For acting like a freak." She flipped through her clothes, all hung neatly and organized by color.

"You didn't act like a freak. You were upset and you handled it, um, unwisely."

She turned back and rolled her eyes.

"Well," I said. "He kind of helped, don't you think? Maybe you should be mad at *him* for getting you wasted and letting his friends give you pills."

She laughed as she pulled something from the closet. "Don't worry about Lucas. Honestly. He's a nice guy." She pulled out another dress, hung it over one arm, and kept flipping. "I was on a mission and there was nothing he could do about it. But I'm okay now. Really, I am." She glanced over her shoulder and flashed a smile. "I can always count on you to have my back. Thanks."

She returned her attention to the closet and pulled out a couple more items. She waved her free hand at me, motioning at me to stand up. "Don't look so sad. This is fun for me. I like playing dress up. And, I want you to go out with Levi. Because you like him."

"But—"

"Butt," she interrupted, turned, and shook her butt at me the way she always did. She laughed. "I'm totally going out with Lucas tonight. Don't look so darn guilty. You remind me of my mother.

A much thinner version of my mother." She walked to me and held up a blue mini dress. "Wrong color." She tossed it on the bed and held up a similar dress in black. "Too boring." She tossed that one too.

"Are you sure you're okay?" I asked softly as she held up a third selection to me. A bronzy tunic.

She sighed. "I don't want to dwell on it anymore. Okay?"

"But—"

"Butt." She turned and wiggled again. "Seriously. Thanks for listening…but I'm done with that conversation." She held up a short-sleeved blouse, pressed her lips tight, and stood back, contemplating the top. "Yes. This one." I took the hanger from her, held the short-sleeved blouse up to my neck, and looked down.

"Well," I said, not really paying attention to the top. I wished I knew how to get her to open up. "Anytime you want to talk. You know that, right?"

She nodded. "You may have mentioned it once or twice." She turned from me and headed back toward her closet door. "Shoes."

I put the top on the bed. "Are you sure you're up to going out with Lucas? After last night?"

"I feel okay. Like my dad says, the best part about youth is that hangovers don't last." She narrowed her eyes at me and said in a mock angry voice, "You sure you want to go out with his cousin? What do we know about him? Other than he's Canadian. My dad says we shouldn't trust Canadians. All they do is talk about hockey and the weather. And flaunt their cheap healthcare."

"Levi plays soccer," I told her. "Not hockey."

"Oh. Look at you, standing up for him." She got down on both knees and rooted around the closet floor, mumbling as she searched.

"He's a nice guy," I said softly.

"So is Lucas," she said with her head inside her closet.

"So nice he let his friends give you pills?" I didn't add anything about them also seeing her topless I needed to tell her, but it didn't seem like the right time. When she was stronger, I would. Not so vulnerable.

"I like him," she mumbled. "Even though he sucks at paintball, which makes him less of a man in your eyes."

I snorted. "Paintball and boyfriends don't mix. Best to keep those things separate."

"Yeah?" She reached her arm far back in her closet. "Levi plays."

"It's woodsball. Totally different."

"Whatever." She pulled her head out of the closet, holding a pair of strappy silver heels. I shook my head no.

"So this is like your first real date?" she said.

My cheeks burned. "I've had dates," I said.

"Okay. Then how about your first date with a boy who you actually seem to like." She stuck her head back inside the closet. "I can't believe he went to yoga. I can't get my head around a boy doing hot yoga," she said, her voice muffled.

"There're lots of guys in the classes," I reminded her.

"I know. But a guy you're into? It seems, I don't know, kind of girly." She emerged again, glancing at me. "Never mind. Sorry. My dad's influence."

"Since when do you care what your dad thinks?"

She shook her head. "You're totally right. I can't believe he rubbed off." She studied me. "You have a pair of cute black shorts, right?" I nodded. "Perfect," she said. "Short shorts, my blouse, and these shoes and he'll be putty in your hands." She dangled a different pair of heels on her finger.

I wasn't sure I wanted him to be putty in my hands. "No," I said. "No way am I wearing those shoes."

She laughed and got to her feet. "You're such a high-heel virgin."

"Well, my life kind of imitates my shoe status."

She waggled her eyebrows up and down. "Well. You're kind of like a balloon. All you need is one good prick." We both giggled. She smacked her lips together, making a loud popping sound.

"Kya!" I said, and my cheeks warmed.

She grinned. "Look at you. All blushy and nervous. Oh my God. If you're not careful, you're going to lose it very soon." She tossed her shoes back into the closet. "Fine. Slutty shoes, you are banished back to the closet."

I giggled.

"Take the shirt," she said. "But don't get any stains on it," she warned.

"You calling me a klutz?" I wondered if she realized she worried more about her clothes than she did about herself.

"Yes," she answered. "I am. From the day we met and you fell on top of me. Klutz."

I giggled again, feeling a case of the uncontrollable sillies coming on. Where suddenly everything seemed ridiculously funny. The tingling in my stomach was a combination of nerves and maybe anticipation.

"And don't let him get fingerprints all over the front of it. Make him wipe his hands before he touches you." She squinted, trying to look mean and intimidating.

Another giggle exploded from a nervous, giddy place inside me.

She ignored it. "Wear your new pink push-up bra," she commanded. "The one that makes your boobs look big."

"You should wear your sports bra, the one that makes your boobs look small," I told her. Kya rolled her eyes but smiled.

"Lucas'll be all, 'What happened to that righteous rack?'" I snorted, imitating his voice.

She pushed me back on the bed and I laughed harder. She bounced onto the bed, jumping up and down. "Yeah, and Levi'll be all, 'Whoa, she must have had a boob job this morning. Score!'" She pumped her fist in the air and imitated Levi.

"I could get some of those watery, jelly things and stick them in my bra. I think my mom had some."

She made a face. Her family did not have to worry about bust enhancements.

"Those squishy things? She wore them to a party once to prove to my dad that bigger boobs would make her more popular with his friends."

"Did they?"

"Of course."

She laughed. "Figures. So Levi'll be all trying to cop a feel at the movie and then he'll pull out a squishy boob and start screaming

because he'll think your boob job was botched and he pulled it off."
We both laughed harder, the uncontrollable kind that hurts your
cheeks and your belly at the same time. I held on to my side, shaking my head back and forth.

"And his hands would be all buttery and salty from popcorn…
so the thing will stick to it…and he'll be all jumping from his seat,
waving his hands around, and screaming, 'Get it off, get it off,'" I
managed to add in, and we both giggled harder.

"And some guy in the audience will yell, 'Serves you right for
trying to get off during the movie!'"

We laughed hysterically until we were almost crying, and then we
were laughing about laughing and it went on and on.

"I have to pee, I have to pee," Kya groaned, holding her stomach
and jumping to her feet. The look on her face made me laugh harder.

After she ran out of her room, I lay back on her bed, letting my
giggles subside with some last-minute hiccups. I breathed deeply to
get myself back in control.

By the time Kya came back from the bathroom, we were both back
to normal. I slid off her bed. She smiled and reached for my hand.
"He better treat you right or I'll kick his ass all the way across town."

"Tell Lucas the same thing."

She smiled and her cell phone rang. She let my hand go and
grabbed the phone. She stared at it and then made a face and put
it down.

"You going to answer that?" I asked.

She frowned, wrinkled up her nose, and shook her head. My friv-
olous mood faded. I almost stopped breathing. My heart thudded.

"Was it…"

She turned away from me. "No," she said, her voice hard. "It wasn't her. She doesn't have my cell number. You should go. Start getting ready for your big night." She went to her bed and picked up her blouse. "Take care of this," she said and handed it to me. She forced a smile. "Have fun. Don't do anything I wouldn't do."

I let that slide. "You want to come over and eat ice cream and Nerds with me?"

"No. The thought of food makes me sick. I'm going to lie down for a while. Cat nap. Get rid of the last of this hangover."

I turned to leave her room. "Hold on a second," she called. She went to her dresser and opened her jewelry box.

She pulled something out and held up her hand. "Catch. You might need this." She threw something at me. I grabbed it. A square, slippery package. A condom. I screeched and threw it back at her. She laughed as it fell to the floor.

"Have fun," she said. "I want to hear all about it later."

I hoped she meant it. That we'd have a gab session and trade stories about our dates. Then she practically pushed me out the door without another word. I chewed my lip.

I wanted to ask her who was on the phone, but she wouldn't tell me unless she wanted to. No use pissing her off or making her even sadder.

chapter fourteen

I took a deep breath and started down the stairs.

"Look at you!" Mom called from the kitchen sink and wolf-whistled while she washed dishes. She grinned and sang, "You're sexy and seventeen." Then she stopped and sighed as she placed a pan in the drainer. "I remember the days when my arms didn't flop in the air like bloated dead fish."

My toned, muscular arms and shoulders were a secret source of pride for me, but not for the first time, I wished my mom could be a little more traditional, a little less stand-up comedian.

"She looks beautiful," Dad said from his chair in the living room that faced the stairs. The chair was well worn and older than I was and had crackling leather, but Dad came from a long line of men who ruled over a man-chair. No one else sat in it and he wouldn't let my mom replace or refinish it. Even though it was out of place with the new furniture, she'd obviously made peace with the necessity of accommodating it long ago.

"Even though the shorts you girls wear these days are kind of obscene," Dad mumbled, looking at me over the top of his reading glasses.

I reached for the hem of my shorts and pulled down.

"Oh, George, they're no worse than the miniskirts in the seventies," Mom said.

"You were a baby in the seventies," Dad said, rustling around the newspaper he was reading and peering at her over it. "In your teen years, it was grunge."

"I miss my Doc Martens and belly shirts," she said. "No, wait, I miss my flat belly. You should have seen my belly before babies, Grace. You could have bounced a penny off it." She plunged her hands back into bubbles to wash another pot. "Anyhow, George, you should be immune to short-shorts, considering you worked with prostitutes for a living."

"Seriously?" I said to both of them as I stepped onto the hardwood. They looked at me as if they'd forgotten I was there.

"I wasn't the one to imply in any way that you look like a prostitute," Dad said, but he laughed.

"Sorry," Mom said. "You look grown-up. Lovely. Nothing like a hooker." She wiped her hands on the tea towel draped over her shoulder.

"Judith." Dad lifted his paper up in front of his face to hide.

Mom giggled and clapped her hands together. "This is your first date with this boy! Do we like him?"

I refused to play along and ignored her.

"If I was a good mom, I'd turn this occasion into a scrapbook page."

"You burn yourself anytime you get near a glue gun," Dad called from behind the newspaper.

She laughed, probably at the thought of herself armed with a glue gun. Some of her friends had a scrapbooking club and she tried to keep up, but she was hopeless at it.

"Mom! Do not embarrass me in front of Levi." I walked into the living room and plopped down on the loveseat opposite my dad, sitting up stiffly so as not to wrinkle my clothes or mess my hair.

"Oh! We do like him!" Mom threw her hand over her heart and sang out, "Oh Levi, Levi. Where art thou, Levi?"

"Mom." I gave her my dirtiest look.

She slowly stopped laughing and stared at me with a mock-serious expression. "Have I ever in my life embarrassed you?" She dunked her hand back in the soapy water and pulled out the drain stopper.

"Can you try to control her?" I asked, turning to my dad.

He glanced up from his paper.

"Me?" Mom interrupted. "Your dad's the one who's going to give him a pat-down before he lets you get into a car with him."

Dad slowly folded his newspaper and put it down on his lap. "No. I have finely honed self-restraint skills. I'm comfortable with Grace's instincts. If she thinks a boy is nice enough to go out on a date with, then I trust her judgment." He pushed down on the leg rest of his chair and sat up straight. "Besides, I called in a favor with some boys on the force and had a check done on Levi Jordan Lewis. I know everything about him, including the kind of gun he prefers to use in woodsball."

"You did not?" I shouted, wondering if Jordan really was Levi's middle name.

He chuckled and picked up his cup of coffee from the end table beside him and sipped.

I turned back to the kitchen. "Mom! Is he serious?"

"What'd I tell you?" She walked from the kitchen and came and sat on the couch beside me, picking up the remote and switching on the television.

"Oh my God," I yelled. They both looked at me with the same innocent expression.

"Gracie," Dad finally said, and laughter was audible in his voice. "I'm kidding. Indie told me he plays woodsball."

Mom giggled. "Look at your face, Gracie. We're teasing you. Relax."

For a moment, I envied Kya and her uninvolved parents. The doorbell rang. I froze.

Mom jumped up. "Do you want me to answer the door?"

"No." I pulled on her hand and she slowly sat back down. I stopped, turning back. "You two behave," I said in a loud whisper and hurried to the front door. My heart banged around my chest region and I patted my hair, licked my lips, and then opened the door.

"Hi." Levi smiled down at me with his ultra-white teeth. He looked perfect in plaid shorts and a plain white T-shirt. I remembered reading somewhere that impressions were made in the first ten seconds or something. If so, I was a goner.

Thud, thud, thud.

What was it about this boy that made my heart patter like a paintball splat? I leaned in closer so I could smell him. What was I? A dog?

"You look great," Levi said.

I smoothed down the front of my shirt. Kya's shirt. "Thanks." God, I sounded like a dork. "So do you." I held the doorknob for support, trying not to stare at how his thin shirt emphasized his firm chest and stomach. He even had on cool flip-flops. When had I become this shallow?

"Are you going to invite him in to meet us?" Mom called from the couch.

I glanced over my shoulder and gave her my most serious "do not mess this up for me" look.

She smiled and got up and I turned back to Levi. "Come in. I apologize in advance for my parents." I held out my hand, he walked past me, and the scent of fresh soap drifted in the air. Definitely not a good time to imagine him in the shower. Naked. I breathed in deeply and turned, praying for nothing embarrassing to happen.

Fortunately, Mom didn't race to the door giggling or grab her camera to take pics. Instead, she walked over slowly, like a regular person, and shook Levi's hand, acting far more normal than expected. She didn't sing him a weird song or tell him an embarrassing story about me, or even ask him what his parents did for a living. I had to give her credit. She was definitely on her best behavior.

She asked Levi how he liked Tadita and he gave a polite answer. Dad pushed himself up out of his lazy chair and sauntered over to the front foyer, joking about how Levi's head almost hit the chandelier. Since he only had a couple of inches on me, Dad believed he'd been ripped off in the height department. He promised me in his next life he'd be a much taller man.

"You're in our new league at Splatterfest?" Dad asked, though he already knew the answer.

"Yeah. I wasn't very good," Levi answered. "I didn't last longer than a few minutes in any game. It's different from woodsball."

"Well, Grace can give you some pointers," Dad said.

"Maybe Levi doesn't want pointers." I glared at my dad, telepathically telling him to not brag about my aggressive game or how much I loved kicking boy butt.

Levi smiled. "No. It's okay. Maybe I do. I'm more interested in speedball now."

Mom tee-hee'd behind her hand, and the only reason she didn't get a dirty look was because she was standing right beside Levi and he'd see me and might think it was meant for him.

"Well, Grace can help, or Indie, Grace's brother. Or Kya. Maybe we can get you into tournament play," Dad said.

I opened my eyes and shook my head at him. "Don't get carried away, Dad. Levi didn't say anything about tourneys."

The thought of Levi in tournaments didn't appeal to me at all. For once, I wanted to be a girl, not a girl trying to prove I was as tough as a boy was.

"Actually I play soccer," Levi told him. "So I'm hoping to make the school team. Tryouts start next week."

Dad was nodding and about to say something when the doorbell rang and we all turned.

I stared at it without moving. Mom gave me a smile as if I was a slow child, and she squeezed past me and reached to open the door.

"Hello, James!" she said. "Are you coming to call on me?"

From outside, James mumbled something I couldn't hear.

"She has a young man here taking her out for a date. Would you like to come in and duel to the death for the fair maiden's hand?"

"Mom," I groaned and glanced at Levi, trying to convey my horror at the words that came uninvited from her mouth. "She's kidding."

"James," I called, moving my head to peer around my mom's shoulder. "Come on in."

James stepped in the door. His ears were bright red. A whoosh of wind followed him and he pulled the door closed.

"Hey, Grace," he said but his eyes automatically went to Levi. He nodded.

"You remember Levi?" he said.

"Sure."

"'Sup," Levi said.

"The market index is up. The value of the euro is up. And from the look of things, you are up for some serious points for taking care of our damsel in distress. Though with Kya, that's kind of a perpetual state of being. But way to go."

"James," I warned.

Levi didn't bat an eye.

"Hello, James," my dad said. "What did Kya do now?"

"Nothing." James glanced at my dad and then me. "Actually I'm here to see if I could call in a favor." His expression was sheepish. "Again. My mom has a doctor's appointment tomorrow and I totally forgot about it. It's at nine and I'm supposed to work at ten. It should be quick. Just a check-in and a prescription refill. I'd only be an hour late by the time I get her back and everything. I'm really sorry for the short notice."

"I can take your mom." My mom touched his arm and smiled. "Then you won't get in trouble with your mean boss and won't lose any money."

Dad snorted. "If Judith can't make it, you can absolutely take the time. Indie can cover for you. Or Grace." He glanced at me but I rolled my eyes, knowing Mom was on it.

"No, it's not a problem," Mom said. "I'd be happy to take her. We need to catch up."

"That's awesome," James said, staring at my mom with love in his eyes.

I glared at James. "Is your phone broken, James?"

"My phone is in perfect working order, but thanks for your concern, Gracelet." He rocked back on the heels of his Converse runners.

Levi glanced around at all of us, not quite getting the vibes.

"He came in person because he was hoping for snacks," I told him.

"Smart boy. Homemade cookies fresh from the oven," my mom said. I didn't bust her and let Levi know homemade meant premade cookie dough she bought at the grocery store and cut into slices. Everyone else knew.

"I thought I smelled something delicious." James smiled and slipped off his shoes and pushed them to the side with his foot.

"I smell something slightly less appetizing," I said as he slipped by Levi and me and headed to the kitchen.

Dad followed. "I might as well join you. No one likes to eat cookies alone. Get us some milk, would you, James?"

James turned and winked as he headed to the cupboard to grab two glasses. "Don't hate on me for hogging the baked goods."

"That's not what I'm hating on you for," I called.

He grinned.

I turned back to Levi. "Okay," I said. "We should get going or we'll miss the show." I wanted to hurry him out before Mom forced him to sit down for milk and cookies too.

Mom managed to sneak in a few quick questions while I slipped on a pair of sandals with modest heels. James and Dad were in the kitchen scarfing and I waited while Levi finished explaining to Mom why his parents were in China for the year. Finally we escaped.

"Thank God," I said when a door separated us from my parents. Even though it was almost seven thirty, warm air brushed my skin along with the warm breeze. The sun still brightened the sky. I tilted my head back and soaked up the rays.

"Don't worry," Levi said. "They weren't so bad. You're lucky my parents are in China. They'd have dragged you inside and pulled out home movies. We would have ended up eating popcorn and hanging out with them all night."

"Well, I know my mom barely resisted making you sit down for milk and cookies." I smiled to myself because he'd inferred that, if his parents were around, he'd introduce me.

"Well, at least she had your friend to feed." There was a twinge of something in his voice. Jealousy?

"James is a good friend. Though he was kind of acting like a dog marking his territory, wasn't he?"

Levi laughed. "A little." We walked down the driveway toward his car. "I take it he's pretty close with your whole family."

"Yeah. I told you before, he's our third. Mine and Kya's. We've hung out together forever. Kya and James have consumed many empty calories at my house. My mom likes to pretend she bakes and she likes to feed people. James has a sixth sense for knowing when she has something in the oven."

He shrugged. "He's lucky. That's cool."

"Yeah. My parents collect people. James because his mom is sick. And Kya because her parents are idiots."

Levi opened his mouth to ask something when a loud smash came from Kya's house. We both looked over. There was giggling, fumbling, and Kya yelled out, "Oops, I'm a klutz." Then she spotted us. "Hey, Skanklet. Hey, Lucas's cousin!"

Tonight I kind of wished my friends lived farther down the street, maybe even on the other side of town. Kya waved as she walked out of the garage and down the driveway toward us. She had on a loose halter dress and the silver heels she'd offered me earlier. Lucas followed, grinning widely but it looked silly and vacant. I suspected chemical substances floating amid the fluid in his head.

"What's with the noise?" I called.

She giggled. "I tripped over the treadmill Dad bought Mom for her birthday. It's collecting dust and cobwebs in the garage." She threw out both her arms and spun in a circle, laughing. "Remember? It caused a huge fight because she thought he was hinting for her to lose weight." She chuckled, and even though her parents weren't currently on the top of my favorites list, I winced, knowing how self-conscious her mom was about her weight. Lucas laughed and threw an arm around Kya's neck and pulled her close, and they walked toward us.

"Dude," Lucas called to Levi, "look at you. All dressed up." He grinned. "I'll give you a soft six, my friend. Seven if you undo one more button on your shirt."

"It's a T-shirt, asshole," mumbled Levi under his breath.

I seconded his sentiments. They reached us and we were parallel on our driveways, only a strip of yellowing grass separating us.

"What's up?" Levi asked and I could already tell by his voice that he was trying to be polite. He nodded at Kya.

Kya said, "Thanks for looking out for me. I was totally out of it last night."

"Yeah," Levi said. "I got that."

Kya pointed at the two of us. "You're adorable," she giggled. "You two are adorable. All dressed up and going out on a date." She shook a finger at Levi. "You take care of my Skanklet or you answer to me."

"Kya." I sent her a loaded look but the glaze of her eyes suggested neither she nor Lucas were going to notice subtle messages.

Lucas laughed and pulled her tighter to him and they both almost tripped. "You think they're adorable? Then we're hot." He leaned down and kissed Kya deep on the lips, as if they were a couple who'd been together for months. I didn't have to use my imagination to guess what had gone on in Kya's house earlier. Another one of Kya's relationships on speed drive. Premature consummation.

Their lip-lock went on a little too long, and Levi cleared his throat. "Okay. Well. We're heading out to a movie," he said and put his hand on my back.

We walked to his car and he opened the passenger door for me. Kya and Lucas managed to untangle themselves as I lowered myself inside the car. Levi held the door open.

"You're not driving, are you, Lucas?" Levi called to his cousin.

Lucas pulled Kya close, wrapping his arm around her neck. It looked uncomfortable. I was surprised she didn't shove him away.

"Nope." Lucas laughed. "Kya and I are walking to a party a couple blocks away. You two should ditch the lame movie idea and come with us."

"Yeah," Kya shouted a little too loudly. I glanced at the front door, waiting for my parents to stick their heads out to see what the noise was about. "Come on, Gracie, it'll be fun."

"No thanks," Levi said and closed my door.

The window was down though and I shouted out to her. "Don't forget we have paintball tomorrow. Be careful, Kya."

Levi walked around the car and opened his door.

"You too." Kya opened her mouth. "And don't piss that guy off. Lucas said he got in trouble with the police. That he has a temper." Lucas put his hand over her mouth and she laughed and wiggled to get away from him but he pulled her in tighter.

I glanced at Levi as he climbed in the driver's seat, but he appeared not to have heard. He smiled and started up the car.

"Grace!" Kya called. I looked over. She held her hand up in the air with her fingers entwined. "Don't forget."

I lifted my fingers and held them out the window, saluting her.

"What was that?" Levi asked as he backed out of the driveway. I brought my hand back inside and placed it on my lap.

"Nothing." I sighed, watching Lucas and Kya walk arm in arm down the street, leaning against each other for support.

"A secret handshake?" he teased.

I shrugged, bothered by the glassy look in Kya's eyes and her obvious intimacy with Lucas. Already. I glanced sideways. "Best friends."

"Sorry." He smiled. "I didn't mean to sound judgmental. You two seem so…different."

I laughed, but it was unnatural and strained, and sounded off even in my ears. "You mean because she's so beautiful and so… Kya…and I'm her boring tagalong?"

"Whoa." He reached over and tapped my knee with his hand. "Not even close. I don't think you're boring. Not even a little. Getting wasted and, well, whatever she and Lucas are up to. That's not how I see you."

His hand lingered on my knee. I loved it there. I glanced out the window. The breeze blew my hair around. I spotted two little girls on the sidewalk. They were about ten, wore flowing summer dresses, and skipped down the sidewalk hand in hand. Based on their blissful expressions, they were best friends in the whole world. I smiled, wishing I'd known Kya when we were that age. Before boys mattered. Boys other than James. Before that horrible man changed her forever.

"I think there's a lot more to you than you let on," Levi said. "And that's not an insult. I think you're strong and very interesting. No offense to Kya," he added quickly.

He pulled his hand from my knee and I had an urge to grab it and put it back. His words tickled my insides. I felt like it was the first time a boy really looked at me. The real me.

"Kya is strong too," I said. "She's had to grow up fast, deal with stuff. And yeah, she messes up sometimes but she's only trying to deal. You know? Deep down, she's a really good person."

"Well, so are you. Deep down. And on the surface too. Give yourself some credit." He turned on the radio and then adjusted the volume to low. "It kind of seems like you've made it your job to protect her. I hope she knows how lucky she is."

I dropped my eyes to my lap. In some ways, it was as if he'd seen me naked. Somehow, I'd told him more than I intended. Or he really did pay attention.

"Also. Just so you know, you're beautiful too."

I made a face. "I look like Anne of Green Gables. My skin's so white it glows in the dark."

He laughed. "To me, you look like a young Nicole Kidman. And your skin is perfect."

Tingles exploded my entire body, making me feel awkward and tongue-tied. My cheeks warmed. He made me feel mushy and in need of a cold shower. Stat.

"The fact that you don't even realize it." He shook his head and bit his bottom lip. "I'm amazed you haven't been scooped up already."

"Kya's the one everyone's interested in," I managed, my voice husky and unfamiliar to my ears. I glanced at him; his cheeks were blotchy too, and my heart thudded harder. He was embarrassed, putting himself out there. And I admired him even more.

"'Fraid not," he said. "Maybe guys are afraid of you. You give 'stay away' vibes, but trust me, I think you're worth extra effort. And I'm okay with other guys being scared off." He grinned and it was so cute I wanted to lean over and kiss him. Except he was driving. And that might kill both of us. And I'd never initiated anything with a boy in my life.

"No offense to Kya but she's more like an appetizer. You're a full-course meal."

"Wow," I said. "I don't know whether to thank you or be insulted that you compared me and my best friend to food." I dropped my gaze to my hands wringing around in my lap, my cheeks full-fledged forest-fire strength.

He laughed as we stopped at a red light. "You make me nervous. I didn't mean to compare you to food. I know she's been through a lot. But I want you to know, you're more than a sidekick. Way more."

I held my breath, terrified and thrilled. No one else had ever said that. Saw me that way.

"Okay." He glanced over and grinned. "My dad told me that the best way to get a foot out of my mouth is to bite down and shut up." He rubbed the back of his neck. I smiled at him, he breathed out, and the tension in the air shifted. Suddenly I could breathe properly too.

The light turned green and he drove off and we were quiet, but it was a comfortable quiet. He turned right, pulled into the theatre parking lot, and found an open parking spot right away. When he pulled the keys from the ignition, he turned to look at me. "Thanks for coming."

"Thanks for asking."

We were both grinning like idiots as we climbed out of the car.

"So, Kya seems to like your cousin. What's he like?" I asked as we walked across the lot.

"You mean is he a nice guy?" he asked.

I nodded.

"He's okay. I mean, maybe not the sharpest shooter on the paint-ball team. But he's harmless." He smiled down and held out his hand. "Do you mind?"

I giggled like a moron but shook my head. He took my hand in his and rubbed his thumb over mine. The sensation ran from my finger to the bottom of my stomach. I ducked my head down and smiled. An image of Kya's sad face flickered, but I couldn't ignore the immediate pleasure of the boy touching me.

"I think he likes her. I mean, after you told me what happened, I told him not to mess her around. I didn't say why or anything, but told him if he messed her up that I'd punch his lights out. And he assured me he wasn't screwing her around."

I nodded, not yet capable of speech. All I could think about was his hand and mine. The touching.

"You okay?" he asked.

I nodded.

"I gave him shit for letting his friend give her pills. He said he didn't realize it until after."

"Good." I thought about Kya's breakdown and then her giddy happiness with Lucas not so long ago. She was on an emotional roller coaster. Up down. Up down.

We reached the theatre and he held the door for me. "Hey, no offense, but I don't want to talk about your best friend anymore," he said and silently I agreed. "Shall we?"

We walked into the theatre, me floating across the air, believing every girl had to be staring at our hands, jealous of my incredible luck. I glanced around, hoping to see people from school, but of course, nobody was around when I was attached to this amazing new boy.

Levi insisted on paying for my ticket and then reclaimed my hand as we went to the concession line. I offered to pay for the snacks but he insisted.

I didn't argue and waited in line with him, disappointed when he had to let my hand go to grab the large popcorn and supersized drinks. He grinned and handed me a huge box of Nerds.

"How'd you know?" I gushed as he handed the Nerds to me and my grin expanded even wider.

"I pay attention," he said as we walked into the theatre.

We sat close to the front.

"So you and Kya have paintball tomorrow?"

I nodded. "A tourney. At the Outdoor Palace."

The lights dimmed and coming attractions appeared on the screen. When the movie was on, I managed to laugh when I was supposed to. I ate my Nerds and popcorn but my entire focus was on the friction in the air between our knees. My body tingled with awareness with Levi sitting so close to me. Our arms touched on the armrest and I missed the gist of the movie. When the credits rolled, I had little idea what it had even been about.

"Did you like it?" Levi asked as we stood.

I nodded and it wasn't a lie.

"Me too." He placed his hand on my back. I wanted to take his hand but was too shy to make the move.

We walked out of the theatre into dark but warm night air. He held the car door for me when we reached it.

"I want to get to know you better," he said as I crawled back inside his car. It both thrilled and terrified me. In a weird way, it almost made me feel like I was cheating on Kya. It was a completely different dynamic. He was a boy and she was my best friend, but I frowned. She needed me. I didn't want that to end. Maybe, I realized, just maybe, I liked having her need me.

I wasn't ready to give that up for anyone. Even a boy like Levi.

chapter fifteen

So how far did he try to go?" Kya wiped crumbs off her mouth. She'd filled her belly with my mom's cookies and then came up to knock on my door so I could chauffeur her to the paintball tourney. She picked up a tube of lipstick from my dresser and rubbed the reddish-orange color over her lips, and then sat on my bed and pursed them up and made kissy noises. "Or should I ask how far you *let* him go?"

I reached over and grabbed the lipstick from her hand. "This is my mine." Sharing hygienic products with Kya was not at the top of my favorites list. "And you don't need to get all made up for paintball."

"Whatever." She went back to the mirror, picked up my brush, and pulled it through her hair. "I want to look good when I mow down the other teams today." She turned to me, her eyebrows high up on her forehead. "Well?"

"Well what?" I tugged my hair into a ponytail and avoided looking at her. I tried not to focus on the lump forming in my stomach and bent down to my gear bag, shifting through to make sure I hadn't forgotten anything.

"Are you saying he didn't try anything?" Kya sounded surprised.

The lump traveled up to my throat as I groped through my gear bag.

"Not even a kiss?"

"Kya." I'd lain in my bed last night wondering the same thing. Why he hadn't kissed me good night when he'd dropped me off. I'd thought about it all the way home, expecting it, and anticipating it, worrying about it. Then when he dropped me off…nothing.

A tremor shook my hand. Did I have the total wrong idea about Levi?

I grabbed a thin Lululemon headband from my bag and wrapped it over my hair. I glanced at Kya's reflection as she studied me in the mirror.

She squished up her nose. "Well, maybe he's looking for someone to hang out with? Like as friends? Or, hey, maybe he's gay?"

I stood up and my expression must have given me away.

"I mean no, he's probably the type of guy who takes things slow. It's fine. Don't worry."

"You think so?" I fought to keep my voice level, to keep the desperation out of it. "I mean, there were signs it was more than friendly. He held my hand."

"He held your hand?" She came over and sat on the bed, pulling me down beside her, the brush still in her other hand. She elbowed me in the side. "Oh my God. You really like him, don't you?"

I grunted and stood up from the bed, thinking about the things he'd said to me. Our emotional connection. The feel of my hand in his warm bigger hand. So why no kiss?

"He's a nice guy," I said softly, and opened a drawer to grab some more headbands to toss in my bag in case I got some headshots. I hated when my headbands got covered in paint, and I liked to have fresh ones on hand. I tucked them into a side pocket on my gear bag.

More than nice. He's amazing. The first guy who really saw me. Not you. The first guy to make me feel special.

"Nice?" She jumped up, reaching for my side, and then tickled me, watching me in the mirror, but I wiggled away from her without cracking a smile.

She grabbed my arm. "Lucas said you should be careful. That he was in trouble with the cops. For beating a kid or something. For no reason."

I frowned. It didn't really sound like the person I knew.

"Did he say anything to you?" she asked.

I shrugged.

"Well. Just be careful." She let go of me and brushed her hair again, slowly. "Remember. Boys are stupid. Throw rocks at them." She smiled. We'd both worn David & Goliath T-shirts with that saying all through eighth grade. She stopped wearing hers first.

I plopped down on my bed, watching her. What else did she know about Levi? "Did Lucas say anything more about him?"

"Only that he has warts on his feet. And he picks his nose in the car." I smacked her. She laughed out loud.

"You always know what boys want," I said, and sighed.

She put the hairbrush down on my bed and patted my leg. "Well, from me they only want one thing, Skanklet."

She jumped up. I thought about her and Lucas. How they'd been all over each other and kind of rumpled up. I knew I should ask what happened but didn't have the energy to make this all about her. Not yet.

"Do you think he likes me?" I asked, hating how it made me sound. Weak and vulnerable.

She lifted a finger. "He asked you out?"

I nodded.

She lifted another finger. "You're hotter than the temperature of my feet after a few rounds of paintball."

I rolled my eyes.

"What? They get hot in those boots." She lifted a third finger. "You are the nicest person in the entire world. How could he not like you?"

I groaned. "But—"

She turned and shook her tush at me. "Own it, Skanklet, own it."

I wished I knew how.

She turned back with a smile. "All right then. If you want to know for sure, next time you go out with him, wear the padded bra. I noticed you did not have it on last night."

"I'm surprised you noticed anything."

She folded her arms across her much more abundant chest. "I'm only trying to help."

"This isn't about the size of my boobs."

She rolled her eyes. "Of course not. You would have a much deeper connection."

I frowned. I didn't want to think that he thought of me as a series of body parts. I wanted it to be more.

"What about you and Lucas?" I asked to take my attention off that train of thought. "What's up with you two?"

I wanted to know what they talked about. If he seemed to see inside her, to things that she didn't show the outside world.

She grinned. "Let's say that we got to know each other really well." Then she giggled. "Lucas and I did it. In my parents' bed."

"Oh my God, Kya. Why would you do that?" This conversation was not going the way I wanted. At all.

Her smile disappeared and she stared at me for a long moment, a sour expression on her face. "Why not? I like him. He makes me feel good."

"But your parent's bedroom?" I tried not to gag. "And you haven't been going out very long."

"So? You're judging me too?"

I bit my lip. "No. But I do want you to...you know...look after yourself."

"I used a condom if that's what you mean."

I shifted uncomfortably on both feet. "No," I said quietly. "It's not."

I was bursting with the desire to go over every detail of my night. Analyze everything Levi had done and said. I wanted to know what she thought. Did he like me? Was he going slowly because he wanted to get to know me? Did he want to be my best bud? What could I do to find out the answer to these questions and more? What could I do to make him like me more? As a girl.

But it would sound petty and childish compared to what Kya had to deal with. So I swallowed all the things I wanted to ask. She studied her nails and we were both quiet for a moment, an uncomfortable silence hanging between us like a dark cloud. Then she looked up. "Maybe Levi has a girlfriend back home?"

Her comment dug right into my bones. What about the hand-holding? He wouldn't ask me out and pay for everything if he already had a girlfriend, would he? Was this merely a friend thing that I wanted to make into more?

I opened my mouth to ask, but she'd scrunched her face up and covered it with her hands. "I didn't mean for it to happen so fast with Lucas. We had a couple of drinks and got carried away." She sniffled and sank down on my bed again. "Like it always does. Why do I always do this, Grace? Am I a slut?" Her eyes filled with tears.

All my questions about Levi slipped to the background.

"Oh, Kya," I said, and sat with her, my arm over her shoulder. "You're not a slut."

She sniffled and her lip quivered, but I took a big breath and decided to give her a dose of reality. It might help. "But maybe you make it about the sex so it doesn't have to be about anything else. You know?" She stiffened under my arm, but I kept going. "I think Lucas really likes you. You."

She sniffled and slid away from me and pulled a Kleenex from the box on my dresser. "But why? Why would he like me?"

The puzzled look on her face hurt my insides. "Why wouldn't he? Give yourself some credit." I went to her side and put my head on her shoulder. "You're amazing."

"Thanks." She didn't move and we both stood like that for a moment, breathing.

"You're the best thing that ever happened to me. You're my best friend," she said.

I hugged her harder. "I know. You're my best friend too."

She pulled away and wiggled her butt and then hooted. "And we're friggin' hot," she yelled.

"Cool it on the ego trip," Indie shouted from the hallway.

We looked at each other and laughed. "Hopefully that's all he heard," she said.

I glanced at the alarm clock by my bed. "If we don't leave soon, we're going to be late." I picked my gear bag up from the floor and slung it over my shoulder. "You okay?"

"I'm fine. Really." She showed me her teeth.

"Okay," I said. "Let's go then. Where's your stuff?"

"I loaded it in the car. You left the doors unlocked, so I put my stuff in the hatch before I came in."

I nodded and opened the bedroom door, waiting for her to go in front of me, and then followed, closing my door behind me.

We walked down the stairs and saw Indie, now in the kitchen shoveling cookies in his face.

"Yo, Indie, 'sup?" Kya said.

"I was chilling until I heard you yelling about how hot you are." He took a sip of milk. "You two going balling?"

"No," I told him as I adjusted my gear bag on my shoulder. "We're going to the beauty salon and these are our supplies."

"Well, you need all the help you can get." He grinned and shoved another whole cookie into his mouth. "Hey," he said, showing us his crumby cookie. "I'm going to be starting at the academy September first."

"Finally!" I said. "I mean that's awesome, it really is!" I added, genuinely happy for him. He'd been wanting to go to the police academy since he graduated high school, but in Washington State he not only needed to be twenty-one, but Dad also insisted he get a bachelor's degree first so he could advance up the ranks faster. Then, when he had the age and the education, Dad wanted to make sure he'd also invested a lot of time volunteering. Even his work at Splatterfest plumped up his resume, working with and mentoring youth.

"Dad thinks I'm finally ready." Dad didn't like us to do things the easy way or without purpose.

"Have mercy on Tadita," Kya said. "Indie Black as an authority figure. It will never be the same in this town again." She walked closer to him and stole a cookie from his pile. "Does this mean you can get me out of speeding tickets soon?"

He laughed. "Nice try, Kya. You should be worried about me being a cop, not excited. I'll be able to monitor your illegal activities from a close range."

"Nah. You'll have my back." She grinned and bit off half the cookie. "Anyhow, I hope you're not planning on living at home. Kind of embarrassing to be a state trooper who still lives in the basement at his parents' house."

"He doesn't even live in the basement," I added as I walked toward the front door.

"I'll be living on my own as soon as I start drawing a salary."

"Awwww. But we'll miss you," Kya said as she followed me.

"Speak for yourself," I said. I slipped on flip-flops and smiled at Indie from the hall. "You'll do great," I called as we headed out. "Congrats."

"You know it," he called as the door closed behind us.

At least one child in our family was bursting with high self-esteem.

The bright sun hit my face and I searched my purse for my sunglasses. The noise from a lawnmower filled the air. I glanced over and saw James pushing the new lawnmower his dad had bought before shipping off. He said he didn't want Indie to have to do our lawns anymore. Awfully big of him. It wasn't his fault he wasn't around, but James already had so much more responsibility than other kids.

James spotted us, waved, and shut the motor down.

"God, it's annoying the way he's always lurking around," Kya said under her breath.

"Kya," I said. "He lives next door and he's mowing his lawn. He's not lurking. And even if he was, he's your best friend."

"You're my best friend," she mumbled.

"And so is James." I waved to him and yelled, "Hey, how's it going?"

"Good," he called as he walked to the front of the lawn. "You two in a tourney today?"

"Ding ding ding," Kya called. "Someone get this man a prize."

He stared at her for a moment and then turned away. "Have fun." He went back to the lawnmower and pulled it back on. The roar burst into the quiet warm air.

I shook my head at Kya, leaning against the car waiting. She jumped in the passenger seat while I went to the hatch and loaded my stuff on top of hers. After I arranged the equipment, I got in the driver seat. She stared at me as I pulled my seatbelt over my shoulder. I stared back, squinting slightly.

"What? I was nice to him," she said.

"That was nice? You act like you don't even know him. You two are pissing me off. Make up already. Seriously. You better get along before the Lavender Festival. We are going together and we are having fun." I glared at her but she didn't say anything.

"Right?"

"Yes, sir," she said.

"What did you say to upset him anyways?" Outside the window, James mowed perfectly straight lines, his head down, his body language droopy and sad.

She lifted her thumbnail to her mouth, chewed, and glanced out the window at him. "Maybe it's what he said to me?"

"Well, what was it then?"

"What?" She turned back to me, rubbing at her nose, peeved.

"What did he say to piss you off?" I growled, aggravated with both of them.

She went back to her thumbnail and ignored me.

"Kya!"

"Nothing. It was nothing."

"Then stop acting so pissy."

She rolled her eyes. "Are you going to start this thing?" I crossed my arms and glared until she finally sighed and did up her own seatbelt. When she snapped it shut, I put my key in the ignition and started it up.

"You're the only person I know who makes me wear a seatbelt," she mumbled.

"I shouldn't be." I shoulder-checked and put the car in reverse. "Besides the annoying bell that goes off, it's respectful."

"I respect you. You don't need to make me wear a belt to prove it." She pursed her lips at me, pretending to kiss me.

"To yourself." I corrected. "Respectful to yourself. You're worth protecting."

She stuck her tongue out at me and I smacked her leg and then drove to the Outdoor Paintball Palace. I think we both made a silent truce to get along on the drive to the outskirts of town. I loved the lush green hills and views of the blue water, but Kya had grown up there and was almost oblivious. Soon enough, we were laughing and gossiping about the players we'd be matched up against. Lola would put us with a couple of other guys we played with in tourneys. Kind of our unofficial team for the summer.

"We can handle any guy out there," she said. "Team BBS. Buds before studs."

I whooped and minutes later, pulled the car into a field. Cars were parked all over it. Loud music pumped from different vehicles with open doors and trucks with guys sitting in the back. All that noise competed with a rock song playing over the main speakers in the speedball arena. We piled out of the car and pulled our gear from the hatchback. A referee walked by and nodded at Kya and me as we headed toward the play area.

Lola stood near the concession area near the entrance. She wore a neon pink shirt advertising NexGen Pods with her shorts and trademark purple high tops. The colorful look worked on her. She had a timer hung around her neck like jewelry and a clipboard tucked under her arm. She lifted her free hand and motioned us over.

"You're not playing?" I asked Lola when we got closer.

"Pulled my groin taking a dive," she said. "At the practice you missed last weekend." She squinted her eyes to glare at me. "Not so cool," she said.

"I know," I told her. I side-glanced at Kya, but she was waving to someone on the other side of the field. "Yeah. We're sorry," I said and knocked my elbow against Kya.

Kya dropped her gear on the ground at my feet. "Hey, Lola. Totally sorry we missed it. Hey, can you watch this for a second? I really need to pee. Too much coffee this morning." She shot her lip up in half a smile. "I'll be right back."

Kya took off and Lola and I watched her go. Then Lola turned back to me, shaking her head. "So what happened? It's not like you not to show. You disappointed me."

I dropped my gaze to the ground and kicked at some loose pebbles. "I know. I'm really sorry." I didn't want to tell her that the real reason for missing started with K and ended with drinking.

"Being a pro takes hard work. College league just as much. You want to have a chance with the Grinders, you can't make excuses. You show up." She narrowed her eyes and flipped back her hair as a sudden gust of wind blew it in her eyes.

"I know. I do, take it seriously, I mean." I bit my lip, not wanting to lie about why I missed practice but not wanting to blame Kya either. "There was kind of an emergency. A family thing. It won't happen again."

It had been circumstantial, after all. And a crisis. And Kya was almost family and she'd needed me.

A silence hung over our heads and a couple of regular tournament players jogged toward us, already dressed in their full gear. Peter and Mike. They stopped when they spotted us.

"Hey, Lola, Grace," one called. "Looking fine today, ladies." The two boys stepped closer.

I clunked knuckles with both of them. "Fine enough to kick your butts."

This was my comfort zone with boys. I could handle testosterone-charged guys strutting their masculinity before a game. When we first started playing tourneys, the boys used to think they were going to hose us down with paint, but they'd learned quickly that we were tough. Legit.

Lola laughed. "That's my girl. Best not get her all riled up, boys. You know that's when she plays her best."

I grinned, happy to see her mood shift to one more pleasant.

"You do like to kick boy ass, don't you?" Peter said.

"Only 'cause you like to get your ass kicked," I answered.

A buzz of static cracked from the arena speakers, hurting my eardrums.

"You're one heck of a soger, I'll give you that, Miss Black," Peter said.

"Soger?" I asked.

"Paintballer with mad skillz."

"Aww," I smiled. "Look at you, sweetening me up. Do you think we should get married?" I joked.

He punched me lightly on the arm. "You're like one of the guys to me, Grace. And I ain't marrying no dude."

I punched him back. Hard. "Lucky for you that didn't hurt my feelings."

He laughed as he rubbed at his shoulder. "Can't say the same thing about my shoulder."

I grinned. "I didn't know you were so homophobic."

His friend laughed. "We don't judge. But look around. Mostly straight-man territory."

I glanced around at the mostly male crowd. The few girls that were scattered about were probably girlfriends and honestly were dressed kind of provocatively, even with the unusual heat. "That is stereotypical on so many levels."

He shrugged. "Like I said, we don't judge." Music on the speakers was interrupted by the crackly voice of an announcer calling for the first teams to get ready to play.

"That's us," Peter said. "Good luck, Black," he said. "See you on the field." He made a motion of shooting paintballs at me and I pretended to catch them in my hand and pop them into my mouth to eat them. The two laughed as they headed off toward the arena.

"Be afraid," I called, slipping on my comfortable paintball persona. I smiled, watching them leave.

"So everything's okay?" Lola asked.

I glanced back at her. "Yeah. Fine. I really am sorry about missing Sunday. I hope you'll invite me back. It won't happen again."

She nodded. "I forgot my sunglasses. I need to go find an extra pair." She brought her hand up to her eyes to block out the sun. "Things okay with Kya too?"

I hesitated and then smiled. "Sure. I mean, she's got some personal stuff going on but she'll be fine." It was as much as I could say.

She nodded. "Okay. Well, listen. I want you to work it out there today. Okay? Show me you want it. Okay, Grace?" The sun passed behind a cloud and she brought her hand down.

"Yeah. Of course. Kya will too."

"We'll see what Kya does out there. Problem with her is that she has it but she doesn't always bring it. I don't think she wants it as badly as you."

The speakers crackled again and a roar went up from the people sitting on the bleachers waiting for the first game to start. We both glanced over.

"I'll take heart any day. I like your consistency, Grace. You're valuable every game and you communicate. And whenever you find weaknesses in your game, you adapt."

"Whoa, thanks," I said, looking back at Lola. She usually wasn't so lavish with praise.

"No thanks needed." She tilted her head, studying me. "You know how sometimes people have blinders when they love someone? Like everyone else can see something but that person can't?"

My cheeks warmed but I nodded slowly.

"Like the girl whose boyfriend treats her like crap? Everyone tells her to leave him but she keeps making excuses for his behavior."

I nodded again. "Um. Yeah." I shifted back on my heels.

She nodded, her eyes trained on the field. She didn't saying anything for a second. "Don't be that person."

I opened my mouth, trying to think of a retort, but my tongue was useless as a blocked marker.

"I'm going to split you and Kya up today," she said. "Put you on opposing teams. I want to see how you two do individually and against each other."

Another cheer went up in the bleachers and I glanced over and saw the Thrashers dressed in full gear, prepping to go out for the first game of the day. "Are you serious?" I pressed my lips together to keep the shock off my face. "But we always play as a team."

"Well, we're going to try something new." She pulled the clipboard from under her arm and checked it. "Kya will play with Steve, Coop, and the D'Ailly brothers."

"Steve Blender?"

She nodded and I groaned.

"Jotham and Justin are cool, but Steve?"

"I know he's an ass, but you're going to have to deal with guys like him in the college league all the time," she said. "And I want you to play with our new female player, Chantelle D'Ailly. And yes, she's Jotham and Justin's sister, in case you're wondering."

I raised my eyebrows. I'd heard rumors about her, but she'd never been to Splatterfest and I'd never met her or seen her play live.

"She's kind of a newb," Lola said. "But she has serious accuracy and heart galore. I want you to play with her on your snake side."

My heart sank. I had nothing against the girl. I'd heard some good things about her, but Kya and I were a team. Her on snake side, me on Dorito. Salt and pepper. Left and right. Nerds and ice cream.

Lola lifted her hand to her forehead to block out the sun again as it emerged from behind the cloud and glanced toward the concession stand. She pointed a pink fingernail. "She's over there." I glanced where she pointed.

Chantelle had her back to me but she was tall and athletic-looking with a long brown braid hanging down her back. She turned as if she sensed us watching and smiled. She was cute. I recognized her from around town. She went to the other high school.

"This is her first outdoor tourney. She's been playing speedball with her brothers mostly. I want to split her from them too. See how she does on her own."

Chantelle waved and smiled and I lifted my hand and acknowledged her.

"Did you hear Jotham's traveling with a semipro team to Huntington Beach this fall?" Lola asked as she waved to Chantelle.

"I heard."

"And Justin is young but he'll be going pro too someday. I have high hopes for Chantelle."

"How old is she?" I asked.

"Seventeen. She'll be a senior next year."

Hmm. I wondered if she had NCPA aspirations. College level all-girl teams were rare, especially one that rocked as hard as the Grinders.

"Oh, I almost forgot. One more thing." Lola reached into the backpack slung by one strap on her shoulder. She dug inside it and pulled out something. "Would you mind wearing a camera today?" Without waiting for my answer, she handed me a headband with a small camera attached to the front of it. "I want to get some footage for a new webcast I'm putting together. It will be seen by Grinder eyes, so play fierce."

"You want me to wear the camera?" I asked, dangling it on my hand.

She nodded and her forehead wrinkled up. "That a problem?"

"Why me?"

She glared at me. "Because I want you to. I want you to show off a little, Black. And show off Chantelle too. She's good. The Grinders are interested in her too."

"Usually Kya wears the Pro Cam," I mumbled, pushing my luck.

"Not today." She pressed her lips tight and her eyes flickered with challenge. "You don't want to do it, Grace?"

"No. Of course," I said, feeling like a bit of a traitor to my BFF.

"Good."

There was a flurry of pops from the arena and a roar from the crowd. The first game was underway. I hadn't even noticed the countdown. The music volume went down a notch.

"There're only two spots with the Grinders next year. Your job is to make sure one of them is yours. Worry about yourself." Lola scowled at my sour expression. "Kya's your friend, she's not your responsibility."

"I don't know," I mumbled.

"How bad do you want it?" She looked toward the arena and then at her watch. "We're playing Capture the Flag today. Resurrection."

I nodded.

"Kya gets a little predictable in these sequences. Maybe catch some of that on tape. I want her to see it. See if she can learn something and apply it."

I nodded again, wanting to stick up for Kya, but knowing I'd pushed my luck enough. I ducked down and tucked the camera in my gear bag.

"Show me what you can do. Lots of chatter. Take some chances. Think on your feet and remember you're wearing the cam. Take a leadership role, okay?" She gestured with her hands, imitating a run-through. "Show me your strengths. I want you to want this."

She clapped me on the back. I spotted Kya skipping back to us, looking happy and carefree. How Kya handled this news could go either way. She got closer, dance-walking to the rhythm of the beat blasting from the concession speakers.

"'Sup, Lola?" Kya said, her mood seemingly improved by the emptiness of her bladder.

"You two need to suit up." Lola checked her clipboard. "I was telling Grace I'm splitting you two up today. To shake things up a little, you're going to play with Steve and the D'Ailly brothers today, Justin and Jotham."

Kya stopped boogying her hip and stared at Lola, her mouth open, her eyes narrowing. "Are you kidding?"

Lola looked her right in the eyes, standing straighter and using her height to her advantage. Kya was tall, but Lola was taller. "Do I look like I'm kidding?"

They stared each other down and then there was another screeching blast of static from the outdoor mike. "Not so much," Kya said.

I let out the breath I'd been holding. Lola relaxed her straight stance a little.

"But Gracie and I are a team, Lolls." She flashed her most flirtatious smile. "Why break up a good thing?"

Lola didn't smile back. "It'll be a good thing for you to play with Steve after the ball-bouncing match you two had last week. Work with him, not against him. Show me what you've got in the restraint department, kid. I need to see more of that and less heat."

Kya's smile faded. "That guy believes in teamwork as much as a freaking broken paintball."

"Maybe you're right, but he's not the only one. You need to learn discipline if you want to play with the big boys. He'll help you with that." She grinned. "Never mind the face, Kya. Think how much it'll piss him off that he's helping you." She pushed a finger into Kya's shoulder. "This could be useful for you in paintball and real life too. Take advantage of the opportunity."

Kya bit her lip. At least she was fighting her natural instincts. In spite of everything, that was an accomplishment.

"Come on," I tugged Kya by the arm, wanting to get her away before she did or said something she'd regret. "You'll be fine. Show Steve who's boss. We need to get dressed."

"Could you watch our gear for a second?" I asked Lola. "We left our markers in the car."

Lola nodded, glancing at her watch again. "Fine, but hurry. I've got lots to do."

"Are you friggin' kidding me?" Kya said when we hit the parking lot out of Lola's hearing range. "She's breaking us up? Making me play with Steve friggin' Blender."

"Try not to piss him off," I said. "She's watching closely. And you know she's the eyes of Betty Baller." Betty Baller was the coach and scout of the Grinders. I opened the hatch and pulled out my gun case and Kya reached in to grab hers.

"There's a new girl out today," I said as I slammed down the hatch.

Kya went completely still. "Who?" She turned her head.

"Chantelle D'Ailly."

"Never heard of her." She was lying. If I'd heard of her, so had Kya.

"The D'Ailly brothers' sister," I said.

"Yeah? Well, just because her brothers can play doesn't mean she can." The audience burst into a cheer and the announcer called the end of the game. Kya hurried ahead of me back, her marker over her shoulder. She bent to pick up her gear.

"After you suit up, I'll give you a vest to wear," Lola said to Kya. She turned to me. "Want to come meet Chantelle?" It wasn't really a question.

"Blender will be your frontman," Lola said to Kya, and pointed to the left. "Your team is over there. They know you're playing with them, so go get reacquainted when you're dressed."

I gave Kya a level glare to tell her to shake off her anger and do what Lola said.

She nodded and headed for the girls' restroom to change.

• • •

"In resurrection, I like to peek out from the bunkers a bit, tease the other team, let them see me and fire at me," I told Chantelle as she pulled on her jersey.

Chantelle nodded. "Perfect." She smiled. "My younger brother is kind of a hoser because he has a wicked hammer that shoots thirty balls per second. He likes to use it, so don't get in a pissing match with him. Take him out first if you can."

"Is he accurate? Bad shots use up a lot of ammo." I checked a pod to make sure it was full of paint and not blocked.

Chantelle smiled. "He's okay. And Jotham will cover him. So take him out too."

"Okay." I hesitated and then took a breath and blew it out. "Kya is good at crawling down the snake to get you to gunfight your way out. Watch that." My stomach tightened.

She smiled. "You mad at yourself for ratting out your best friend?"

I pulled down my mask and adjusted the camera.

"It's okay," she said. "I like to win too."

We headed out to the field. Time to go take out my best friend.

• • •

Kya was quiet. She barely looked at Chantelle or me as she loaded up her gear in record time. Chantelle stripped off her clothes. "Wish they had showers in here." There were streaks of paint in her hair. "You played great, Kya," she said.

"Thanks." Kya's team took us out first and we met up once more and lost, but she still seemed pissed off. She'd cool off after she had a chance to gripe.

"Maybe we could hang out sometime. The three of us. I don't know any other female players," Chantelle said as she pulled on shorts.

"Yeah. Maybe." Kya lifted her gear bag and slung it over her shoulder. "You're really good," she said to Chantelle. "And I don't say that to many people."

Chantelle smiled as she tugged on a tank top. The smile lit up her already pretty face. "Thanks. You too."

Kya nodded and turned to me. "Blender's cleaning my marker for me. I'll go get it and meet you at the car," she said. "Throw me your keys?"

I tossed them at her and then sat on the bench to take a breather.

"Is she pissed at me?" Chantelle asked when the door shut behind her. She went to a mirror and pulled some dried paint from her hair.

"Nah. She gave you a compliment. That practically means she loves you." My cell phone rang, signaling a message, and I jumped to pull it from my bag. I glanced down at the text and smiled.

Hope you had fun today)

Chantelle smiled wistfully, nodding at my phone. "Boyfriend?"

A grin took over my face. "I don't know."

She pointed at me. "But look at you. You like him! Who is he?"

"Levi Lewis," I told her and giggled. "He's pretty amazing."

Chantelle got comfortable on the bench beside me and spent the next ten minutes quizzing me about Levi. "He totally likes you," she said after hearing about the movie and even the non-kiss good night. "He was probably nervous."

"You think?"

"Totally. I have two brothers, remember? And their friends are always at our house. Some of them, even the hot ones, are shy. It's hard for some guys to make the first move. Especially if they really like you and don't want to screw it up."

I stood up. "Thank you for saying that. I think I love you." I ignored a twinge of guilt and the voice in my head wishing Kya had reassured me like that.

"He sounds amazing," she said, and sighed. "You're lucky."

"Yeah?"

"Definitely."

"You have a boyfriend?" I asked her.

"I wish."

"I know someone you might be interested in," I said, thinking of James.

"Really?"

"Let me work on it," I told her. "Okay. I have to get to Kya."

She stood and picked up her gear bag. "Yeah. It's awesome you have a girlfriend to play paintball with. I'm jealous."

Her, jealous of me? I threw my bag over my shoulder.

"Don't be," I said without thinking. "Things aren't always the way they seem."

My choice of words surprised me.

Was I trying to tell myself something?

chapter sixteen

I saw Kya and James every day at work, but with the rainy weather, we hardly had time to talk. Rain meant better business at Splatterfest. Dad must have been rocking his rain dances in his back office. Kya spent most of her free time hanging out with Lucas, the way she always did in the beginning stages of a relationship. Poor James was busy with his mom, who was having a bad flare-up.

When the day came for us to go to Seattle, the sun finally came out and I spent most of the morning at work texting Levi. We'd been texting at least three or four times a day. We were getting to know each other and we'd had coffee together again without being interrupted by Kya. He even showed up for another yoga session.

But still nothing had happened between us. As in lip-locks. Or groping. My head was confused, my body a rage of chaotic hormones. Did he like me? I had no idea how to read the signs. I wanted to ask Kya, but she was busy with Lucas. A couple of times, I thought about calling Chartelle for advice, but that felt like cheating. James wasn't any help at all when it came to relationships.

After work was finally over, Kya came to my house to help me get ready. She primped me, pulled me, sprayed me, and even lent me some clothes. When I started down the stairs, Indie was in the kitchen and he glanced up and frowned. I descended slowly, clutching the railing for support. The kitchen reeked of popcorn and he opened the microwave door and pulled out a fully popped bag.

"You look like a little kid playing dress-up," he called as he dropped the bag of popcorn on the counter and reached for a bowl.

"You look like a grown-up who lives with his parents and has a tapeworm in his belly." I kept my chin high and my expression regal as I continued sauntering slowly, trying not to fall over in the heels Kya insisted I wear. I nixed a shopping trip. The dress I'd borrowed from her was tight and short. Truthfully, I felt like an imposter.

"You want her to look like a little kid, Indie," Mom said. She stood at the sink, drying dishes that couldn't go in the dishwasher. "Look at her. She looks so grown-up I bet some of your friends would ask her out."

"God, Mom." Indie ripped open the bag of popcorn and dumped the contents into the bowl. "The thought of my friends checking out Grace makes me want to vomit."

"Good," she said. "Because your job as older brother includes keeping them away from your little sister. Especially the cop types. They're the worst."

"You should know, you married one." He shoveled a handful of popcorn into his mouth and plunked himself down at the kitchen table, watching me attempt to walk.

"I married a good one," Mom said. "Some get corrupted or let the groupies go to their heads. And into their pants. Don't be one of them." She waggled her finger at him and then dried her hands on her pants.

Indie laughed. I scrunched up my face. "Mom. Seriously."

She smiled as she picked up a large silver bowl and tucked it into a cupboard.

"Kya looks pretty hot," Indie said, and I glanced behind me. Kya was now working the stairs like a beauty queen doing a pageant walk, even using the railing to stretch out her strut. Her dress looked like someone had gone after the hem with scissors. It barely grazed her thighs. It also hugged her butt and everyone raved about her butt. She could be a butt model. That's probably why she liked to shake it around so much. From what I saw checking out mine in the mirror, my butt was flat and boring as if someone whacked it hard with a two by four.

Mom went to the table and snapped a tea towel at Indie. He laughed and rubbed at his arm. "Owww. For a girl who is best friends with my little sister, hot. Like my own sister but not quite. That kind of hot."

"Thank you for clarifying. Kya, you're stunning, and, Grace, you're beautiful." She whistled. "God, weren't you two running around in tutus and rubber boots a few days ago?"

"Um, no," Kya said. "I wouldn't be caught dead in an outfit like that." She walked over to Indie and stuck her hand in his bowl of popcorn.

"Hey," I said. "I really did wear that."

"Of that I have no doubt." I gave her the evil eye but she laughed.

"I love you, Grace. But you have no idea how to accessorize. Rubber boots with a dress?"

"I was five," I said.

Mom laughed. "You were an individualist," she said. "She was ahead of her time."

Mom threw down her tea towel then and glanced down at herself. "But when did I get this old body? Where did all *my* youth and hotness go?"

Indie and I exchanged a look, knowing how the rest of the sentence would go.

"Oh, that's right. I gave birth to two children," she said.

"You look pretty good for an old gal," Indie told her and shoved another handful of popcorn in his mouth.

I tried not to laugh as she gave us both a faux dirty look. "Damn right I do." And then she clapped her hands together. "Okay, girls. Ready to go?"

Kya nodded and Mom pulled a cooler bag of snacks from the fridge, even though the drive was only two hours. I tiptoed closer to the front door where I'd put my overnight bag. Mom didn't even mention that our shoes might be ruining her hardwood. Dad would have had a fit seeing us walk in high heels in the house. He probably wouldn't be so forgiving of the short dresses either. Good thing he was at jury selection.

Mom slung the strap of the cooler bag over her shoulder. "And watch it, missy," she said to Kya, eying her from her high heels to the top of her curled black hair. "I am the wife of a cop. I have good instincts. I have no qualms about embarrassing you. Remember, I know how to make people cry." She walked toward me. "Especially boys who ogle."

"She's not kidding." I plopped down on the bench beside the front hallway closet and pressed my knees tight. Mom put the cooler bag down beside our overnight bags that seemed to be waiting patiently to be carted off.

Kya giggled and swiped a handful of Indie's popcorn. "Don't worry, Mrs. B. I know how to make boys cry too," she said with her mouth full.

Mom didn't say anything, but I saw a hint of sympathy in the way she pressed her lips tight.

"Did you borrow that from Kya?" Mom asked, turning back to me. The dress was shorter, tighter, and blacker than anything in my closet.

"How did you guess?" Kya called from the kitchen.

"Maybe you're less of an individualist," Mom said, but before Kya could be offended, she continued. "So short. Dresses are so short these days. Please tell me you girls are wearing underwear."

"Mom!" The things that came from her mouth shouldn't surprise me, but she still managed to shock me sometimes.

Kya giggled.

"God, Mom, I'm eating," Indie said.

Mom put her hand over her mouth and giggled. "Sorry. That was entirely inappropriate. I've seen pictures of too many famous teens who forgot to put on underwear." While I closed my eyes to rid it of images, she continued, "Don't tell your father I said that. He'll put me away."

"Again?" I asked.

"Dad stopped trying to institutionalize her years ago," Indie said. "Futile, I think he said. She'd only escape."

Mom and Kya giggled.

"How on earth did such a conservative man marry a woman with such a foul mouth?" Indie asked, imitating Dad's voice.

Mom waved her hand in the air as she went to the front hall and slipped flat sandals on her feet. "Oh, hush. I'm only having fun. And your dad loves me despite my potty mouth. Without me, this family would lack spontaneity." She grinned. "But sorry, girls. That was a little over the top. Please erase that comment from your memories." She stepped over to the bags.

"If only I could," Indie called from the kitchen.

"Don't worry, I grew immune to scarring from your comments years ago." I hobbled toward her.

Mom shook her head. "Women went through so much to get equal rights and now we're back to flaunting and sexualizing ourselves. It seems like a step backward in so many ways."

"We don't need the women's lib lecture, Mom." I tugged down my skirt for good measure.

Kya strutted toward us, not at all deterred by her shoes. "We're showing we can do it all. Dress sexy but still demand respect. Anyhow, it's a good disguise, Mrs. B. None of the baller guys will suspect that we can kick their butts. Then we hose them down."

My feet hurt already. "If only I can walk in these heels for an entire night."

Mom glanced at us both. "Why you two had to get all gussied up before our drive to the city I still don't understand."

"We want to go straight to the party as soon as we get there," Kya reminded her for the millionth time. "Looking hot and ready to mingle."

"More like finding Betty Baller to suck up to," I clarified, poking Kya in the arm.

"I'm glad you want to impress the Grinders and not the boys," Mom said, and squinted at Kya. She turned back to me. "Look at you in high heels! You're actually taller than me with those on."

"Ballet slippers or flats wouldn't do these outfits justice," Kya said. She stopped in front of the mirror on the front closet door and whirled in a circle.

Mom sniffed the air. "You ever have on perfume? You smell delicious. Like vanilla sunshine."

"She's the vanilla, I'm the sunshine," Kya said. "Will you take pictures of us?" She reached in her purse and handed my mom her phone and her purse to hold.

"So you can post them online for creepers who stalk teenage girls?" Mom said, squinting at the camera functions as Kya grabbed me around the waist, posing hard and using me as a prop. "Those really are short skirts." Mom held the phone up and snapped a couple of photos.

She was right. If we wore these to school, we'd be sent home for dress-code infractions, but it seemed best not to point that out.

"Maybe I should come to the players' party with you girls." She snapped another photo while Kya posed like a superstar. "Of course, I don't think my yoga pants and T-shirt will pass the dress code."

"Key word for the party is player, Mom," I said. "And no offense, but I've seen you play paintball and it's not pretty."

Kya giggled and took her phone and purse back and flipped through the pictures.

"Well, you two girls need to be careful. Maybe not in the paintball arena, but at the party. You may think you're playing dress-up but you both look grown-up. And very beautiful." She bent down to pick up her bag. "Honestly, you could wear something more comfortable and change when we got there," she mumbled.

"We'll be late as it is." We'd both worked later than we wanted.

"There will be other girls there," Indie said, as he got up from the kitchen table and tossed his empty bowl in the sink instead of the dishwasher. "But they might be wearing bathing suits and sashes and serving drinks." He laughed.

I stuck my tongue out at him. Kya ruined my moment by striking another sexy pose.

"Should I pack my bikini?" Mom called back. "I could make a sash."

We all ignored her.

"The Grinders are going to be there," I told Indie. "They get respect. That's why we're going, remember? There will also be a few other girls trying to secure a spot on teams."

"Just warning you, Grace, girls are treated like ornaments by some of those guys. The players' party might be bad," he said.

"I think we can handle it," I said, and glared at him.

"Like we're not used to that," Kya said to back me up.

"These girls will be fine," Mom told him, and then she opened the front door.

"We rule!" Kya called.

"We'll be back tomorrow night," Mom called to Indie. "Tell your dad I'll text him when we get to Seattle."

"Why don't you text him to tell him that?" Indie called back.

"Why don't you do as I ask?" she said. "Bye, Indie." She headed off to the car. Kya and I picked up our bags and followed.

Outside, Kya handed over her phone for more pictures and Mom dutifully took a couple more shots of us putting our luggage in the hatch and then tucked in her own small overnight bag and cooler bag.

I heard a familiar little bark and saw James walking toward us on the sidewalk, with his Chihuhua mix, Brian, on a leash trotting beside him. James stopped. I waved as Mom slammed down the hatch. Kya bumped me to the side with her hip. "Come on. We should go."

"We have time to say hey to James."

"He's probably getting an erection from seeing you in that outfit," Kya whispered in my ear, low enough that my mom couldn't hear. She smiled fakey-fake at James. 'Hey, James," she called, and strutted to the passenger door.

"Shut up," I called to her ass. Her exquisite model ass.

"Grace Elizabeth Black," Mom said.

I frowned but turned to James. Kya giggled and climbed into the front passenger seat and closed the door behind her.

"Hey, James," Mom greeted him. "How about these girls, huh?"

"Wow," he said as he reached the driveway. "You look…amazing, Grace."

Mom started humming the song. "Both of them do," she said and turned, looking for Kya and frowning when she saw her already in the car. "They're going to be majorly outnumbered. I wish you were coming with us to look after them." Mom bent down to pat Brian.

James smirked. "Have you checked out my muscles, Mrs. B? Kya and Grace can probably handle themselves far better than I could. Besides, I'm not a player, so I wouldn't even be able to go to the party anyway."

"So not a player," Kya called from the passenger seat. The window was rolled all the way down. She lifted her arm out and flexed, poking a finger into her bicep. "Sick. Right, James?"

He rolled his eyes, but at least they were talking.

Mom cooed at Brian, picked him up, and rubbed noses with him. James and I exchanged a look and he laughed. Mom and his little dog would nose-smooch for hours if we let them. She loved dogs but couldn't get one because of Dad's allergies to dander.

"You must be pumped to meet the Grinders," James said.

I nodded happily. "Yeah, but I still wish you were coming along."

"Not my thing." He glanced at Kya, but she'd pulled down the mirror in the visor of the passenger seat and was wiping lipstick from the corners of her mouth.

"Have fun," he called. "And good luck! Dazzle 'em with your charm."

"We will, James!" Kya called, and flipped up the visor. She smiled and it was actually genuine. My heart did a happy skip.

"Thanks!" I said to James. "I'm pretty nervous."

"Nervous." Kya made a loud hmmph sound from inside the car. "They'll be signing up for the Grace Black fan club."

"How could they not love you, Grace?" James said. "You're the real deal."

"Thanks. Hey, did I tell you I found the perfect girl for you?" I asked him.

"You're already taken," Kya called from the car.

We both ignored her. "Her name is Chantelle. She plays paintball, and she's super cute. And smart. Really, really smart." I had no idea if that were true, but it seemed like a good selling point for James.

"I don't need you to set up sympathy dates for me," he said, and turned his attention back to his dog still in my mom's arms.

"No sympathy. She's awesome. I think you two would hit it off."

"Sure. Whatever," he said as he petted his dog's head.

I glanced at my mom. "Come on, Mom, let the dog breathe. It's time to go." She reluctantly put Brian on the ground. "Can I set it up?"

James shrugged and I took that as a yes.

"You want to drive?" Mom asked. "I'll sit in the back and read."

"Sure!" I smiled at James, waving, and then wobbled in my heels toward the driver side.

"See ya," I called, and slipped inside the driver's seat. "Hey!"

James turned around.

"We're still on for the Lavender Festival next weekend, right? The three of us."

Our annual tradition. My favorite event of the year. A hokey little carnival with local crafters and musicians. A small town event but I loved it. Dad had given all three of us the whole day and night off.

James shrugged.

"James Edward McTavish," I yelled. "You are coming and that's final. Or I will kick your butt."

He smiled. "My butt quivers with fear, Grace. We'll talk. Have fun. Good luck."

Mom slipped into the backseat and fastened her seatbelt.

Kya groaned. "I have no idea why you love that stupid festival so much."

"Don't let her fool you," Mom said. "Grace is a softie."

I turned my head to glare at her and she laughed. "Sorry, Grace. It's true, honey. You came out nurturing. And you're not nearly as narcissistic as the rest of us."

"Thank God for that," I said.

"Much more like your dad."

"She's not nearly as hairy though," Kya said. "And she looks better in a skirt."

"Whatever," I said to both of them. "We are going to the Lavender Festival and you'll like it," I told Kya.

I started the car and glared at Kya, waiting. She stared back and finally rolled her eyes and did up her seat belt.

"Thank you," I said, and slid my own on and backed out of the driveway. James stood on the side of the driveway with his little dog and waved as we drove off.

"Aww. He looks like one of your dad's sad little monkey pancakes," Kya said, watching him in her side-view mirror.

"Poor guy," Mom said. "He's probably feeling left out of the girls-only weekend."

"I asked him to come," I said.

"I told him we'd be talking about our periods and bloating and cramps the whole way," Kya said with a laugh.

"You're evil," I told her.

Mom leaned forward to give me instructions on where to turn to get to the highway and provide me with driving tips, as if I'd never driven on the expressway before. I rolled my eyes at Kya but she grinned, her head back against the seat, enjoying herself a little too much.

"Are you sure you can drive in those shoes?" Mom asked.

"We should send her back," I said to Kya.

Mom laughed and leaned back. "I trust you but I have to fulfill my motherly obligations. At least some of them. And without me, you wouldn't be going."

I turned to give her a quick smile. She may not be the mom who gave out hugs like sunscreen on a sunny day but I didn't question her support, as bossy and weird as it might be at times. I focused back on the road. And here she was now, sacrificing her weekend so Kya and I could go to Seattle.

"I can't wait to meet the Grinders." I reached to turn on the radio. A pop song blasted from the speakers and I turned it down, checked for cars in the rearview mirror, and then moved into the next lane.

Kya nodded. "The party is going to be epic. We're going to be the hottest girls there."

"That's what I'm afraid of," Mom called from the back. "You'll be like little lambs going to slaughter. Turn left up there, Grace."

"I know," I called, and put on my signal.

Kya turned to my mom. "So not a lamb. I'm the wolf in lamb's clothing. But I promise to give a tongue-lashing to any boy who looks at your daughter the wrong way."

I made a choking noise as I steered onto the highway. "They'll be too busy looking at you. You inhale attention the way Indie inhales asthma meds. As if you need it to breathe."

Kya pretended to be offended for two seconds. "I don't need boys' approval. Besides, I have a boyfriend." She grinned at me and then glanced back at my mom. "So does Gracelet."

"She does?" Mom said, sitting forward in her seat again.

"I do not have a boyfriend." I frowned and checked my rearview mirror as a semitruck came roaring up behind us.

"Don't let those big trucks intimidate you," Mom said, turning her head. I did my best to ignore the truck trying to drive right up my ass.

"What about Levi?" Kya said in a singsong voice. The truck moved to the left lane to pass me and I relaxed my grip on the steering wheel. "He hasn't kissed her yet, but she wants him to," Kya told my mom.

"Oh my God, you are not talking about this with my mom."

"Why not?" Mom called from the back, her voice singsong happy.

"Let's talk about your love life instead," I said to her.

"Okay!" Kya said and turned to my mom. I caught the wink with my peripheral vision. Kya and Mom giggled under their breath.

"La la la la, not talking about this," I said, and turned up the music louder.

We drove for a while, bopping our heads, singing, and listening to my mom belt it out from the backseat. When a commercial came on, I turned down the music. "So number one goal is to meet Betty and the Grinders and show them how awesome we are," I clarified.

"Of course." Kya turned to stare out the window at a field of horses. Her favorite animal. She'd taken riding lessons when she was a kid and still talked about it.

"Not to flirt with paintball boys." I put on my signal to pass a slow-moving tractor in the lane ahead of us.

"Maybe a little?" Kya said.

"I'm already visualizing putting duct tape over your mouth." I smiled and she stuck her tongue out.

"Nothing says love like a little duct tape," Mom called. "Ask your father."

"I do not want to know about that," I said.

Mom snorted and she and Kya laughed and laughed and laughed until I was forced to join in.

When we finally arrived in Seattle, the GPS talked us to the hotel next to the convention center. We checked in and went straight to the room to freshen up. I ran to look out our window and discovered a lovely view of the back parking lot and trash bins.

Kya and I dropped our stuff on the floor, pulled out our makeup bags, and hogged the mirror in the bathroom to fix ourselves up. When we came out, Mom had changed into her bathing suit and put on an oversized cover-up to head to the swimming pool. As much as she complained about getting old, she looked great.

She stood and tucked a book under her arm. "Try not to come back too late, okay? Not past midnight?"

"How about one?" Kya asked.

"12:30," Mom said. She sighed. "I haven't been sleeping well lately, another lovely side effect of menopause besides horrifying cramps and fits of rage. I might take a sleeping pill."

"Way too much info," I told her as I slid on my shoes.

"You might as well hear about it. It's your destiny," she said.

"Our cue to go," I said to Kya. She laughed as she put on her heels and we did last-minute checks of each other as we headed to the door.

"You have your tickets?" Mom asked. I patted my purse.

"Good luck!" she called. "Be good."

"Depends on your definition of good," Kya whispered as we headed down the hallway.

I frowned at her back as I tried to negotiate the floor in my shoes. She better not have any ideas of getting into trouble. But history wasn't really on my side.

chapter seventeen

The VIP party was held in a ballroom in our hotel, with a formal dinner followed by an after-party in the same room. On the main floor, we asked the concierge for directions and he walked us to the nearby party room, intrigued when he found out we were paintball players. When we reached the noisy hall, the concierge nodded his head and left us. "Have fun."

I took a deep breath to collect myself. The room was huge, much bigger than I'd imagined, and the noise level already high. We walked into the crowd. I peeked inside the gigantic ballroom and my stomach flipped. White flowers spilled from oversized vases placed at entrance doors to the ballroom. Colorful balloon centerpieces rose up from tables around the room. At the front was a head table decorated with fresh flowers and cool ropes that looked like they were made from paintballs. Beside the head table was a huge screen and beside it a podium with speakers. Off to the left, a DJ was set up and at the other side of the room, I saw a portable bar that people were buzzing around.

The party spilled out into the hallway. Portable bars were set up in two corners in the wide hall, and all around us people chatted and laughed. I gawked around at good-looking girls in short-shorts and tight shirts with Spyder logos carrying trays of food and stopping to serve people around us. The walls of both the ballroom and the hallway were covered in paintball sponsor banners.

I walked slowly behind Kya who cruised the area, smiling at strangers as if she were the guest of honor. Without her experience in heels, my movements were slower. The ambiance of the crowd and the excitement in the air sucked some life from me, but it seemed to have the opposite effect on Kya, energizing her. Lots of eyeballs checked us out, and Kya lifted her head higher and strutted harder.

"We should find our table," I whispered to her, glancing around and recognizing some faces from paintball tourneys and waving, but everyone looked so much more glamorous in dress-up clothes.

Even though it was a player's party, there were obviously sponsors and spouses attending too. Some older women in cocktail dresses and older men who couldn't possibly be players milled around, mixed in with the obvious players, some with dates on their arms, but many grouped with their teams, traveling solo.

"Oh my gosh, this is like being on the dessert bar at a buffet," Kya said with a happy smile as eyes passed over us. "The best-looking desserts."

I ignored her, pulling my dinner ticket from my zebra purse and glancing at the table number listed on it. I peeked inside the ballroom, spotted some table numbers, and figured out the proximity of where we would be sitting. "Come on, we're that way."

"Wait," Kya said. "We have almost half an hour before we eat. Let's wander a little more. Oh. Check out those hot guys checking us out." I glanced over and saw a group of twenty-somethings gathered in a circle in front of another portable bar. Two girls in the group wore dresses as short as ours but had noticeable ink on their legs. I didn't recognize them. Four guys stood by, wearing dress pants and dress shirts. Two had face piercings; the other two were more conservative and they were the ones checking us out.

"Let's get a drink," Kya said, stopping on the spot.

I almost crashed into her and frowned, but she tugged my arm, pulling me in the direction of the bar. "Just get a soda or something, Grace. Relax. Come on."

The sudden movement threw me off-balance and I tripped completely out of one of my shoes. It flipped onto the rug like roadkill and I hobbled for it, lopsided. Kya threw her head back and laughed a deep, throaty laugh, watching guys noticing her.

With warm cheeks, I bent down, trying to slide my shoe back on without giving everyone a free peep show of the underwear I was wearing. Mom would be proud. By the time I stood up, the two guys were approaching.

"Be cool," Kya whispered in my ear. "Here's our story. We're college students. We can say we work at Splatterfest, but we don't live at home."

We used to play this game all the time. Making up stories to tell boys we didn't know. But that was at the mall or movies and with boys our age.

"We can't do that here," I whispered back. What if they knew the girls on the Grinders? The girls standing with them could be players. I didn't want to end up looking like an idiot.

The first to reach us, an older dude with slicked-back hair and a button-up shirt that needed one more button, beelined straight for Kya. "Hey," he said. "You ladies work here?" He practically wiggled his eyebrows up and down.

God. Did he think we were the entertainment?

"NO!" I said. Loudly.

His expression changed and he grinned, but I could almost read the words forming in his head.

Paintball groupies.

"NO!" I said again.

Kya widened her eyes and gave me a stern look. "Actually, we're ballers."

He and his friend who'd stepped beside him and was eyeing me up and down laughed a little too hard, like she'd made some really funny joke.

"Seriously. We play," I told them. I opened my mouth to trash-talk a bit, but Kya put her hand on my arm and interrupted. "We also work at Splatterfest. In Tadita," Kya told them, and grinned as if she'd revealed winning lottery ticket numbers. "I'm Kya, this is Grace."

At least she used our real names.

"The place the cop owns? I've heard of it. Some good ballers have come out of there," slicked-haired guy said.

Kya nudged my side with her elbow, so I pressed my lips closed and said nothing.

"I'm Michael. This is Richard," the slicked-back hair one said, not taking his eyes off Kya. I glanced at the other guy with his tight, curly hair, rather beady eyes, and facial hair that should have been shaved off. In my humble opinion. He grinned at me a little too lasciviously.

"We're reps for Dirty Paint. The best paint in the biz." Michael leaned down and said something in Kya's ear and she grinned at him like he was a delicious piece of chocolate cake and not some old guy with greasy slicked-back hair and a perverted slope to his mouth.

Richard stepped closer to me and stuck his hand out. "Nice to meet you."

I forced a smile, feeling uncomfortable and self-conscious and wishing they'd go away, but reached out my hand. "Ditto." He lifted my hand to his mouth instead of shaking it and kissed my fingers. His lips were rough and sloppy wet and I pulled my hand back quickly. Awkward. I attempted to smile, like his gesture wasn't wet, creepy, and contrived.

I tugged down on my dress, glancing to Kya for help but she was already in her element, flirting up a storm with Michael. They walked away, and feeling stupid. I followed like a kid being dragged to the dentist. Richard matched his steps with mine.

"So. What do you do?" Richard asked in a pinched voice. Great. I'd been paired up with my socially inept equal. "When you're not playing paintball?"

Is this how older people interacted with each other. Really? I silently cursed Kya and fake smiled at Richard.

"Um, I'm a student," I said.

"State University?" he asked.

No. High school.

I smiled and shrugged noncommittally.

"What year?" he asked.

"Coming up on my last," I said, trying not to technically lie or dig a hole too deep.

"My alma mater. I graduated a few years ago."

Not from my high school. I smiled, thinking about how old that made him. 26? 27? Way too old for me. Way too old for Kya to be flirting with his friend.

"Huh," I said, looking around the room, trying to spot Betty Baller. I saw a couple of other women who had the look of ballers, but didn't recognize them.

His gaze stayed on me. Staring.

"Uh. Are you in a league?" I asked to be polite.

"Nah. I played when I was younger but I travel a lot now, with my job. Sales, you know."

"Huh. I thought this was a party for players only." I tried not to make it sound as rude as it did in my head.

"There's a lot of corporate here, since we pick up most of the tab." He chuckled as if it came out of his pocket personally. "Those girls work for Alpha Wear." He nodded toward the girls they'd been standing with and I pretended to smile along with him.

"Huh," I said again, keeping sight of Kya and Michael ahead of me at the portable bar, still head to head in an intimate conversation like they'd known each other forever.

I pressed my lips tight and tugged on my earring.

Richard turned to me as we reached the bar. "Drink?" he asked.

"Um. Coke? Thanks." I wished he would take his friend and

disappear. This was supposed to be my night. My night to find the Grinders, not two random sales dudes.

"She's not a drinker," Kya said. I glared at her, sensing mocking in her tone, but she kept her eyes on Michael.

"So. Do you go to many shows?" Richard asked me. God. He sounded seriously lame.

"I wish," I said. "This is my first and only because it's so close to Tadita. I'm here to meet the Grinders. Betty Baller. I really want to play for her team."

He rubbed his chin and narrowed his eyes. "But they're a college team."

My cheeks warmed and I glanced around the room, trying to think of a response.

"Gracie would switch schools for them," Kya cut in. "She wants to play for the Grinders because they're all-female. She secretly wants to be a contract killer," Kya said as Michael handed her a martini glass. Filled with something bluish.

I lifted my eyebrows. "Apparently not so secret anymore."

She winked as she sipped her blue concoction. I had an urge to flick it from her hand. Watch it splash all over the floor.

"After you graduate from college?" Michael asked me.

Kya opened her eyes wider and then lowered them to her drink. "Of course."

"And what about you?" Michael turned to Kya, nodding at her drink. "Careful, that's a double."

"Perfect." Kya flipped back her hair and took another sip. "Career-wise, I'm keeping my options open."

"You should go into sales like us. Get a job with Spyder or something. The perks are great." He grinned and lifted his drink in the air. "Free drinks!"

"Totally." Kya put her glass down on the table by her hip. I stared at it. Empty. I'd had two sips of my Coke.

I glanced over at a huge clock on the wall by the bar.

"This is so much fun," I said, narrowing my eyes at Kya. "But we should find our seats."

"We still have twenty minutes or so." She didn't look at me and she giggled. Not an entirely sober giggle. Sparks shot out from her pupils as the alcohol kicked in. She was a fricking lightweight who liked to pretend she was hardcore.

I pulled on her arm. "Come on, Kya. I'd like to see if we can find the Grinders before the after-party."

Michael grinned but slid his hand over mine and pulled it away from her. "I heard Betty Baller is going to be late. Her plane got held up or something. I'll introduce you after dinner if you like. Don't worry. We'll get you to your seats before they serve the first course."

He turned his back to me and stepped up to the bar, leaning forward to put in an order. Great. He knew her. If I had to explain to Betty why two sales guys thought I was in college on another team, I would strangle Kya. I needed to think about the choices I made for my friend.

Kya turned to Richard while his friend got her another drink. "So you get lots of free stuff?" Not exactly a beater around the bush, my friend.

"Sometimes," he said.

Kya giggled as if he'd delivered the punch line to a great joke. "Free paint? Awesome!"

"Yeah. But I don't play, so…" He took a sip of his drink.

"Well, I know some players who would love free paint." Kya winked and Richard glanced around the room, apparently finding her as lame as I found him. Michael handed Kya another blue martini. She missed my dirty eye and slurped half of it back.

I steamed as Michael stepped even closer to Kya and the two of them flirted harder. I gave up even trying to make conversation with boring old Richard and we awkwardly watched the crowd while Kya and Michael carried on. When he handed Kya another drink, I got fed up and walked to the dining room by myself. Kya and Michael followed and Richard dragged behind them.

At our table, a couple of younger guys sat with older men. I sat in my assigned seat, smiled and said hello, ignoring Michael, who pulled out Kya's chair and placed a blue drink on the table in front of her. He leaned down and whispered something in her ear. She giggled and whispered back in his ear and then laughed overly loud.

Richard excused himself and left for their table, which thankfully was on the other side of the room. The people at our table watched while Kya flirted. I died a little inside, smiled apologetically, and then pretended the contents of my purse fascinated me. Finally, Michael reached down to give Kya a good-bye hug and she hung on a little long.

"What's their problem?" Kya asked in an overly loud whisper when she noticed everyone staring at her as Michael strutted off to his table.

I shushed her as she giggled and gushed too loudly about how hot Michael was. Two older men joined our table, taking the last seats. One man sat beside me, the other to his left. They had on golf shirts with matching logos on the chest pocket. I wondered if all the sponsors would stay for the party afterward.

"These are great seats!" I said to the man beside me, determined to ignore Kya's already half-drunken state. "So close to the head table."

He politely agreed and introduced his friend. I introduced myself but ignored Kya who was babbling to the man on her other side.

"I'm starving!" I said with too much enthusiasm. "I'm looking forward to dinner."

He asked who I played with and it turned out he knew my dad. Great. He told me about a video demo that would play after dinner, before the speeches and awards, about a new generation of paintball guns his company made.

Kya was regaling her seatmate with a rundown of her best snake side moves. As the servers carried out the first course, she stood. "I have to pee," she announced to the entire table. Her martini glass was drained.

I glared at her, but she held her head high, wiggled out of her chair, and moved expertly in her heels, leaving me alone with strangers. A moment later, the master of ceremonies, a funny and articulate pro baller, welcomed everyone and showed some webcast clips about the future of paintball on the screen. Waiters in black and white fanned out around the room, placing a plate of greens in front of everyone.

I told the waiter to leave a plate for Kya and glanced around, nibbling on my salad, distracted. The men beside me kept me entertained with stories about their business, but when the servers came to clear the salad plates, Kya still hadn't returned. I wanted to ignore the worry and my building anger but pulled my phone from my purse to see if she'd texted.

Thinking about you and hoping you're having a blast.

From Levi. Despite everything, my heart tripped on happiness. I wished Levi were beside me having dinner, not Kya. Where the hell was she? I sent him a noncommittal smiley face and tossed my phone back in my purse.

The main course came out but I barely tasted the few bites of chicken and vegetables I managed. The man beside me told the table funny and interesting stories he heard from his son about life on the pro circuit, but halfway through the meal, I pushed my plate away and excused myself. I got up and walked carefully around tables in the crowded room, conscious of my short skirt and wobbly walk.

When I reached the now empty lobby, the sounds of cutlery clinking and loud voices and laughter grew a little more muffled. I headed toward the bar where we'd met Michael and Richard. The bartender nodded but no one hung out around him. I started to get worried and hurried toward a sign that indicated restrooms were around the corner.

I stopped when I rounded the corner.

On a leather couch in a narrow hallway that led to the restrooms, Kya was on Michael's knee. Giggling. Stroking his hair. He had an arm around her, and in his other hand, he held a beer. Kya sipped a drink, draped over him looking drunk and ridiculous. On a couch beside them, sat Richard, his legs crossed, sipping an amber liquid from a short clear glass.

A wave of rage propelled me over faster than I thought I could walk in heels. Kya spotted me and grinned, waving happily, keeping one arm draped around Michael. He stared down her shirt, grinning. I wondered if he was sober enough to see the fume coming out of my ears.

"What the hell, Kya? What are you doing?"

"What's it look like? Having a drinkie poo." She snickered and planted a kiss on Michael's lips.

"We decided to meet up to have another drink," Richard said. "She said you were coming." I glared at Michael and Kya, not even acknowledging Richard's existence.

"The only thing you missed was dinner. Including an awesome video with footage of the Grinders." I pulled her by the arm and she detached from Michael's face.

"I didn't miss that." She pointed up at the wall behind me. I turned to see a TV screen with a live shot of the podium and a clear image of the screen. "We saw the speech and videos. We had a great view from here." She giggled and threw back the last of her cocktail. "I'm not hungry."

I gritted my teeth. Was she kidding me?

"I ate alone. Worrying the whole time what happened to you." I reached down and pulled on her arm again, trying to get her up off Michael's lap.

"No loss. The food at these places always sucks." Michael laughed and reached for my hand. "I'll get you a drink. My expense account takes care of all our liquor needs."

I pulled away from his hand and snarled at him.

He lifted both hands in mock surrender. "Whoa. Take it easy. We're only having fun here."

"This is my birthday present!" I said to Kya, ignoring him. "And you're ruining it."

"It's your birthday?" Michael asked. Alcohol obviously made him less than observant about my mood. Or blissful enough that he didn't care. "Happy birthday. Someone get this lady a drink." He lifted his drink in the air to toast me.

I glared at him and crossed my arms. "Yeah. I'll be eighteen. In two weeks. Not legal to drink yet. Sorry. Both of us are in high school. Not college."

Michael's mouth dropped open. Richard laughed, happier than I'd heard him sound all night. "Eighteen?" He laughed harder and lifted his drink up. "That is awesome."

Michael frowned. "Eighteen's legal though, right?"

"Legal for what, exactly?" I thought about taking off my shoes to use as a weapon on him.

"Dude," Richard said, standing up. "She's ten years younger than you. She's younger than your little sister."

I glanced at Richard, finally appreciating him. "Exactly."

Richard chuckled to himself. "Come on, dude. High school. You want to be her prom date? That's sick. Even for you." He stuck out his free hand and pulled Michael to his feet as Kya untangled herself, her expression confused. Richard clapped Michael on the back, ignoring her as they walked away, disappearing around the corner back to the busy dining area. Richard's laughter echoed behind them.

Kya straightened herself up. "There go my free drinks," she said. And hiccupped. "But I forgive you."

I stared at her. Her slightly smudged makeup. The slack expression. The unsteady body language. "Forgive me?"

The monitor crackled on the TV and I looked up and saw the MC back at the podium.

"Are you freaking kidding me? You lied to get free martinis and you sat out here drinking with some guy you don't even know, instead of sitting inside with me. Having supper, meeting sponsors. Getting ready to meet the Grinders."

The MC announced that awards would be given out shortly and that a video of game highlights would run while everyone enjoyed dessert.

I pulled Kya up by the arm and dragged her, trying not to slip in my shoes.

"You're a party pooper. And I have to pee." She pulled back in the opposite direction and we crashed into a girl walking out of the restroom.

My eyes opened wide.

I stared at the girl. Horrified.

chapter eighteen

S orry," I mumbled, recognizing her face and the purple streak in her hair. Linda something. One of the Grinders. I wanted to cry. She was a sick player. One of their best.

She lifted an eyebrow and I smiled apologetically but I didn't know what to say other than, "Hey."

Kya giggled some more. We both looked at Kya for a minute. The glossy eyes. The stagger in her steps. Her chin drooping down.

"Better take care of your friend," Linda said, her voice not unkind.

"Yeah," I said. "Some guy bought her a bunch of drinks."

"You Grace Black?" she asked me.

"Yeah." I nodded, fighting dueling pleasure and embarrassment that she knew who I was.

"Woo hoo." Kya threw her arms up and punched the air. "Grace Black. Miss Perfect. Look at her. So freaking perfect." Kya slurred and put her head on my shoulder with a sloppy drunken grin. "She can do no wrong, my Skanklet. Unlike me."

"Kya." I untangled myself and smiled at Linda but my lips quivered.

I wanted to cry for Kya, but I wanted to cry for me too. This wasn't the way this night was supposed to go. I wanted a rewind button.

"Something tells me you're going to be holding her hair back for her in there," Linda said. "Isn't that what you girls do for each other?"

I shook my head but she'd already started to walk away. "Good luck," she called.

Not me, I wanted to tell her. I'm not like that. I led Kya into the restroom, wondering if Linda had ever needed to look after a friend in this condition. If she understood.

I pushed hard on the bathroom door and it bounced back and slammed my finger.

It hurt and my eyes filled. "You're ruining everything," I hissed at Kya as she stumbled into the stall.

She leaned against the door and sniffled, but snot ran unattractively down her nose. And then her eyes opened wider and tears gushed out. She dropped her head down. "I'm a terrible friend," she wailed. Her voice broke and she sniffled harder.

I sighed but didn't contradict her as she used her palm as a Kleenex.

"I suck."

She sobbed louder.

I wanted to tell her off again for ditching me alone at the table. Embarrassing me, never mind herself, in front of a top-ranked Grinder. For screwing up. Publicly.

I pushed her gently back and closed the door behind her. She was already blubbering and babbling and there was no use trying to talk sense in her current condition.

"You don't suck. Just go to the bathroom," I said quietly.

She fumbled around and locked the door and while she was in

the stall, I went to the mirror, reapplied lipstick, and blinked at my reflection.

At what point do you walk away from someone who involves you in their screw-ups? I knew in many ways she merely acted the way she thought the world expected her to. Or the way she felt. Messed up. The damaged girl inside her won out sometimes. The damaged girl emerged from too much blue liquor. A few seconds later, she started singing and then she finally emerged from the stall, still pulling down her dress.

"You okay to go back to the party?" I asked. "They're doing awards and speeches and then the mingling will start." I stared at her, wondering if she could keep it together. I wanted to meet Betty. I was willing to take the risk.

"Yesh." She grinned and slipped her hand inside my elbow crook.

We walked slowly back to our seats. I kept my eyes ahead while she giggled and begged me not to be mad at her in an exaggerated whisper. When we reached our table, I smiled and slid into my seat, relieved that someone was at the podium speaking and we didn't have to make excuses.

A waiter walked by and Kya held her hand up to order a drink, but he asked for ID and she pouted as he promised to bring her a soda. Pretending not to notice, I kept my attention on the speaker.

When Betty Baller was called to the podium, I clapped extra loud and sat up straighter. She delivered a great and inspiring speech about women in paintball and how we could help the game and work with the men. I looked beside me to see if Kya got the message. Her head was on her chest. She'd fallen asleep.

The image of pressing my hands on her throat did not seem an unreasonable one. I wanted to stay. To make an impression. A good one.

The man on her other side lifted his eyebrows, his lips pressed tight. I sighed. I had to get her out of here. What else could I do? Best friends looked after each other.

So much for making my way over to the Grinders table and introducing myself. So much for the speech I'd prepared for Betty. I needed to get Kya out of there.

I grabbed her shoulder and shook hard. She opened her eyes, groaning and grumbling. "Come on, Sleeping Beauty," I whispered, and helped her get to her feet. She was coherent enough to get up, so I waved off one of the men who offered to help, glancing over at the table where Betty Baller returned after her speech. The table was lined with girls from the Grinders, including purple-haired Linda. Betty Baller's eyes narrowed and one of the other girls leaned over and said something, but I quickly turned my back, pretending not to see them.

Supporting Kya as discretely as I could, we worked our way through the ballroom and finally out the door into the still empty lobby. With my lips pressed tight, we walked back the way we'd come in. When we passed the concierge, he discreetly turned his head. Kya mumbled and apologized to me as we headed to the elevator. When it arrived, we got on and she started to cry when it moved.

"Everyone hates me. I can't do anything right." Her voice echoed in the tiny square space.

"Oh, Kya," I sighed, watching the numbers as they slowly moved up the floors. Genuine sympathy seeped into my anger, but Kya probably wouldn't even remember this in the morning.

She exhaled loudly, tipping back and forth on her feet. "I'm an asshole. You shouldn't even be my friend. I don't deserve you." She sighed. "James is right. I ruin everything." Her tears streaked mascara down her cheeks, adding to the messy "girls gone wild" thing she had going on.

"You're definitely a mess right now," I told her in a soft voice.

"All the time." Fresh tears leaked from her eyes. "No one loves me. Why would they?"

I stepped closer and put my arm over her shoulder. "I may not be happy with you right now, but I still love you."

She shook her head and laid it on my chest. "No. Don't love me. Don't."

"Shhh. Shhh." Part of me wanted to yell, "Quit screwing up." The other part of me wanted to hold her closer and tell her everything would be okay.

Finally, the elevator reached our floor and the doors slid open. I pulled her outside to the hall. She stared at the carpet as if the geometric pattern mesmerized her. Her shoulders slumped and her head drooped. Then she glanced up, her eyes shiny.

"She called again. She talked to my mom."

The elevator door shushed close behind us. I put some pressure on her elbow, to get her moving.

"What did she say?" I whispered.

"She asked my mom to ask me to help her."

I took a deep breath. No one had helped Kya. God knows. Look at her now.

"What did your mom say?" We walked slowly down the hallway. She stumbled a little and I steadied her, checking the door numbers. Our room was further down.

"She told her no," she said louder, her voice hard, and she pulled away from me.

"Well. What do you want to do?" I asked.

"What I want is not to be." Her voice sounded raw and hollow. She looked at me. "Don't look so scared. I don't want to kill myself but let's face it, it would be better for everyone if I'd never been born."

I stopped. "Kya. That's not true."

Her face collapsed, drooping as if she hadn't slept in weeks. Muffled laughter from inside a hotel room rang in the air. Deceptive hilarity.

"Kya, your parents can be assholes, but they don't think that. They don't." I pressed on her back to get her moving.

If I thought it would help, I would have turned around, gone back down the elevator, and driven two hours to her house, woken up her parents, and made them tell Kya they loved her. Made them tell her they were sorry for what happened to her. And that they didn't think it was her fault. She was buckling under the weight of her guilt. She'd done the right thing, taking the guy to court. Her parents never stepped up to convince her that no matter what the judge said, they thought she was innocent. She needed to hear that.

But they wouldn't say it. I couldn't make them.

Instead, they cursed, drank, and ate their feelings away. By not dealing, they were causing a bigger wound.

"What do you want to do?" I asked softly. "About the girl?"

She choked. "Nothing. Exactly what was done for me. Nothing."

I pulled her close and we reached our room, I tried to imagine what I would do in her shoes. I didn't know. Why should Kya face him again after the outcome last time? As much as I felt badly for the other girl, Kya was my person. She came first.

She hiccupped.

Super.

I put my finger to my lips. "Mom is probably sleeping. Try to be quiet," I whispered.

"Sorry." She sighed. "Michael was hot, wasn't he?" Her voice was hard and angry.

"No," I said softly. "He wasn't hot. He was old and gross. And you deserve better than a guy who gets you drunk to try to score."

She snorted. "As if he needed to get me drunk."

"You don't have to sleep with guys," I whispered, "to make them like you."

She stared at me for a moment with heavy eyelids. "You don't get it, do you, Gracie? I sleep with them so they won't like me."

My heart broke for her a little more.

chapter nineteen

O h, sweetie," I said.

She snorted again. "Sweet as a dill pickle."

She stood straighter and swallowed repeatedly, as if to keep back a puddle of black emotions. "Don't tell Lucas I was flirting with that guy. Okay?"

"I don't plan on telling Lucas anything."

She nodded but she looked crumpled.

"You okay to go in?" I asked, and stuck my hand in my purse, searching for the hotel card.

"Give me a minute," she said, and sniffled.

I swiped the key in the door. "I'll see if my mom is still up," I whispered. She bent over, breathing deep, and propped her back against the wall. I lifted my finger to let her know I'd be a second, pushed open the door, and stepped inside. As soon as the pattern on the carpet changed from hallway to room, I kicked off my ridiculous shoes. My feet silently cheered. The heavy door slipped behind me and shut.

"Shoot," I whispered, staring at it. Then I tiptoed around the corner toward the two queen-size beds.

"Hey!" a voice called.

I grabbed my heart. "Geez. You scared me."

Mom sat cross-legged on a bed, watching TV, the volume turned off.

"You're early. How was the dinner?" she said when she saw me. She squinted past my shoulder. "Where's Kya?"

"Uh." My bottom lip quivered. "She's coming. Um. The dinner kind of sucked. And she's kind of upset."

Mom's face wrinkled up, showing her concern. "Really? You were so looking forward to it, what happened? Why are you back so soon? Where is she?" she repeated.

I bit my lip. Mom uncrossed her legs and stood. "What's wrong? What happened? Where is Kya?"

"She's fine. She's, uh, in the hallway." I kind of wanted to leave her there. "Composing herself."

"Why?"

I looked at Mom. Of all the times in the world to act maternal, she'd pick this moment? "Promise not to get mad?"

She frowned. "That is not a good question to ask, especially when you're a teenager."

I nodded. "I know." I took another deep breath. "Kya..." I paused, not sure what to say.

"What?" She took a step toward me and then another and reached for my hand.

I chewed the inside of my cheek. And decided to go with the truth. God. I seriously needed some lessons in parental deception.

"Some guy kept buying her drinks," I said, aware that my strategy consisted solely of trying to lay the blame on him. "They were strong. And she doesn't handle liquor very well. So, she's kind of drunk. And upset."

Mom sighed loudly, dropped my hand, and walked past me to the door. "That child is more than a small handful."

"It wasn't her fault, Mom."

She had her hand on the doorknob but turned back. "Grace, she made the decision to accept the drinks on her own. And she drank them."

My mom. The hard ass.

"I'll talk to her and bring her inside. Take off your dress. Change into something comfortable." She opened the door. "Oh, Kya." She mumbled something else I didn't hear.

I went to the door to hold it open. Mom slipped an arm under Kya's underarms and helped her inside, muttering things in her ear.

Kya was mumbling back and crying softly again. Mom and I helped her to the empty bed and sat her down. Mom pulled off her shoes and pushed her gently back, pulling away covers and tucking them around her.

"This one can sleep in her dress," she said to me. Kya closed her eyes, falling asleep immediately or, more accurately, passing out.

"Thank God one of you is responsible." Mom turned back and patted my arm. "I guess I can thank your dad for that too."

"Probably," I agreed, and went to my overnight bag, took out my pajamas, and went to the bathroom to change and wash my face and brush my teeth.

When I got back to the main room, Mom was sitting on her bed, watching Kya.

"I worry about this child," she whispered.

My heart ached a little, the way she kept an eye on Kya with such concern. I had a teeny bit of Kya in me after all, wishing for more from my mom. How many times when I'd been younger had I wished she would have been more affectionate? True, she was always there for me, but more often than not with a joke instead of a hug or a kiss. That's just the way she was. I thought I'd accepted it.

I nodded. "I worry about her too."

She held out her hand and pulled me down beside her and we both stared at Kya.

"But not you," she said.

"You know me. The responsible one."

She paused. "You're a good kid. Better than I was at your age. That's for sure."

"The Dad influence," I said.

She nodded and stared at the floor for a minute. "I haven't always been the kind of mom you needed." She sighed. "Your dad told me over and over that I don't show enough. How I feel. It's hard for me. To express myself that way. I hope that hasn't been too awful for you, having a mom like me. My sarcasm is such a defense mechanism. I never learned how to deal with my feelings like you do."

I shook my head and opened my mouth, my cheeks flushing.

"It's okay. Let me finish. You're sensitive and you take on people and their problems. Like Kya." She sighed again. "But be careful you don't forget about yourself." She smiled but it didn't reach her eyes. "I admire you. I don't know that I showed you enough."

"I have plenty of issues of my own, don't worry," I told her.

She smiled but it was lopsided. "They probably stem from not being hugged enough as a child."

I pushed lightly on her arm. "Or being dropped on my head," I joked. "Whatever, Mom. You could have done a lot worse. A LOT." I smiled. "You're a good mom. I'll keep you."

"No." She wiped under her eyes. "I'm happy you haven't resorted to this." She gestured at Kya. "Don't."

I blew out. "Not my style." The air conditioner flicked on with a loud thump and a whir.

"Thank God," Mom said. "It's so humid in this room. I'm hot-flashing all over the place."

We smiled at each other and sat in silence for a moment, listening to people in the hallway opening doors and laughing. And then it was quiet again. Just the whir of the air conditioner.

"Alcohol makes things worse when people use it to cope." We didn't move, squished up side by side, our knees touching. "I don't want to preach but I know. I used to do that. When I was younger. Drink too much."

"You never told me that before," I said quietly.

"Well, I haven't needed to. Honestly, I'm so proud of you. The way you handle yourself."

I wanted to ask more, but she stood, apparently done with the conversation about her boozy teen self. She patted the bed and moved to the other side, pulling the covers back for me to crawl under. "Sleep with me. If Kya gets sick tonight, you don't want to be the one she lands on."

She went to the bathroom, brought out a white, stiff towel, and laid it beside Kya's head. Then she turned off the lights and snuggled under the covers, slipping in beside me. It had been a long time since I'd slept in the same bed as her. But it was oddly comforting.

"The guy who raped her," I whispered, stretched out on my back staring at the ceiling. "He did it again. To another girl." I puffed my pillow up and burrowed my head into the middle of it.

Mom inhaled sharply, also on her back, but turned her head to me. "How do you know?"

"She phoned Kya. At home. And then her mom. She wants Kya to talk to her lawyer. Kya's been really messed up from the calls."

"Poor Kya." Mom said. "Half the problem is the way her parents handled it," she whispered. "So much like mine."

I held my breath. The air conditioner clicked off and the silence startled me.

"She went to a few sessions with a therapist, didn't she?" Mom whispered.

I nodded in the dark even though she wasn't looking at me. "A couple times and then her mom had her eye surgery and couldn't drive. Her dad wouldn't take her. She never went back."

"I remember." She reached over and ruffled my hair. "She's going to deal in destructive ways until she comes to terms with it."

I blinked in the darkness.

"She won't," I said. "Get help, I mean. I try to talk to her. But she doesn't want to. Ever. The only reason it came up was the girl calling. It set her off."

My fingers went to my ear, twirling around my earring.

"Who was the boy who bought her drinks tonight?"

"I don't know. Some guy. Guys like Kya. She can get them to do whatever she wants. She flirts a lot." I stopped before I said more.

Mom exhaled loudly. "People deal differently. Flirting is part of trying to take back power."

I nodded in the dark and twirled my earring round and round in my ear.

"It's about control." She sighed. "Some girls shut down. Others get promiscuous."

A single tear dripped down my cheek. "I feel bad for her, Mom. But…" I swallowed and took a deep breath. "But I'm mad too. She wrecked our night. You know? We were supposed to use this night to impress the Grinders. She made a fool of herself and ditched me for some stupid guy and his drinks, and I had to look after her instead of getting to know the Grinders. And Betty Baller was there."

"It's okay to be mad," Mom said, ruffling my hair. "You have the right to want what you want."

An ache in my chest that lingered since dinner mutated and grew. "But I couldn't leave her there."

"No. Not really. But you need to think about things, Grace. What you're willing to give up to get what you want." She clucked her tongue. "But first you have to know what you want."

I wanted to make the Grinders. But I couldn't walk away from Kya to do it. Could I?

"What would you do if you were me?" I asked.

"I don't know what you can do. Other than caring." She patted my head and rested her hand on my forehead. "I had a friend. In high school." She paused and took her hand away. "She was incredibly promiscuous as a teen, a mess through her teens really. She was raped when she was young. But she got therapy and got on track and she's now happily married with a family."

"That's awful," I said.

"It is. But the good news is she made it out."

We were both silent for a moment. The room whirred with unfamiliar sounds and smells.

"You're a good friend. But it's important to go after what you want." She exhaled slowly. "Kya takes up a lot of air in a room. And you've always let her. Maybe I have too."

"I want Kya to be okay," I said.

On the bed beside us, Kya snored softly.

"I know." Mom smiled. "I think she will be. In time. And what about you? Don't lose sight of your own goals."

"Hmm," I said, pondering. My goals had always included Kya. But what if they didn't?

Mom yawned and then flipped onto her side, facing me. "Hopefully, Kya's using protection. You too. I am far too young and foxy to be a grandmother."

"Mom!" My cheeks burned so hot I'm surprised my pillow didn't smoke.

"You planning on joining a nunnery?" she asked.

I buried my head. "I heard the outfits are nice."

"Seriously, Grace."

"Seriously, Mom. Not going there with you."

After a moment, she giggled. "Okay. Truce. No safe-sex talk tonight. Just, you know. Be careful."

Kya snorted loudly and I looked over, but she was deep in her inebriated sleep.

Mom and I giggled. "I hope she feels terrible in the morning," Mom said, and flipped over onto her side.

"Me too," I agreed.

I sat up with a sudden urge to check my cell phone. I grabbed my purse from the bedside table and reached for it. When it powered on, the message indicator flashed.

"You're actually going to text that boy right after our sex talk?" Mom mumbled but didn't roll over. "Please don't be sexting."

I reached over and smacked her lightly on the butt and she giggled.

Hot yoga sucked without you.

The message from Levi changed my mood. I smiled in the dark, forgetting my friend and her problems for a lovely moment.

And then Kya cried out.

I watched over her as if she were my toddler, even as a twinge of resentment nestled into my head. For some reason, I thought about my mom complaining about all the burping and clothing and feeding she used to do for us when we were small.

She always said she'd never change having us, but she wouldn't want to do it again.

I think I understood her sentiments a little better.

chapter twenty

Kya got out of bed and grumbled something to my mom about hopping into the shower while I lay half asleep on the bed. Mom was already up and sitting at the little desk across from our bed, drinking coffee and reading the paper, fully dressed and made up. I pretended to be sleeping to avoid talking to either of them. When Kya emerged from the bathroom followed by a puff of steam, but smelling and looking much better than she did going in, I finally sat up. She'd blow-dried her hair and put on makeup and walked around the corner into the main part of the room, seemingly bent on acting as if nothing out of the ordinary happened the night before. She smiled at me as she plunked her ass down on the edge of her bed.

"So," Mom called, looking up from her paper. "How's your head?"

Kya ducked her chin and stared at the floor. "It's been better, but I don't feel too bad."

I hid my grin. No burying it under the rug the way her parents would have. She wouldn't be able to pretend nothing happened in this hotel room.

"No more repeat performances from you, missy," Mom said to Kya.

"I'm really sorry," she said. Her eyes filled with tears and she sniffled, still studying the pattern in the rug. "It was really stupid."

Mom stood up, walked over to the bed, and sat beside her. "Can we chat for a moment?" she said to me.

I slipped out of bed, grabbed my bag, and went to the bathroom to shower and give them privacy. I didn't particularly want to be a part of that conversation anyhow.

After I finished primping in the bathroom, I emerged and Kya and Mom were still perched on the bed, but they were hugging. Kya looked at me and wiped her eyes as Mom let her go.

"You look nice," Kya said. I glanced down at my jeans shorts and Splatterfest T-shirt knotted at the bottom because of its huge size and shrugged. "I'm going for comfort. You look nicer. Even with your hangover," I added because I needed to.

She wore a glittery red tank top with tan shorts and low heels and her hair looked great, her makeup flawless. Her cheeks darkened slightly and she glanced at my mom who nodded as Kya stood. "I'm sorry, Graceling. For putting you in that situation last night," Kya said, her voice cracking.

I nodded, freshly remembering my exposure to the sad little girl who still lived inside of her. "I know," I said softly. She came over and hugged me.

"All packed and ready to go?" Mom said, retrieving her own bag from on top of the dresser. Kya gathered up her fake Prada purse and slung it over her shoulder.

I slipped on laceless sneakers and we all grabbed our overnight bags, did a last minute room check, and then headed out, down the slow elevator to the hotel lobby for a free continental breakfast. Mom and I loaded our plates with buns and muffins and fatty carbs. Kya popped a Tylenol with her coffee and nibbled at half a bagel as we filled our faces.

"Hangovers are an appetite killer, aren't they, Kya?" Mom said.

Kya smiled sheepishly. "I know, Mrs. B."

"God. I sound like my mother." Mom shook her head and went to get a refill of coffee.

Kya glanced across the table "I really am sorry. About last night. Ditching you at dinner."

I nodded, not ready to forgive her entirely but also feeling tugs of sympathy.

"Your mom is handling it pretty amazingly," she said.

"Because you're not her daughter," I said. And she feels sorry for you, I added in my head. "But please don't get drunk in front of her again. Until we're at least thirty. She likes to pretend she's cool and I don't think she can handle being the responsible one again for a long time."

Kya grinned and then Mom returned to the table with a to-go cup of coffee, and the three of us checked out, loaded everything into the car, and walked over to the convention center. As if by unspoken agreement, we tucked away memories of the night and prepared to have a most excellent adventure.

The tradeshow floor was huge. Rows of booths ran farther than I saw from the entrance. We put on our lanyards and headed into the crowd. Sales guys operated equipment booths and players young and old roamed up and down the aisles. Music, shouting, and laughter jammed the hot air in the room. Someone shoved a map and list of events in my hand and I scanned it for the Grinders booth.

A festive, even joyful vibe drifted in the air, with shouts from players we recognized making me feel like a minor celebrity. The ickiness in my belly was buried under the feel-good vibes floating around. Webcasts of games blasted from a booth to my right and I recognized the D'Ailly brothers and Chantelle on the screen. I yelled and pointed to Kya and she nodded, but she was moving toward the Empire Ax booth, eyeing the latest gun that wouldn't even be released until September. Lights flashed, noise levels accelerated, and some of the adrenaline I loved about the game pumped into my veins.

We moved, distracted and as hyper as little kids in a candy store. Mom was an awesome sport, following us from booth to booth, meeting paintball people and answering questions about Dad and checking out new equipment with us. It wasn't her world but she was playing along like a pro. When we passed by a booth with Richard and Michael in it, we veered around it widely and they didn't appear to see us.

Finally, we turned a corner and headed toward the Grinders booth. I stopped and took a big cleansing breath and grabbed Kya's hand, squeezing hard. She twisted away.

"Sweaty," she said, scrunching up her nose.

"You can do this," Mom whispered in my ear. "Just be yourself." She patted my back, discretely mouthing "good luck," and wandered off in a different direction to give me privacy. I glanced at her as she left, saying an inner prayer of thanks that she knew me well enough to give me space to schmooze on my own.

I walked. Strutted really. Shoulders back. Head held high. The way Dad taught me. In the booth, I spotted Betty Baller under the Grinders banner. She saw me as I got closer and raised her hand. "Grace Black!" she called. "I knew I recognized you. Come on over."

I ignored the shooting balls of nerves in my belly, pasted a big smile on my face, and walked. I glanced behind me, but Kya had stopped to talk to someone and wasn't following. I frowned but wiped it off as I swiveled back to Betty.

"There you are!" Betty said as I reached her. She looked younger up close. And pretty. Smooth dark skin. Amazing green eyes that looked right inside me.

I stuck out my hand and she grasped mine with both hands. "Awesome shirt," she said. "And so good to see you. I've heard so many great things about you from Lola," she told me, and then pulled me in for a quick hug.

"Thanks," I said as we broke apart. "I've heard so many great things about you too. And the Grinders!"

She nodded, smiling at me. "I recognized you at dinner last night, but you disappeared and I didn't see you at the party."

I glanced behind me for a second, looking for Kya, and then quickly back at Betty. "Yeah. My friend Kya wasn't feeling so great, so I took her to bed early." My face warmed.

"That's too bad," Betty said. "You could have met Ciara Janaye. She was at the party signing autographs and hanging out."

"No way." I cursed Kya in my head. Ciara Janaye was one the most famous female players in the world. She was from Brazil. Her poster was on my wall at home and another huge one papered the wall at Splatterfest.

Betty pulled over a couple of players who were in the booth dressed in Grinder Gear. Pink and orange suits of awesome. I recognized Linda, but she was on the other side of the booth chatting with a girl about my age. The girls were awesome, funny, and full of great advice and practice tips. We chatted for a few more moments and they said wonderful things about Lola's webcast I'd shot with Chantelle. I beamed, thrilled they'd seen it, knew who I was, and thought I had mad skills.

I babbled about some of their games I'd watched online.

"I can't wait to see you play live," Betty said with a smile.

We chatted some more about Lola and then Betty asked about my dad and Splatterfest. She was amazed they'd never met, but said she was sure they'd be seeing each other a fair bit in the future. My heart skipped happily with those implications.

"What are your marks in school like?" she asked. I told her I had a solid grade point average in my junior year and was going to work hard in my senior year and wouldn't have any problem making the grades needed for college.

"That's awesome, Grace," she said. "I get a good sense you'd fit in well with my girls and Lola thinks so too. I'm really hoping to invite you out to a game this year, to hang out with the girls, get a feel for who we are and how we play. I'd love to have you practice with us. See how you interact."

We chatted for a while longer about her team and what she liked in her players. She was nicer than I'd imagined and easy to talk to, and with every word, every inch of me wanted to be on her team. Linda walked over then and bumped me with her hip.

"Hey, Grace! I looked for you after dinner but didn't see you around."

"Yeah. Kya wasn't feeling so great"

I ignored the knowing look on her face and looked around for Kya, wondering what she was doing. She should be over here sucking up. This was the main reason we were here. To network. Make a good impression. Yo. This was the moment. Happening without her.

I spotted Kya at the far edge of the Grinders booth, batting her eyelashes at a tall, handsome dude wearing a Grinders T-shirt. I frowned and raised my hand in the air to flag her over but she didn't see it. One of the other Grinder girls made a joke and I turned back.

I nodded my head, no idea what they were talking.

"I heard there's another girl in Tadita we want," one of the Grinders said.

"Yeah. Kya! She wants to play as much as I do. We play really well together. She'll be right over," I piped up.

We all glanced over to where Kya was making eyes at the painter dude.

Betty pressed her lips together and tapped her fingers over them. "Actually I think we're talking about another player. Chantelle D'Ailly. Lola said she showed a lot of promise." She glanced toward

Kya. "Kya needs to take herself and this game a little more seriously if she wants to make the Grinders."

"She's an awesome baller," I said. "She loves the game."

"Hmm. Well. She needs to show it. I know you're friends and I appreciate loyalty, but she's got to prove she has what it takes off the field as well as on. She's really strong, but we need a team player who represents the Grinders."

Behind us, the Grinder girls laughed and we both turned to see a little girl dressed in a colorful tutu with a T-shirt and cowboy boots, talking a million miles a minute. A daddish guy was behind her, grinning.

I turned back, wondering if Lola mentioned the incident with Steve and the bonus balls to Betty. More than likely, from the sounds of it. My stomach turned. I stared at Kya but she didn't look over. What the heck was she doing? She seriously needed to leave her flirting for another time. I pressed my lips tight, panic making them dry.

The Grinder girls oohed and aahed, apparently captivated by the little girl in her tutu.

"She can," I told Betty. "She's got some family stuff she's dealing with right now. She's kind of off," I said quickly. "Bad timing, she's a little distracted." I narrowed my eyes at Kya and she finally glanced over, as if she sensed us talking about her. Then she threw her head back and laughed at something painter dude said. Perfect.

"I understand. I do. But players gotta learn to leave personal stuff off the field," she said. "When we're out in public, we're representing the sport, but also the school. And corporate sponsors. Most college athletic teams have a strict no liquor during the season rule, and we're one of them."

"Yeah." I nodded my head. "That's cool. I mean, good. Not a problem."

"Not a problem for you?" She smiled and glanced back at Kya and painter dude.

I returned a weak grin. "She's really great, she really is."

"Well, my boyfriend seems to like her," she said.

My features must have revealed my absolute horror that Kya was flirting with Betty's boyfriend because Betty laughed. "Don't worry. I'm only kidding. I mean, Keith really is my boyfriend, but I'm not worried. I trust him. It's no big deal. He can handle girls like Kya."

The hair on my arms stood up. Girls like Kya? Oh man. Not good. Not good at all.

I lifted my hands up to my mouth like a megaphone. "Kya," I shouted loudly. I think it startled Betty but Kya looked over. I narrowed my eyes and tightened my mouth, motioning for her to join us. Kya glanced at the handsome dude, he smiled at Betty, nodded, and said something, and then they both walked toward us.

"I'm looking forward to talking some more," Betty said. "And keep those webcasts coming! I have your contact info from Lola. So we'll chat again, okay?"

"Awesome." I smiled but wanted to kill Kya with my bare hands.

Keith reached us first and he slid his arm over Betty's shoulder. "This is my girl," he said to Kya. "Betty Baller."

Kya smiled.

"This is Keith, he plays for the Paparazzis," Betty said to me. "This is Grace. The baller I've been telling you about."

He reached out to shake my hand. He had a wicked tattoo on his arm of a jacked-up paintball gun. "The Paparazzis?" I asked, impressed. He nodded. "Cool." I turned to Betty. "You know Kya." I sent Kya a telepathic message to act charming and smart.

"Nice to meet you in person," Kya said to Betty. "I've seen lots of your footage online. You and your team are awesome."

I nodded, silently urging her to keep talking, to bond. I wanted Betty to see the real Kya too, the girl I loved, but Betty was already looking past her and waving at someone who'd entered the booth. I followed her gaze. An older man in a dark suit reeking of money raised his hand in the air.

"Sorry, I gotta talk to this guy. He's a potential sponsor." She patted Kya's shoulder and then slipped away from us, her boyfriend at her side, his arm still draped over her shoulder.

Kya watched them walk away. "Her boyfriend is pretty cool," she said, but her voice was flat. "He's going to play against Jotham in Florida." Across the booth, Betty and Keith grinned while the older guy used his hands to tell an animated story.

"Why were you talking to him? You should have been here meeting Betty."

Kya lifted a shoulder and brought her thumbnail up to her mouth, glancing over at the other Grinders. "I thought you'd want some time with her first. You know. Let her see how awesome you are."

I scowled. "What about you? You have to make a good impression too."

Kya kept chewing her thumb but didn't look at me. "I didn't think she'd be too happy with me after last night. I remember running into Linda outside the bathroom. I didn't want to ruin your chances."

"Oh, Kya," I said. "You messed up, but you can undo it. You have to prove you want this. Show her who you really are." I grabbed her arm and tugged her toward Betty and Keith. "That old guy won't talk forever. We'll wait until he's done. You need to talk to her again. Let her see how cool you are. And dedicated to the sport."

Kya tugged her arm back and narrowed her eyes. "I'm sorry. I feel like crap. My head hurts. I'm tired and schmoozing with Betty Baller isn't something I feel up to." She walked out of the booth. I followed, biting my tongue to keep from giving her a lecture about her drinking.

"Kya." I grabbed her hand in front of an outfit booth. "Come on. You need to do this."

She shook her head. "No, I don't."

"What'd you say to her boyfriend?" I crossed my arms, peering at her.

"Nothing horrible. Don't look at me like that."

The way she was acting lately, I had no idea what she might have said. Overhead on the speakers, a deep voice announced a product demo was taking place at the main stage. A group of teen boys rushed past, pushing each other trying to get to the front first. I suspected the demo going on involved girls in skimpy outfits.

"Seriously. We were talking paintball. He was telling me about his team. They're fricking good."

"I know." I watched the boys disappear into the crowd. "He plays for the Paparazzis."

"Excuse me for not studying everyone's portfolio." She made a face at me. "School doesn't start for a few more weeks."

"But this is important! This was our chance to make an impression." I didn't have to point out she hadn't made a good one.

"Maybe I've gone along with you without thinking about what I want."

"You're only saying that because you're hungover."

She spun on her heel, storming off, and I watched as another man joined Betty and Keith. A lineup was forming. With a sigh, I hurried off after Kya.

By the time I caught up with her, Mom had spotted us and rushed over to see what Betty said. Some of my excitement returned but I avoided looking at Kya as I gave my mom a play-by-play, and left out the parts about Kya's bad attitude.

Mom clapped her hands and then declared that she was starving and needed lunch. While we lined up at a concession to pay too much for a hot dog and soda, I pulled out my phone and texted Levi. He texted back immediately and my heart dinged with glee. I sent James a text to let him know that I'd talked to Betty but didn't mention Kya's behavior to him either.

Kya kept her head buried in her phone and Mom carried on a conversation with a woman standing behind her. When she left to go use the restroom, Kya put down her phone and reached for my hand.

"You did great with Betty," she said with a shy smile. "That's the real reason I got the tickets. For you. Not me." She smiled wider. "Don't worry about me, okay?"

I tucked my phone back in my purse. "I do worry about you. I want you to be with me at college, but—"

"Butt." She turned and wiggled her butt at me, but it was unenthusiastic and I didn't even smile. She stared out at the crowd walking the trade floor and then looked back at me. "I know you want good things for me, Grace. I do."

Mom rejoined us and we finally got to the front and ordered our food. We walked for a moment, trying to find a table, but that was impossible so we kept walking while we ate.

A blob of mustard dripped from the hotdog onto my shirt. My Splatterfest white shirt. I groaned. Kya laughed and handed me one of her napkins.

"I'm such a klutz," I mumbled.

"You get that from your father," Mom said with a smile because she was always covered in food stains herself.

"That's another reason I love you." Kya wound her free arm around mine. "You're so in tune with your faults."

I frowned down at the yellow stain right in the middle of my left boob. "I'm a loser," I groaned. "Thank God we talked to Betty already."

Kya made a face. "You're not a loser, you're a trendsetter. It looks like a paintball splat."

She unlocked her arm from my elbow and dipped a finger into her hotdog bun, smeared it with mustard and pressed it against her own shirt. I sucked in a breath. She'd spent a big part of her paycheck on that sparkly top.

Mom laughed and then happily stuck her finger in her hotdog bun, but she hated mustard and instead wiped it with a blob of ketchup. She smeared it over her T-shirt but it was black and it didn't even show up. We all laughed.

Our moods lightened, our tanks filled, we got into the groove again, cruising around peeking at new equipment and seeing more familiar faces. With lots of positive attention, Kya's spirits rose and she seemed almost back to her old self.

"I'm glad I came with you girls," Mom said. "Despite your shenanigans last night."

Kya's ears turned red.

"I like seeing you in this world," Mom said. "I've always kind of wondered if it was too macho or a good example for you girls, but I like you here. Blazing new trails. There're not many places where women are still in the minority. You're doing us proud, girls."

"Ugh, Mom, no. Not another speech about how in your day you had to fight for equal rights." I held up my hands in defense and she glared at me and then grinned. "Fine. But you girls have so much to be grateful for—"

"That we don't even know about," Kya and I finished with her.

The three of us laughed and then Mom stopped to admire the work of a tattoo artist who had a booth and was displaying some artwork. Kya put her head on my shoulder.

"Should we ask your mom about our BBS tattoo?" she asked as we watched Mom flip through a book of sketches.

"Uh, now's probably not the best time. We're not completely in her good books yet."

Kya leaned her body against me. Her skin warmed me but it was slightly sticky, and under her vanilla body spray, I detected the slight scent of last night's alcohol sweating from her pores. Behind us on a wooden bench, a guy made a creepy comment to a friend sitting beside him, but we stayed glued together and ignored them.

"I'll make it up to you. I'll get on Betty's good side. And Lola's. Don't worry, okay, Skanklet? It'll be you and me next year. On the Grinders team. Kicking ass and taking names," Kya said.

"We belong on that team," I told her. "Both of us."

"You bet your sweet ass."

One of the creeps behind us whistled. "Talk about sweet asses," he called.

Kya and I both spun around.

He nodded his head and puffed up his chest. With his faux mohawk, he kind of looked like a peacock strutting his feathers. "Hey, ladies. I know how to make you feel real good."

I raised my eyebrows. "So you're leaving then?"

Kya whooped appreciatively and the guy mumbled something about us being lesbians while his friend razzed him and they got up and shuffled off.

"Forgive me?" Kya asked, walking to the bench and plunking down on it. Traces of last night's binge lingered in her tired body.

I wanted to forgive her. I did. But I wanted her to care too. About making the team, yes, but I wanted her to care about herself. And truthfully, I wanted her to care more about me.

"Don't give up on me," she whispered, and for a second, her mask slipped off. Pain shone in her sad eyes, but something else too. Fear.

I had an image of her on a lifeboat, hanging on to it by her finger-nails. I was slipping too. And truth stared me in the face. As I strained to pull her in and keep her afloat, she was starting to drag me under.

chapter twenty-one

J ames and I glared at each other over the counter at work. He was
working on something at the computer. I was in front cleaning
the glass. Kya was in the arena with Indie, cleaning up.

"I'm not going to sugarcoat things for you. You do that on your
own. Anything Kya does, you have an excuse for her. Including
ruining your trip to Seattle."

"I wasn't telling you so you could condemn her. I told you because
I'm worried about her."

Our conversation about her behavior in Seattle was not going
the way I planned. James didn't feel bad for her at all. He thought I
should have left her with the sales guy from the get-go.

"That's not what friends do," I said.

"Exactly," he said.

I sighed. Clearly, we couldn't have a rational talk about Kya. I
was getting sick of it. He needed to know the truth and I was sick
of holding it back.

"I'm going outside to do the windows," I told him and left.

I scrubbed at the windows to get rid of some of my frustration
and then took a break. My face was tilted up to the sky outside the

front of Splatterfest, my eyes closed, enjoying the warmth of the sun when something startled me.

"Grace?"

I spun around, caught taking a break. Then when I saw him, a smile turned up my lips.

"Hey!" I said. "Hi!" My heart thumpity-thumped and the grin on my lips stretched up and an urge to dance tingled in my feet. So much for playing it cool.

"So you got home okay?" Levi stood so close to me I smelled his slightly soapy scent. His hair was wet on the ends. Good grooming habits. I glanced at his face and my hormones swooped into action. My physical reaction to him was much more than friendly, if there'd been any doubt in my mind.

"How was the trip?" he asked, one hand awkwardly behind his back.

I glanced behind me at the building that currently housed Kya and bit my lip, wondering what to tell him. We'd texted of course, but I hadn't filled him in. Split-second, I decided I didn't need to. I didn't want a reaction like James's.

Instead, I made googly eyes at him and told him a little more about Betty and the other things we'd seen at the show, leaving out the parts involving Kya's meltdown. The tightness in my gut loosened. My insides smoothed. Telling Levi the good parts brought back some of the excitement I'd been robbed of.

A goofy smile with a will of its own possessed my face. I looked around the empty parking lot. "You're early. Your league doesn't start for about forty-five minutes."

"I came to see you," he said simply.

My cheeks reddened. "Oh."

"Actually, I brought you something." He pulled his hand from around his back and held up a colorful box with a silver flower sitting on top of it. He held it out and I put down the Windex and took the box. Nerds. I lifted the flower to inspect it. It was heavy and the material seemed very familiar. I laughed.

"Is this made from duct tape?"

He grinned again. "Yeah. My dad taught me to make them when I was a kid. He's kind of a rogue duct-tape crafter."

"Very cool." I grinned down at it.

"I never made one for a girl before," he said.

Music. The words floated into my ears like music. Blushing, I looked into his eyes and we stared at each other, grinning. Swoon. He took a step closer to me. His lips were so close all I had to do was tilt my head up to kiss him.

"And Nerds," I babbled to break the spell. I shook the box, as if the sound of my candies rattling around could shake off lusty thoughts. "My favorite food in the whole world!"

He laughed but didn't take his eyes off me. "I'd hardly call Nerds food."

"I beg to differ. They're kind of a food group all on their own." Shaking the box produced magical tunes. "Thanks."

"You look great," he said softly.

I glanced down at my XL Splatterfest T-shirt hanging to the bottom of my bright pink spandex shorts. "No, I don't." My voice cracked.

"No. Really," he said with a grin. "Very couture."

"Couture?"

"My mom's into fashion. She tosses that word around all the time. I don't even know what it means."

I laughed again. "Well. It doesn't mean this."

The front door opened with a whoosh and we both stepped out of the way to avoid getting hit.

"Oh my God!" Kya yelled as she pushed through. "Your brother and James are driving me crazy!" She stopped when she saw Levi. "What are you doing here? You're way early, dude."

"Hey, Kya," he said. Unlike most boys, his face didn't light up when he saw her.

"Aren't you supposed to be hosing down the bunkers?" I asked, opening my eyes wide to give her the hint to go away.

"I pretend to work, your dad pretends to pay me," she said, and held up her hand to block the sun from her eyes. "I already did. Don't get your panties in a knot." She rolled her eyes at me. "It's nice out here. I should have taken window-cleaning duties." A cloud passed over the sun then, it darkened, and the temperature instantly cooled on my skin. She dropped her hand from her eyes.

"Why're you here so early?" she said, turning to Levi.

I frowned. I'd never be rude like that to one of her boyfriends. I shivered. Oh! My cheeks flamed, realizing I'd called Levi my boyfriend. Coffee, hot yoga, a movie, and a ton of texts, and I'd labeled him my boyfriend?

"I came to talk to Grace." He didn't smile at her.

Despite the friction between them, my embarrassment faded and a new glow lit up my insides. A plane flew noisily over our heads and we waited for the racket to pass. A hazard of having Dad's paintball place so close to the airport. Sometimes it sounded like we were on the runway.

Kya grabbed the flower from my hand. "This is cool," she said when the noise from the plane engine died down. "It's made from duct tape? Where'd you get it?"

"I made it for Grace," Levi told her

"Cool," she repeated. "I approve."

"I'll sleep better tonight," he said.

Kya lifted her eyebrows and pressed the flower in my hand. "Nerds? Someone is paying attention." She stared at him but he didn't flinch. She turned back to me.

"James and Indie are driving me crazy in there talking about Minecraft. They're grown men. Well, Indie is. My head almost exploded." She made the sound of a bomb detonating and flicked her hands in the air. "I should go back inside," she said. She opened her eyes wide at me and went back through the front door.

"Is she okay?" he asked.

"Who knows?" I instantly regretted the way that sounded. "I mean, she's fine."

He took a step closer to me again and I held my breath and made myself stay still. "I really didn't come here early to talk about Kya."

"Oh?"

"Grace?" he said, his expression suddenly serious.

"Yeah?"

"There's something I've been meaning to ask you. It's driving me crazy."

"What?"

He leaned down until his lips were inches from mine. I stared at them, my brain woozy and useless.

"I wanted to know..." he said softly. He licked his top lip. "I've been worrying about wrong signals. You're hard to read." He reached over and brushed my hair back. I held my breath, afraid to move. Willing him. Do it. Don't. Do.

"I know this is weird, but I'm going to ask straight out." He let out a breath and it smelled like peppermint gum. "Can I kiss you?" he asked.

And somehow, his asking made everything perfect. I grabbed his shoulders, still clutching the Nerds, and they rattled as I pulled him down and pressed my lips all the way against his.

It was as amazing as I imagined. More.

I closed my eyes. His lips were soft. He applied the perfect amount of pressure. I wished it would never end. When he pulled slightly back, I let out a sigh. My entire body felt like it could float away in the light breeze. The sun came out from behind clouds, adding warmth from the outside as well as inside.

"Wow," he said.

"Wow," I agreed, fanning myself with my flower-holding hand.

We grinned at each other.

"We definitely should have done that sooner," he said, pressing his forehead against mine.

And then we were doing it again. We lingered slowly on each other's lips, exploring and nibbling. At first, the kisses were soft and slow, and then a whoosh of intensity weakened my entire body and he opened his mouth wider. He made a growling sound in his throat as a car pulled into the parking lot, honking the horn over and over. We stepped away from each other and laughed, glancing over at the car.

"I'd better stop," he said, pushing back his hair and grinning. "But we need to do that again. Soon. In private."

I nodded, biting my lip.

Two guys emerged from the car then, whooping in appreciation. I glanced at them, almost thankful for the virtual cold shower.

"Gracie, you hussy," one called.

I gave him the finger. One of our regulars. He laughed and made kissy sounds as they walked past us and went inside.

"You busy tomorrow night?" Levi asked, and he shoved his hands in his front pockets, grinning kind of bashfully.

"Shoot. I mean, yeah. The Lavender Festival is on. Kya, James, and I go every year. It's kind of our tradition. Just the three of us." I seriously wanted to ask him along, even though we desperately needed trio time alone. I bit my lip to stop myself from inviting him.

He nodded. "That's cool. What about Sunday?"

I paused. "Uh. A paintball tourney. Mini one. But I don't want to miss it. Lola's putting it on at her outdoor place. She told me to come."

He nodded. "No, that's okay. I get it. Okay. One more shot. How about tonight? Are you working late?"

Two birds chasing each other swooped down close to us and then flew up to the roof of Splatterfest.

I grinned. "Until ten."

His lips turned down in disappointment. "But league play ends at nine."

"My turn to close up."

"Oh." He paused. "Well. Maybe I could stick around? If it's okay. I mean, if you want to go get a bite to eat or something after?"

I smiled down at my shoes. "I'd like that." When I looked up, he had a big grin on his face.

"Okay. Good," he said, as if he were super cooled out.

We smiled at each other like idiots.

"I should go inside. You can hang with me at the front while everyone checks in if you want." He nodded and bent and picked up my Windex bottle and cloth for me, and held open the door. I walked through it clutching my flower and box of Nerds as if it were a bouquet.

Loud pops crackled from the arena when we walked in.

"Sorry," I heard Kya yell.

"Kya. Be careful," Dad yelled back. "You almost hit James in the head."

Kya made a wiseass comment and James said something that got lost in the distance.

"Job hazards," I told him as we headed toward the front counter. I pulled out a stool and put it in front of the counter.

Levi kept me entertained while I got the computer system ready for the boys coming in. Dad must have heard Levi was around because he came out front to chat. I cringed a few times as he tried to act all cool and uncoplike with Levi and mostly failed at both. Finally, Kya came out to help me get organized and Dad went back to his office. Boys drifted in. When Lucas came, Kya dragged him off to the coat room for a whispered conversation.

"You think she and Lucas are fighting?" Levi asked as I made a note in the computer about buying new paintballs.

I glanced up, thinking of her making out with the old dude at the party. "I don't know. She never said anything. But who knows? Why?" In the coatroom, I saw their heads close together, deep in conversation.

"He told me he invited her to have dinner with my aunt and uncle and she said no. I think he was kind of hurt."

"Really?" I guessed Kya didn't want to meet his parents or be subjected to scrutiny. Parents of boys were not really her scene. I picked up my box of Nerds and poked my thumb in the opening. I held it up but he shook his head.

"She didn't say anything when you were away?" he asked.

I pretended to be engrossed in something on the screen. "No," I said. "Nothing." I spun around from the computer then, poured out a handful of Nerds, and tossed some in my mouth.

"Mmmm. Nerds."

"He's bummed," Levi said, watching the two of them. "He really likes her."

I crunched my Nerds without responding. James poked his head out of the training room and waved his hand.

"Hey," I said. "Everyone's checked in. You better go suit up. Your team is playing the second round."

Levi sucked his cheeks in and then blew out. "Okay. Here goes nothing."

"Good luck!" I called, watching him walk to the change room, seriously mesmerized by the fit of his jeans. He held his fingers in a peace sign over his head, grinned, and then disappeared inside.

James tapped the microphone in his hand and lifted it to his mouth. "Test. Test." It crackled and loud feedback squealed from the speakers in the arena.

"Indie, turn down the volume," he yelled, and started off toward Dad's office, still flicking the top of the microphone with his finger.

"You've been injected," Kya said, and I jumped a little and turned. She leaned against the counter, her arms crossed, watching me.

Lucas stormed by, following Levi's footsteps but moving faster. "Injected?"

Lucas vanished into the change room.

"Stung in the ass by the love bug. Jones came in and said you were making out with some dude in the parking lot."

I hid my smile under my hand and pretended to cough. No use denying it.

"You've taken things up a notch?" she asked.

I giggled. "Yeah."

A loud cheer and laughter roared from the change room. We both glanced over but the boys were still inside.

"Are you and Lucas having a fight?" I asked.

She sighed. "I don't know."

"I am your father." James's voice boomed from the speakers in his Darth Vader voice. No crackles or feedback accompanied it.

"He doesn't bring me my favorite candy. Or make me flowers from tape."

She slipped behind the counter, reached over me, opened a drawer, and grabbed some birthday party brochures.

"Is that really what you want?" I asked softly.

She added the brochures to the display we had on the counter-top. "No." She stuck out her bottom lip. "Yes." She made a raspberry noise with her tongue. "I don't know…maybe."

"They're different guys," I told her.

"And we're different girls."

I pressed my lips tight and wiped down the counter with Windex and a paper towel as she reached for my Nerds and helped herself to some.

"Maybe that's not his style," I said, and held out my hand. She dumped some candies in it. "He likes you," I told her.

"His parents want to meet me." she said, and stuck out her tongue and it was a little orange from the Nerds. "I am so not into that."

"Why not?" I asked.

There was a stampede of feet as the first teams ran from the train-ing room to the back to grab guns and paint. I spotted Levi and Lucas dressed in camo gear, heading for the bleachers to watch the first round.

"Have we met?" Kya asked. "I don't do parents."

"But he likes you. He wants his parents to like you. It's not that big of a deal."

"But—" she said.

"Butt." I stuck my butt out and wiggled it.

She laughed. "You're not allowed to steal my moves." She sighed then and watched with me as James walked around the outside of the arena going over the rules in a Star Wars voice. I loved how unapologetically nerdy he was. The first game began with a few loud pops and music from the speakers pumped out low so the players could hear themselves yelling over top.

"I don't want anything serious," she said.

Levi jumped down from the bleachers and headed to the back to gear up, and he spotted me and waved. I waved back and a smile turned up the corners of my mouth.

"Look at you," she said. "The opposite of nothing serious."

Fireworks popped in my brain. I smiled in his direction even though he'd disappeared.

"I've never seen you like this before, Grace."

I covered my mouth with my hand and blinked innocently.

"Remember…" She lifted her fingers up and crossed them over each other. "BBS."

"Of course," I told her, touching my lips, and the thought of kissing Levi sent goosebumps racing up my arms.

She rolled her eyes and jumped up on the stool. "So, you want to hang out later tonight?" Kya asked. "When you get home from work? I could bring over a movie. Or we could hang in your room and eat Nerds and ice cream?"

"Uh, I can't." Boys shouted and shot at each other in the background.

She pushed her bottom lip out.

"Levi asked me to get something to eat with him after work."

She scowled and part of me battled to invite her along but I fought the instinct. I wanted to enjoy time with Levi. Alone. I longed to attach myself to his lips again.

I walked closer and nudged her with my elbow. "We're going to the Festival tomorrow though. You, me, and James."

She groaned as a flurry of shots blasted from the arena.

"You haven't forgotten and you are NOT getting out of this. We made the pledge and I reminded you."

The Lavender pledge. Five years ago, James, Kya, and I promised to go to the Festival together every year, without anyone else. We'd each eaten a flower to seal the deal.

"Yeah. That was a long time ago. We were thirteen. And stupid."

"Well. Now we're eighteen and stupid. Well, you and I are. James has never been stupid a day in his life. But that's beside the point. We made a promise. We're going."

"James has been stupid." She jumped off the stool. "Is Levi coming?" Her arm banged against the box of Nerds, it fell to the ground, and candies spilled all over the floor. She glanced at me. "Sorry."

I stared at the colorful Nerds scattered on the floor and sighed. "It's okay. And no, Levi is not coming. Did I not just bring up the pledge?" I walked out from behind the counter toward the closet where Dad stored the cleaning supplies.

She sat down again and watched me while I swept the candies into a pile and then onto the dustpan.

"I'm worried about you." she said as I knelt down.

"Why?" I stood and slid the candies into the trash. Putting my hand on my hip, I stared at her, not backing down.

"Just be careful," she said.

"I could say the same thing to you. In a lot of ways," I told her.

In the background, James announced the end of the first round. Woots and whistles blasted the air.

Kya flicked back her hair and peered the other way, pretending to be interested in the activity in the arena.

"Guys are assholes," she said. "Remember that."

Unfortunately, she believed it was true.

"Not all of them. Levi's a good guy."

"There've been stories. We'll see." She leapt up and headed out toward the back. "I'll go see if your dad and Indie need any help."

And then she was gone.

chapter twenty-two

My heart fluttered with happiness and I put my hands in the air and twirled in a circle, even though Kya and James were dragging their feet a couple of steps behind me. The soothing scent of fresh lavender filled Main Street even more than usual. The smell lightened my mood and contributed to my dancing despite the growliness of my two best friends.

They couldn't ruin this for me today. My date with Levi had been wonderful, with lots of kisses to make up for lost time. I'd stayed up late dreaming of more.

The Lavender Festival was one of my absolute favorite things about summer in Tadita. Yes, it was hokey and old-fashioned. There were no fancy electronics or rides or games or flashy displays. But there was food and flowers and I loved every inch of it. Even the weather was cooperating with sunshine and no rain or dark clouds in sight.

As part of the festivities, almost everyone wore purple somewhere on their body. Even James wore a purple T-shirt. Kya had a purple boa wrapped around her neck and both of us wore awful purple feather earrings I bought us a few years ago. I rocked a pair of purple shorts that did absolutely nothing for my skin tone, but I didn't care.

Vendors were set up all over streets closed off to traffic. Jewelry. Crafts. And of course there were flowers. Flower displays everywhere. We passed a cotton candy vendor with no lineup and I stopped and bought the biggest bag of purple cotton candy they had. I ripped off a hunk and shoved it in Kya's mouth until she laughed, getting it all over her face and hands. James dug his hand in the bag and came out with half the spun sugar, smiling like a little boy.

"My kryptonite," he said happily.

The sugar rushed to our brains and my grumpy friends loosened up a little.

"Look!" I yelled.

At the end of the street, there was a contest going on and a parade of dogs on leashes were wearing costumes and trotting in a circle with their owners. Some of the owners wore matching outfits. I spotted a Chihuahua dressed as Yoda. And a wiener dog bride.

"Ahhhh." Even Kya laughed and pointed out her favorites. We howled when a huge sheep dog dressed as Princess Leia rounded up her back to take a gigantic poop in front of the judges. And then a dog dressed as Shrek mounted Yoda, and the little boy holding the leash yelled at the top of his lungs. The three of us cracked up again.

"So," I said to Kya. "We're going to set James up with Chantelle. They will totally love each other. And get married and have babies."

Kya glanced at James. "Hmm. Maybe."

I giggled. "Look how red you are, James. Chantelle can't wait to meet you. I am so stoked."

"Come on. Let's go to the barns to see the horses," Kya said with a skip in her step. Her favorite part of the fair was horses wearing beautiful floral bouquets. Most of the horse owners offered free rides down Main Street.

The barns were past the Recreation Center where one of the ice skating areas was cleared to the concrete floor and used to display fair entries. We hadn't gone inside, but I knew from memory that rows and rows of tables would be set out, lined with entries for contests like best pie or best LEGO creation. Some would have ribbons on them. In eighth grade, I'd won the prize for my home-made flower planter and still had the cherry red ribbon pinned to the bulletin board in my room.

We waltzed past the Recreation Center and then James stopped at another vendor to buy a bag of fresh kettle corn. He walked backward in front of me to offer me a handful and turned quickly and I opened my mouth to warn him but there was a big thunk. I stopped and winced on his behalf. He'd walked straight into a pole. With his nose.

"Ouch." He rubbed his nose and blood covered his hand.

Kya laughed. "Dude," she said. "I think you dented that pole."

"He's hurt." I bumped her with my hip. "You okay?" I asked. We stopped walking and people veered around us. I took his arm and pulled him off to the side of the road. Kya followed behind us.

"I'm fine," he said in a nasal voice, holding his nose.

"You're not fine."

I took the popcorn bag from his other hand and saw that blood had dripped over the top. I wrinkled my nose up and tossed it in a nearby trashcan. Then I pushed James down so he was sitting on the curb. "You okay?" I sat down beside him and pulled off the hoodie I'd wrapped around my waist for later, when the sun went down. I handed it to James. "Press this to your nose." He said no but his nose was bleeding and spilling over his hands.

"Go ahead, James, it's black. And old." Not exactly true. I'd bought it at the beginning of the summer, but we didn't have anything else to sop up his blood with. I put it gently to his nose and he took it and held it there.

"Whoa," Kya said, and plopped her butt on the other side of me. "You have a lot of blood for such a skinny guy," she said to him.

"I can spare it," he said without glancing at her.

"It's not like sperm, James. It doesn't grow back."

"Sperm doesn't grow back. It takes two and a half months to mature in the body."

"Now you're an expert on sperm too? Funny, 'cause it's not like you're exactly going around filling the women of the world with yours."

He glared at her, the hoodie still pressed up against his nose. "Yet there you are, the original donor recipient."

"Would you two shut up," I said sharply. A woman holding young kids by their hands gave me a dirty look as she walked by.

Kya and James glanced at me, seemingly taken aback. Definitely not my Lavender Festival voice. "So not appropriate," I said to them both. "And please don't talk about your sperm. That's gross," I said to James.

"You have no idea how gross," Kya said.

Pain radiated in my stomach. The two of them snarled at each other with something more than anger. It bordered on hate. I wiped away a bead of sweat, looking back and forth between them. "Guys. Come on. We're here to have fun."

That mood was gone.

"He thinks he knows everything about everything," Kya said to me. "He has a pole up his skinny butt. A 'deeply intellectual' pole he is so overly fond of fornicating with. I'm sure he and Chantelle will hit it off perfectly. She's a pain in the ass too."

"Big words, Kya. You get them off a gossip website?"

A woman holding a large glass vase filled with flowers walked by and gave them a dirty look. We were collecting way too many of those.

"How about condescending? You like that word, right, James?"

"Condescending? Do you even know what that means?" he said with a smirk.

"Funny." Kya got to her feet. "You know what, James? I happen to like pop culture and I don't give a crap about politics. Does that make me a bad person? Should I feel like I'm not as good as you are because your overgrown brain is full of shit that bores the crap out of people?"

"Whoa!" I stood up and put my hand on Kya's arm, but she ignored it. She ignored me and the curious glances from people around us.

"I do feel like I'm not as good as you, okay, James. Does that make you feel better? You wear your geekiness so proudly and think it makes you so special. Well guess what? It's as much a cliché as cheerleaders or football players. I'm sick of it. And of you."

She swiveled on her stylish sandals, swooshing the boa that had come loose around her neck. She marched off in the opposite direction of the barns.

"Kya!" I yelled. I glanced at James, but his head was down and he stared at the sidewalk.

"Go ahead," he said without looking up. "Go after her. Take her side, you always do."

"What the hell is going on with you two?" I snapped, keeping my eye on Kya as she set off through the crowd. I wanted to stamp my feet and yell at both of them to stop it. Stop ruining things.

"Why don't you ask her?" he said, still staring at the ground.

And then he got up, still holding my hoodie to his nose, and walked the other way. "I'll clean your hoodie and get it back to you."

I stood in the middle, unable to choose which one to go after, trying to figure out what the hell was going on. And what to do about it.

I had no idea.

chapter twenty-three

When the paintball tourney at the Outdoor Palace was over, I stayed to help clean up. Sticking around to help was professional courtesy more than anything, since Dad knew the owner and they helped each other out when they could. Lola had taken off early to meet her boyfriend at a concert, so there was only me and Don, the owner. Helping Don also took my mind off the fury bubbling inside me. Kya hadn't shown up or answered any of my texts. Mad was an understatement.

When we finished cleaning the bunkers and guns, Don told me to take off. He locked up and headed out to his office behind the arena. If he was anything like Dad, he'd be there for a while, finishing paperwork and other business-owner things I didn't have any real desire to learn about.

He turned up the music on his speakers and I smiled and threw my gear bag over my shoulder, heading out to the field that acted as the parking lot.

Because I'd waited too long for Kya—who stood me up—I'd arrived late and gotten a crappy spot in the field and had a bit of a hike. It was dark, but lights in the arena lit up the lot. As I headed to my car, I saw a bunch of the boys hanging around a hatchback propped open. They laughed over music. A couple of red tips burned in the darkness. Don would be out soon and was not the kind of guy you wanted to piss off smoking illegal substances on his property.

I hesitated, fighting off a panicky sensation about being all alone. But the guys had to be ballers, so shaking off nerves, I kept walking, no choice but to pass them. I lifted my chin and lengthened my stride, shoulders back, fingers gripping my keys. Their faces weren't visible, so it was easier to pretend they weren't there. I could tell they'd seen me but I kept my eyes fixed on my car.

"Hey, it's Paintball Chick," one of them called. It sounded like Steve Blender's friend, Cameron. "Where's the hot one?" he called, and they laughed.

"Kya Kessler," Steve said. "She didn't show up tonight."

"The one with the exquisite ass? She's doing Lewis right?"

"Not anymore. I'm next." Definitely Steve's voice.

I saw their faces. Four of them, all holding bottles of beer. Hurrying my footsteps, I called, "Kya wouldn't touch you with a ten-foot pole."

"You sure about that?" Steve asked.

"You better watch it or Lewis will kick your ass," another guy said.

"He's puking in the bush. He's not going to kick anyone's ass."

Lucas had shown up for his first tournament game. Loud and obnoxious. If he was puking, that meant he'd been drinking. Not cool.

"She's not bad-looking," one of the other guys called.

A flutter of nerves sped my steps up.

"Maybe after a couple of beers," another answered.

"She looks like an elf and she's flat as a board," Steve said. "Ten beers maybe."

The rest of them howled. My stomach tightened, even as I told myself it didn't matter what they said. My cheeks were on fire though. Humiliation sped my breathing up. I put my head down and forced one foot in front of the other, almost at my car.

"I'd do her," another voice said, a hard edge to it. "I'm not fussy." I squinted but didn't recognize the guy. Steve laughed and high-fived him. They were walking closer to my car.

I clenched my hand into a fist, clutched my keys, and didn't say anything. Steve hated me because I kicked his ass in paintball. I wanted to get away. Quickly.

"Not so tough without that Canadian loser around to protect you," Steve said. "He beat the shit out of some dork kid at his old school? Big hero, right?" He took a sip of his beer and didn't take his eyes off me. He'd reached my car and was leaning against the driver side, blocking my way.

"Screw off," I said through clenched teeth. "Get away from my car."

"Aren't you the tough one?" he said. "You like Canadian bacon?" He grabbed himself in the crotch and curled up his lip. "You'll like my meat then."

My heart pounded faster, but I squeezed my fist, trying to remember Dad's self-defense tips.

"I can give you more than bacon."

Steve's voice had an edge that made my pulse race. He stepped aside and held out his hand as if to let me get to my door. I clicked it open and skirted around him, grabbing for the door handle. Fingers dug into my shoulder. Hard. A sound popped out of my mouth and I dropped my bag but my foot automatically kicked back, aiming for his private parts and connecting. I made a fist, threw my elbow back and up, and it connected with his nose. There was a flash and then someone else grabbed me and pulled my arms, locking them behind my back. I stomped on a foot and he oomphed and swore.

Steve grabbed my ponytail and yanked my head back, wiping his mouth off with the back of his hand while the other guy held me. I inhaled deeply with fear and pain, not believing it was happening, and I struggled, but the grip on me was iron-tight.

"Let me go."

Steve ran a finger along my cheek. I jerked my head away but he laughed and then stuck out his tongue and leaned forward, licking my cheek. The wetness, the awful smell, and the horrible implications made me feel sick to my stomach.

Steve reached for his belt buckle and jiggled it around and the inside of my brain froze. I couldn't think. Move. Comprehend.

"Leave her alone," a voice growled from behind me. "Seriously. What are you going to do? Gangbang her in the parking lot? Let her go."

Steve swore under his breath and stood taller, looking past me.

"She kicked me in the balls and gave me a bloody nose." He spit on the ground in front of me. My heart pounded, my breath quickened. "She needs a lesson."

"You scared the shit out of her, what'd you expect?"

Lucas stepped in front of me, putting himself between Steve and me. "Her dad's an ex-cop, Blender. Don't mess with her."

"I thought you left," Steve growled at him.

"I was busy," Lucas said. "Let her go, man," he said to the guy behind me.

"Busy puking." Steve laughed.

Lucas towered over Steve and almost doubled him in width. "Let her go," he said again. "You not only have to worry about her dad and brother, but you don't want to piss Levi off. Trust me."

Steve took a quick step at me and threw his hands up in the air. "Boo!" he screamed.

I cringed but managed to keep from crying out. He grinned an ugly smile, reached out, and squeezed my nipple. It hurt and it made me want to barf.

"Nothing worth playing with here," he said, pressing his face up to mine. His breath was horrible and bile rose up my throat.

"Dude," Lucas said in a low but hard voice. "Let her go. Now."

Steve nodded at the guy behind me and he pushed me by the shoulders so my body slammed into the car. Steve whacked his hand on the hood of the car beside my head.

"Boo!" he screamed again.

Lucas reached over and pulled him away. I met Lucas's gaze. "Get out of here, Grace," he said quietly. "These guys have been drinking."

Shaking so badly I could barely open my car door to get inside, I fumbled and managed to get in and lock the door behind me and start the car. Pressing my foot hard on the gas, I peeled forward out of the parking lot.

I glanced up in my rearview mirror and then drove, holding my breath on and off until I got back into the city. As soon as I could, I pulled over to the side of the road. I put the car in park, dropped my head to the steering wheel, and breathed deeply. In and out. In and out. My hands shook and tears ran down my face but no sound came out. I kept breathing deeply until the shaking stopped.

What would have happened if Lucas hadn't shown up? Deep down inside lurked a niggling feeling that somehow, someway, I'd brought this on myself. That I'd done something to deserve it. Rationally I knew it was wrong, but it was there.

Shame. I thought of Kya. I wanted to cry but I couldn't.

When I pulled into the driveway, I turned the car off but didn't move for a minute, remembering how scared and how defenseless I'd been forced to feel. I got out of the car slowly, thinking about whether to tell my parents. Dad would go ballistic. Indie would probably beat the crap out of him. He might even jeopardize his position with the police.

They might try to ban me from playing paintball with Steve. That would mean no more tourneys. I needed to keep playing with Lola. Consequences mishmashed up in my mind.

I couldn't say anything.

The only person I wanted to talk to was the person I'd been furious with earlier.

I wanted to talk to Kya.

I wanted to hug her a little bit tighter.

chapter twenty-four

D ad left for work early and Indie and Mom were out when I got out of bed. I texted Kya over and over, left messages on her phone, her Facebook, everywhere, but got no answers. Nothing.

Levi texted. I answered without mentioning anything about what happened. I wondered if Lucas would tell him. Would Levi wonder if it were somehow my fault?

After a few hours with no response from Kya, I decided to storm her house and bang on her door. I put on shoes and stomped outside, my legs shivering in the cool wet temperature. I had my head down, deep in thought, and almost collided with James in my driveway.

"James," I said, surprised.

"Hey. I was just coming to your house to see you. We need to talk," he said. He held out my hoodie. "I washed it."

His nose didn't look crooked or broken. I took the hoodie and gratefully put it on over my light T-shirt. "Thanks."

A door slammed loudly and we both turned to see Kya on her porch. She spotted us and shook her head. "Great," she said, and mumbled as she locked her door.

"I've been trying to get a hold of you all day," I yelled, louder than necessary. "You didn't friggin' show up for paintball last night. And now you're ignoring my messages?" I'd never spoken to her with so much fury.

She merely walked up her own driveway clacking her heels on the cement. Her expression stayed infuriatingly neutral. I noticed her favorite skinny jeans looked almost baggy on her. Dark purple circles outlined her eyes. "Sorry. I couldn't make it last night."

"You couldn't make it? You couldn't call me? Text? Send me a friggin' smoke signal?"

She rolled her eyes and glanced down the street. "I just got home a while ago. I had a quick shower and I'm heading out again. I haven't had time." She chewed her thumbnail with the same expression she used on her mom.

James half laughed, half snorted at her ridiculous claim.

"I'm not your parents, Kya," I told her.

She pulled her nail away from her mouth. "I know. They're not as nosy as you."

"Nosy? You stood me up. You didn't even bother to tell me you weren't going to paintball. And what were you DOING last night? Where were you all night? Did you sleep at Lucas's?" I searched her face for clues that Lucas might have told her what happened to me.

She looked puzzled. "Lucas's?" She went back to her thumbnail and looked away. "No. I broke it off with him."

I frowned. "When?"

"After the festival." She shrugged, pretending to be fascinated by a couple of neighbor kids racing around the cul-de-sac on their bikes. "I'm kind of seeing someone new."

James made another sound in his throat. I glared at him and then back at her. "Who?"

She developed a sudden interest in her nails and held out her hand to inspect them. "Steve."

My body froze. I couldn't move and barely breathed as that sunk in. "Steve who?" I whispered.

"Blender."

Then my mouth dropped open. She turned back to the kids on their bikes.

My ears pounded. "Are you kidding?" I asked. The scope of it wouldn't register. "You're not serious, right?" I almost begged.

James made another gurgling sound in his throat. Thunder rolled in the distance and I glanced up at the sky. A storm was brewing. Moving in quickly if the black clouds were any indication.

"He's not bad. I've gotten to know him better since we played on the same paintball team. He's actually generous and kind of sweet." She held up her wrist with a brown leather bracelet wrapped around it. "He gave me this. And some paintball stuff."

My head pounded harder. I rubbed my temples, frowning. "Are you kidding?" I shook my head, furious with her. I'd stood by her through many, many guys, but this was not the same. "You think buying stuff makes him a good guy?"

She shrugged and glanced down the street again. Thunder rumbled overhead. "Whatever. Don't inflict your standards on me right now. I'm not in the mood."

"Steve Blender?" James repeated.

She glared at him and he shut his mouth.

"Did he tell you what he did last night?" I barely managed not to scream. My voice shook with pent-up emotion. I wanted to grab her by the shoulders and shake her. Shake hard to get some sense in her.

"What'd he do?" James buried his hands in his front pockets.

I ignored him, focusing on Kya, agitated by the lack of expression in her eyes. "He did some messed-up stuff," I said through gritted teeth, and clenched my hands into fists, remembering the smell of his breath.

"What happened?" James repeated, anger raising his voice a few octaves.

"He told me." Kya ignored me, stood on her tiptoes, and glanced down the street.

I stared at her. That was the extent of her taking my side? The best friend who I'd stuck by over and over. And over.

Something inside me broke. The storm was tangible in the air. The temperature noticeably dropped.

"What," I asked, my voice shaky, barely controlled, "did Steve tell you?" The hair on my arms stood up.

Kya sighed and finally had the courtesy to look at me. "He said his friends were razzing you. He feels bad. I know you're holier than thou. He said he was a bit drunk but he's sorry he teased you. You take things too seriously."

My hands squeezed into tighter fists. "Teased me? Kya. It was worse, way worse than teasing. He scared me. It was horrible."

She sighed. "You know what? He said you'd overreact. I hate to say it, but he doesn't like you very much." She sounded almost bored.

"Kya. We're talking about Steve Plender," I reminded her.

"I'm not stupid," she said. "I know."

"Are you sure?" I snapped.

She glared at me, narrowing her eyes into slits.

"What happened?" James interrupted with a shout. I glanced at him. His face was bright red. "What'd he do to you?"

"James." I reached for his arm, trying to tell him to wait a minute. Even though he was clearly the better friend and actually concerned about what happened. "Not now, okay?" I said softly.

He cursed under his breath but didn't argue.

Another snarl of thunder roared from the sky, closer now. The lightning wasn't yet visible, but it was coming. The clouds looked like hail was brewing.

"Steve is a not a good guy, Kya. You don't want to mess with him."

"You don't even know him," she answered.

"You're taking his side?" It stung more than she knew, hearing her stick up for him. I closed my eyes to hide my hurt and breathed in deep.

James growled under his breath.

"When exactly did you break up with Lucas?" I asked. "Before you stood me up for paintball or after?" My heart ached. It actually hurt.

She shrugged, not appearing overly concerned by my anger. Or my anguish.

"Before."

"Funny," I said, my voice even lower. "When he was sticking up for me with Steve, Lucas didn't say anything about you breaking up with him."

"Well. I guess he hadn't checked his messages yet," she said, glancing down the street.

I saw a flash of lightning in the distance. I gawked at her. "You broke up with him by text?" Thunder followed, low and grumbly. "Oh. My. God. Kya. That is so not cool."

She focused on her thumbnail. "I didn't want to hurt his feelings."

James snorted. I gave him another look and he rolled his eyes. "She broke up with a guy by text," he pointed out.

"You were too chicken to deal with him in person?" I said to Kya. "Or too callous?"

Her defiant and childish expression changed and her bottom lip quivered. Her eyes filled with tears. She finally looked me in the eyes and I recognized the person I knew. "Don't be mad at me. I've been so messed up since the call..." She glanced at James and stopped.

"When does Grace ever get mad at you?" James snapped.

"Shut up, James," she said, snarling.

I narrowed my eyes at both of them. "You stood me up yesterday, ditched paintball, and now you're going out with one of the biggest jerks on this planet. After I told you he hurt me." I paused to gain some control. "That's not acceptable, Kya. It's just not. You can't go with him." My voice rose to a shout.

"Wow," James said. "I guess she can get mad at you. Will wonders never cease?"

"What's wrong with you?" I snapped at him, even though it wasn't James I was mad at.

The sky cracked with thunder, as if echoing my anger.

"James is still mad at me because we slept together," Kya said. "And now he knows he can never have you."

The air went still.

My stomach dropped.

"What?"

I stared back and forth between Kya and James. He stared at the ground. She stared at him, smirking. I squeezed my hands shut so as not to slap the self-righteous sneer off Kya's face. That was almost incest and made me sick to my stomach. I turned to James. His ears were bright red. His face stiff.

"That's what I was going to talk to you about," he said softly. "Finally." He sighed. "She didn't want me to say anything."

"Blah, blah, blah," Kya said. "Of course you had to tell her."

A headache attacked my temples and dizziness tilted the world on its side. I stumbled on my own feet, trying to stay on the ground as the world as I knew it changed underneath me.

My mouth opened but nothing came out. I had trouble catching my breath. "What?" I repeated, touching my throat.

"Go ahead, James, tell her what happened." Kya crossed her arms and glared at him.

James blinked at her as if she were a ghost. "It was horrible," he said.

Kya snorted. "Don't blame that on me. I wasn't the frickin' virgin who practically cried when it was over."

"Kya!" I yelled truly horrified. I didn't even know this person.

James looked like he was going to cry again.

"What the hell?" I shouted at her.

A car squealing around the corner interrupted our little chitchat.

It sped to the middle of the cul-de-sac, music blaring from an open window.

"Thank God," Kya said.

The horn honked, and when I saw the driver, I recoiled.

"Hey, babe, come on," Steve shouted out the window. For a horrible second, I thought he was talking to me. "Come on, Kya."

One of his buddies jumped out of the passenger seat, opened the door, and got in the back. Steve laughed. "You have wet dreams about me last night, Grace?"

I flicked my middle finger in the air. I spun around to Kya. "You can't go with him."

"Kya," Steve shouted again. "Bring me some sugar."

Kya turned toward the car but glanced back at me, her lips tight. "Don't tell me what to do." She walked away. "Sorry not everyone thinks you're perfect."

I wanted to vomit. "Kya." I ran forward and grabbed her by her arm. "Don't go."

She shook my hand off. My mouth dropped open.

"We have to talk about this," I said.

"There's nothing to talk about. I'm going with Steve."

"Kya," I pleaded, my eyes filling with tears. "You don't know what he did. It was awful. Don't go with him. Please."

"Awful? I wish what happened to me had happened to you. Then you'd understand awful." She ran down the sidewalk.

I looked away as she hopped into Steve's car. He honked his horn and then squealed off before she could even put on her seatbelt. I watched, cold right down to my bones.

I reached for James and held on to his arm as she disappeared out of the cul-de-sac.

"Come on," he said, putting his arm loosely around my shoulder. He walked over the grass, leading me to his backyard.

"She slept with you," I repeated stupidly. "And left us for Steve."

We walked to his old swing set and, without a word, we each took a seat. His dad had cemented it into the ground when James was a kid, and never got around to taking it out. James twirled on his swing and the chain links raveled around each other.

"Am I supposed to forgive this too?" I asked him. Thunder cracked but it was softer. I locked up for the dark clouds, but they had moved away too.

"What did Steve do to you?" James asked.

I shook my head. "Never mind. It was nothing." I watched my feet dangling into the sand under the swing set. "What did Kya do to you?" I whispered.

"Wow," he said. He lifted his feet from the ground, the raveled chains unwound, and he whirled in a circle. "That's the first time you've ever blamed her for something." When he came to a stop, he bent his head, his feet dangling beside mine. He dragged his feet over the dirt.

"That's not an answer," I told him.

He started to wind up the chains again, not looking at me. "The week after school ended. When you went camping with your family. I went to her place to watch her stupid movie. *The Virgin Suicides*. And that part came on when the sister has sex in the field? Kya came over and sat on my lap and..." He stopped twirling. "I don't

need to go into detail. But she started and…it happened…and…"
He shoved his feet to the ground, jarring himself into place. Dust
flew up from under his feet. "I wish I could undo it. It was awful.
She laughed at me." He stood up not facing me and the swing
swung out behind him. "I felt awful and ashamed, and she laughed
and told me I could never have you now that I'd slept with her. Best
friend rule." He didn't look at me. The sky rumbled, but it sounded
far off, less ferocious.

My hand went to my mouth to hold in the pain that wanted to
crawl out. "But you and I are friends." I stopped. "We're friends," I
repeated. I got off my swing.

He turned to look at me and there was pain in his eyes. "It's okay,
Grace. I know you don't feel that way about me. I mean, I've always
known. But you have to know what I feel." He laughed but it was a
bitter sound, like his dog's bark. "Kya's always made sure to remind
me you don't feel the same." He started walking toward the deck. A
bird flew into the birdhouse by the railing.

"Kya says stuff like that. It doesn't mean anything." I stopped,
realizing how silly it sounded. He'd pretty much admitted he did
feel that way. My throat hurt, trying to hold everything inside. The
last thing I wanted to do was hurt James. Too. How could I possibly unhear his confession?

I slowly followed behind him.

"She wanted to put me in my place. To prove to me that I'm like
every other boy she knows. And I was. She called me a stud. She
spit the word at me. And then she wrapped her fingers together
and made that sign you and her love so much. Buds before studs."

"Oh, James." The last thing I'd ever wanted James to be was a stud.

He walked up the steps on the deck. "I'm sorry. I never wanted that to happen with her. I should have been stronger…"

I closed my eyes and breathed in the cool air. The scent of lavender drifted over from Kya's backyard. I walked up the steps, reached for his hand, and then stopped. He noticed, but he pretended not to and instead punched me on the shoulder.

"It's okay. I know what I am to you," he whispered. "Best friend who happens to be a boy. I hoped. Someday. You know." He smiled but it didn't last. "And then Levi came along."

He sat down on a patio chair and I sat next to him.

"I'm not the girl for you," I said. "You deserve someone who feels the way a girlfriend does. You're a total catch. I can't wait to introduce you to Chantelle. I think you'll really like each other."

"Yeah. Sure. Stupid Levi," he said, but he smiled and this time it reached his eyes. "You like him, don't you?"

"Levi is…yeah, I like him. He gets me and…I don't know. It's weird." I wrapped my arms around my knees to stave off the cold. "I don't feel like I deserve him."

"You deserve him. Just make sure he deserves you. Don't let Kya ruin that. She will if she can."

I sighed. "What am I going to do about her?"

"What has she done for you lately? Honestly. You've always had her back, but when has she ever had yours? She stood you up. And she walked away. To Steve Blender."

I didn't want to think about it.

"Remember Kya's trampoline?" I said, looking across the fence to Kya's backyard.

"Yeah." We both stared at the spot where the trampoline used to sit. Ghosts of our best times tumbled around the empty space.

"Hey. What's the difference between Steve Blender and a trampoline?" James asked.

I shrugged.

"You take your shoes off to jump on a trampoline." He grinned.

I groaned at his attempt to joke around. "What the hell is Kya thinking?"

James laughed but it was bitter. "I don't think she's into rational thinking lately."

I thought for a moment.

"There's a reason," I said slowly. "And I think I should tell you." He needed to know. It wasn't in anyone's best interest to keep her secret anymore. He needed to understand. Why I'd always stood by her.

"She was raped," I whispered, my heart pounding.

"I know," he said in a dull voice. He stood up from his chair, shaking his head. "She's unbelievable. You know that?"

My head snapped up, watching him pace. "You know?"

"Grace, she told me." He scratched at his head and pushed up his glasses. "She told me not to tell you." He pressed his lips tight, shook his head. "I suspected you knew, but she asked me not to say anything."

"You knew?" I repeated.

"Yeah. And apparently so did you. She told me you didn't know.

I guess she wanted me to believe that you'd stand by her, take her side because of who she is. Not because of what happened to her."

I shook my head, not comprehending. "When did she tell you?"

He shrugged and plopped back down on the chair. "A couple years ago. Top secret."

Another lie I'd somehow bought into. That I was the only one she'd trusted to tell. Another betrayal. Lumped on top of the others. She'd lied. Blatantly.

"I feel bad that it happened to her," James said. "It explains lots. But she also has to take responsibility for herself and her behavior." He paused. "You have to let her."

The bird flew out of the birdhouse and escaped over the fence. I wished I could join it.

"The difference between me and you," James said, "is that I don't think that it makes everything she does okay. She played us."

"Wow," I said. I had to think. It didn't change what had happened to her, but it did change things.

"I'm done with her," James said softly. "And I think you have to make a choice too, Grace. Figure out what you want without her clouding your view."

My insides squeezed tighter. Breathing hurt. James pushed on his chair and stood. "I should go inside and check on my mom."

I reached for him, afraid to let him go. Afraid to face my choices on my own. "James! I'm scared."

James took my hand gently off his. "You've spent so much time worrying about her, you don't even think about what you need.

And whether she's the best friend for you." He moved away and slid open the patio doors to go inside his house.

"She's my best friend," I called.

"Is she? Maybe you need to choose your friends better. You think about that. Okay?"

"You're my best friend too," I called.

"Am I, Grace?" He sighed. "I hope so. You let me know."

"But…" I called.

He stuck his butt out the door, wiggled it, and then disappeared inside.

I laughed as he slid the door closed.

I'd talk to her. She and James could work through this awkwardness. She'd dump Steve when she knew what he really did. Everything could go back to normal.

There was still hope.

chapter twenty-five

I dozed on and off all afternoon. I'd crawled under the covers as if a flu had invaded my system. Knowing what Kya had done to James physically hurt. Knowing she'd lied to both of us. I was so confused. Did I even know her? I slept instead of thinking.

Then early in the evening, someone knocked on my bedroom door. I flipped on my back, staring at the ceiling. "Yeah?" I called, expecting Indie's voice.

"It's me," Kya said from the other side of the door.

I sat up, trying to remember what I needed to say. I didn't feel ready to deal with her. Not yet. "Come in," I said, only because there was little choice.

"Hey." She walked in my room and shut the door behind her. She caught my eye and looked away as if we were uncomfortable strangers.

"I'm surprised to see you here," I said. Sober, I didn't add.

"Yeah. I left Steve's." She walked over and sat on the end of my bed. "Did you know they took a video of me at his house a couple weeks ago? Topless?"

"I was going to tell you. But you were upset, so..." I shrugged, fighting a guilty wave of conscience. As if I were the one who did something wrong.

She bit her lip. "They showed me. But I got it. And erased it. Thank God it didn't get posted on Facebook or something."

"You're lucky," I said, and pulled my covers around my legs.

"Wow. You're quite the hard ass tonight."

I glared at her and the smile she'd pasted on her lips faded.

"I thought you'd be loaded by now," I said, not backing down. "Maybe a repeat performance for them."

She took a deep breath and licked her lips, pretending to be fascinated with my stuffed sock monkey. She picked him up and held him. "I guess I deserved that."

"I didn't say it to hurt you. I said it because it's true." A surge of anger raced blood to my face, but for once, I didn't try to bury it with an excuse or mince my words.

She sighed, hugging my sock monkey to her chest. "I know."

I sniffed and detected the smell of cookies from the kitchen. I was hungry. I hadn't eaten anything all day.

"I was feeling really down. About fighting with you. And then when I got to his house, they showed me the video. Laughing like it was a joke. It made me sick. Seeing myself like that. So I erased it and left. I walked home. They wouldn't give me a ride. Jerks."

I pulled my knees into my chest and pushed off the blankets. "Why didn't you call for a ride?" I asked out of habit.

"I didn't know if you would come," she said, putting my monkey back on the comforter.

I nodded. She was right. I didn't know either.

"Anyhow. I wanted to see you. You always make me feel better." She reached over and tickled my feet but I moved them away.

"What's wrong?" She smiled. "Come on, Skanklet, you know you wanna get tickled."

The nickname made me cringe, but I pushed my emotions down into the tiny hole in the pit of my belly.

"You're supposed to call me a name too," she said softly.

I shook my head once.

She pressed her hands together. "I thought a lot about you as I walked. And what I've been putting you through lately. And James."

She was pushing all my sympathy buttons, but I sat up straighter, resolving to stay strong. I pictured the way she'd slipped away from me to go to Steve. After what he'd done to me. How much it hurt. After I'd taken her side so many times. I pictured James. The stud.

"You screwed him over," I said. "Literally."

She leaned her head forward, braiding a tiny strip of hair. "I know. It was stupid." She pushed it back and sighed again. "I'm messed up, Grace." She let go of her hair and it fell close to her head. "That girl who got raped. Everything."

"You slept with James before she called. Do you think you can undo it? Or the way you chose Steve over me?"

Her eyes narrowed. "But I came back," she said. "For you."

"You left because he was being a jerk. It wasn't for me." I realized how true that was. I opened my eyes and really looked at her.

She yawned then, covering her mouth. "Sorry. I'm so tired. I've been so upset."

I lifted my chin, not letting myself fall into the trap she was setting. Knowingly or not, this was the part where she'd pull the sympathy card and I'd sign on the dotted line.

"James was our best friend. Is our best friend," I said. "You have no idea how much I want things back the way they were. But James was a virgin. He didn't want that with you."

She laughed then, but it sounded cruel. "Poor James. But he's a big boy. And I'm sure it wasn't as bad as when I lost my virginity."

I cringed but took a deep breath. "I know that, but this is about him," I said slowly.

"The only reason he was upset was because he's frickin' in love with you and he didn't want you to find out about it. I don't know how you fail to see that." She sat up taller, rolling her shoulders back and moving around her neck.

"This is not about me," I told her. "Why would you do that? Why would you do that to James?"

"To James?" She thumped my bed with her fist. "He kind of had to participate, you know?"

I closed my eyes to the image in my head.

"I couldn't stand the way he judged me, okay?" Kya said. "His snide jokes about me and boys. He thought he was so much better. So I decided to show him he wasn't."

"Oh, Kya."

"Don't 'oh, Kya' me. Guys don't look at me the way they look at you. When they see me, all they see is someone to sleep with. They look at you and they see the girl they want to take home to mommy and marry. Like stupid Levi. Bringing you flowers and candy. Too nervous to even kiss you. It makes me sick. You're so freaking perfect. And you never let me forget it."

Both of us stared at each other, our eyes wide open.

"I am far from perfect."

"That's not what Lola says. Or Betty Baller. Or James." She got off the bed. "You know what? Forget it. Forget you. I'm sick of you judging me. Looking down on me. You and James both."

Footsteps creaked up the stairs; our voices had escalated.

"I never looked down on you," I told her.

"No. What about me with James? And Steve? You approve of me going out with Steve?"

I scowled. "You're too good for him. And you shouldn't have gone with him today."

She laughed and crossed her arms over her chest. "You don't own me. What about James? Do you think I'm too good for James too?"

I didn't answer. It wasn't a fair question.

"I didn't think so," she said, and stood, putting her hands on her hips. "You know what? I don't want to be the person you feel sorry for anymore. I don't want to worry about my grades and making that stupid college paintball team and impressing people I don't give a crap about. I'm sick of hearing how I should try to be more like you. All I ever hear is how great Grace Black is. Screw that." She dropped her hands to her side, making fists. "Screw you."

"Kya?" This had gone farther. Faster. I stared at her, willing my friend to come back. The friend I loved.

"Yes?" She put her hands back on her hips but didn't change her snarling expression.

"I'm losing you," I whispered.

"So dramatic, Grace. So dramatic. Maybe I've always been lost."

Footsteps slowly moved down the hall. Indie? I didn't even care if he heard.

"You lied to me," I whispered. I twisted my earring around and around, staring at her. "Why did you tell me that James didn't know you were raped?"

Her eyes opened wider. She glanced around as if she were in a cage and needed to escape.

"Why did you tell us both it was a secret?"

"Screw you. Screw you and your judgmental eyes and your too good for everyone attitude. I don't need either of you. You don't have the right to judge me. You don't know what I go through. Stay out of my life. I *am* lost to you, okay? Don't call. Don't text. Stay the hell away from me. You are no longer my friend."

She slammed my door on her way out.

I breathed out slowly as the sting dug deeper. My heart ached. I'd been shaken to the core. The horrible reality that we were breaking up smashed into my gut. Maybe we weren't romantic. But it was love. And losing her took away my breath.

There was another knock on my door. "Grace?" Indie said. "You okay?"

"NO!" I shouted back.

Too many things had been done. Things that couldn't be undone. I closed my eyes to still the dizziness. When I opened them, I reached for my cell phone.

There was no going back. I'd made a choice.

chapter twenty-six

The sun was still out, but it would set earlier than yesterday and the day before. Early August and we were losing bits of sunlight every day.

Levi had come straight over when I called. He put his hand out as we walked out of my cul-de-sac, and despite everything, despite the negative stuff oozing around my brain, taking it was wonderful. I chose him to turn to.

"That totally sucks," he said as I breathed in the smell of him. "I mean that in a massive understatement way. Kya's on a definite downward spiral if she's hooking up with Steve Blender."

We walked down the sidewalk and approached an old woman with a turquoise and brown skirt billowing around her. She held the leash to a black Chihuahua with a tiny little head and pointy black ears, wearing a miniature bandana with autumn leaves all over it.

"I know." I thought about telling him what Steve had done to me. But it wasn't a good time. There were other things to worry about right now.

The woman glanced back at us and smiled as she stepped aside. "Move over, Fredrick," she said to her dog. "Let these young people pass."

I smiled at her as we walked by. She had inviting eyes. A peaceful feeling warmed me as I brushed past.

"Tell Lucas I'm sorry about Kya," I said to Levi, and waited to see if Lucas had said something about what had happened, but Levi merely nodded.

"He'll live. I mean, he liked her." He stopped as if thinking what to say next. "But they were moving pretty fast. And in the end, she's not really his type."

"She does that. Moves fast in an effort not to be seen." I stopped. There I was. Still making excuses for her. But how could I not?

He nodded. "Yeah, I guess. I feel worse for James." I'd told him the whole story. I didn't want secrets between us. I'd tell him about Steve. But not then.

"They've been my best friends for so long." I glanced up as a streetlight flickered overhead. "It's so messed up." We turned at the corner, heading toward the school.

"It sucks," Levi said. "Losing a friend is hard."

We walked toward a path that would take us through the school grounds. I glanced at his profile. "I like that you don't try to solve my problems or tell me what to do like my dad or brother would. Or even James."

He rubbed his thumb over mine. "I'm not a very manly man, am I?"

"Au contraire," I said, and grinned. I couldn't believe I was flirting.

"Busted. I'm a bit of a mama's boy," he said.

I laughed. Not the impression he gave off at all.

"No. Really. No brothers or sisters. My dad traveled a lot when

I was a kid and it was me and my mom. And then she went back to work. She had lots of strong ideas about right and wrong and how not to act. She ingrained them into my head." We walked past the school play structure. A few young boys about twelve years old were sitting on top of the monkey bars, laughing at something. "Her dad was a man's man. You know? She hated that. She didn't want me to be like that."

I nodded. "No hot yoga for him."

He laughed. "Exactly," he said.

The school path led us to a busier street and we walked down the sidewalk. I noticed the leaves were turning orange on the trees in the middle of the boulevard.

"I don't know if I even know how not to look after Kya," I said softly.

He nodded. "I lost a good friend a while ago. It was different but still awful."

I waited for him to say more.

He sighed. "We were friends since we were kids. His mom was awesome. Is awesome. We went to different schools but grew up beside each other. Our moms hung out when we were young. When my mom went back to work, his mom kind of took over. Sort of like your parents with James."

My heart ached again at the thought of James. I nodded though, understanding what he meant.

"So we were close, but we had separate lives too. You know? We had other friends. He used to talk about girls at his school. The ones he liked."

We walked past a white van almost parked on the sidewalk. We walked around it and I caught a glimpse of our reflection in the window. Our hands clasped together. In spite of everything, my heart pitter-pattered.

"Anyways. I teased him. He had all this info about girls. And he told me he had a girlfriend. That he'd been with her for a while but hadn't told me."

Another couple approached us on the sidewalk. A great-looking guy and an athletic girl. They both said hi and Levi paused until we passed them.

"I didn't believe him so I bugged him, you know, trying to catch him lying, but in fun, right? I thought he was full of it, but not like I really cared or anything. We played video games and stuff, we didn't exactly double date." He paused to catch his breath. "I had braces until tenth grade. And was kind of shy with girls."

I glanced over, trying to picture it. Two joggers ran toward us, we dropped hands, and Levi stepped in front of me to let them pass. When they were gone, he took my hand again and matched my steps.

"Anyhow, he got defensive. Said he'd prove it to me. That he had a girlfriend. I asked why I couldn't meet her. He said she had strict parents. So I bugged him, asking to see pictures." He swallowed. "It was stupid. But for some reason, I pushed it. I meant like a class photo or them standing arm in arm. Something. A couple days later when I was over at his place, he was acting all proud, patting his pocket, telling me he had pictures." His voice cracked and he cleared his throat. "So he took me outside and he pulls out his cell phone. I think he's going to call her, get her to talk to me or something, but then he turns the phone on and shows me a picture." Levi took a deep breath and ran his fingers through his curls. "He had a bunch of pictures. Of the girl. Giving him a blowjob. He took pictures."

He coughed and shook his head while I grimaced. "That wasn't the worst thing, though. He had other pictures. And she was a kid. I mean, young. I asked how old she was and he grinned, all proud, and told me she was twelve It was a kid he used to babysit. He said when she turned twelve he'd taught her to give head. He said that. He was her babysitter. Her babysitter." He dropped my hand and wiped his hands on his pants. "I lost it. I mean, I started hitting him. And he's small. He dropped to the ground but I kept on going. I couldn't stop until his dad came outside and pulled me off."

I reached for his hand and squeezed it hard. "Neighbors had already called the police. His dad threatened to press charges and his mom looked at me with big, shocked eyes. When the police came, I didn't say anything but I told his mom in private to check his cell phone. And to never ever let him babysit kids again.

"The police wanted to charge me, but his mom didn't let them. When my mom came home later, I told her what happened and we both cried." He closed his eyes for a second. "I never saw him again. A few weeks later, his mom and dad put the house up for sale. They moved away."

He stopped then, and I halted beside him as he stared at a car parked in a nearby driveway. "I asked my mom to get a hold of the girl's parents. I still wonder if we should have told the police everything. I mean, they were there. Other kids found out I beat him up. But no one knows why. I didn't tell anyone what I saw on his phone. Not even Lucas. He doesn't know why I did what I did."

I squeezed his hand. "It's hard to know what the right thing to do is sometimes."

"But maybe he should have been charged? Maybe that was the right thing to do? What if he does it again?"

"I don't know," I said. "I'm sure his parents made sure he got help?"

"My mom said the girl got help. Her parents were really good."

I nodded. "What could you do besides that?" I asked. "You were a kid too." An urge to cry tightened my throat. How were we supposed to know the right thing to do?

Levi glanced around the street. "We should turn back."

I nodded and we reversed direction and switched hands we were holding.

"Kya hates me." I dropped my gaze to the street and tried not to cry.

"Grace," he said, "she doesn't hate you. You didn't do anything wrong."

I watched a robin fly onto a nearby lawn. He ducked his head down and came up with a worm. I wondered how he'd known how to find it.

"I'm supposed to be there for her. Forever," I said.

"Says who?"

"The second F in BFF means forever." A motorcycle whizzed

from nowhere and sped past us. I looked at his profile. "Maybe I can be a friend from a distance."

"Sometimes you have to let people go. Even if you love them," he said.

I watched the back of the bike as it disappeared around a corner. Maybe looking after Kya really had been a substitute for going after what I wanted. Maybe I could let her go and start thinking about myself.

"Maybe I can't be there for her anymore. But I don't think I can stop caring."

Without warning, Levi leaned down and pressed his lips on mine. I stopped walking. All of a sudden, I didn't care so much. About anything.

"You can't stop being you. But sometimes new people come in your life for you to care about," he said, and kissed me again. He grinned, swinging our joined hands up in the air, and bumped his hip against me. "So. Do I get to help you celebrate your birthday tomorrow?" he asked.

"How'd you know about my birthday?" I asked.

"I pay attention."

I smiled even though the reminder of my birthday made my heart ache. "I have monkey pancakes in the morning." My birthday tradition included breakfast. It had always been Kya, James, and my family. In my heart, I knew Kya wouldn't come, but I wasn't ready to give up yet on James.

"I also have a paintball game in the afternoon." I tilted my head. "But I'm free in the evening."

"Thank God." Levi grinned. "My aunt and uncle are out of town. I already forbid Lucas from being home. I was really hoping I could make you dinner for your birthday."

"You cook?" I asked.

"Like I said. Mama's boy." He bowed at the waist. "At your service. Of course we're talking BBQ hamburgers?"

"It sounds perfect." Something like hope turned up the corners of my lips.

chapter twenty-seven

On the morning of my eighteenth birthday, I woke up with a heavy heart. Every year since we'd moved to Tadita, Kya and James would be bouncing on my bed already.

Had James decided not to accept me as a friend? Was he asking for a different choice than what I'd thought? I honestly thought James would be around. Especially on my birthday. James loved birthdays.

Guilt mixed with anger and then turned to sadness. Was it my fault for not feeling the same way about him? I'd thought our friendship was strong enough to take almost anything. Was I now toxic to him the way Kya had become to me? Was he better off without me in his life? The questions brought tears to my eyes and made my nose ache.

I'd never wanted to hurt either of them.

"Monkey pancakes are so great," Mom sang downstairs. Her voice drifted up to my room and added to the emptiness in my heart. I dragged myself out of bed. Indie brushed past me in the hall.

"Hey. What up, birthday girl?" he said, and pretended to karate-chop me.

I didn't answer or even crack a smile.

"You okay?" He dropped his hands to his sides and frowned.

"No." I went back to my room and shut the door.

A few seconds later, he knocked softly.

"Go away, Indie," I said, not caring that my behavior was more fitting of a ten-year-old than an eighteen-year-old.

My best friends were lost. It sunk in and it stung.

Indie walked away from the door. The ache in my heart expanded. I flopped on my bed and stared at the ceiling, feeling a pity party for one coming on.

Soon my door opened again and Mom stuck her head inside. "Can I come in?" She walked in before I answered.

"I'm sorry you're feeling sad on your birthday," she said.

"I miss them." I kept my eyes on the ceiling, wishing I could go back. When things were easier and the three of us would be bouncing on the bed, waiting for monkey pancakes from my dad. "Especially James. But Kya too. No matter what."

Mom leaned against my dresser and I sat up and crossed my legs on the bed.

"Kya was never your problem to fix," she said.

"Maybe. But I'm worried for her. I mean, I'll always worry. Even if I can't be there for her anymore."

"You're growing up," Mom said, and moved closer, sitting down on the end of the bed. "You're doing the right thing, Grace. You have to look after you. Kya's a strong girl. She's going to be okay."

My feet were chilled. I got up and went to the dresser, opened my sock drawer, and pulled out my yellow SpongeBob socks, a gift from James last Christmas. I sat on the bed beside her and pulled them on.

Mom smiled. "That's my girl. Embracing your inner weird."

"You're the one who started the sock fetish in this family." True.

There was another knock on the door and Dad stuck his head in. "Girls only or can I come in?"

"Come in," I said.

Dad bounced in and kissed me on the forehead. "Happy birthday." He sat on the bed beside Mom, watching me. "You okay?"

Sighing, I shrugged. "I will be."

"Of course you will."

"It's hard losing a friend. Especially your best friend. It's okay for you to symbolically wear black for a while." Mom reached over to ruffle my bedhead hair even more.

"But maybe not today. Not on your birthday," Dad said. "I will happily join you in a Ben & Jerry's binge to make you feel better."

"Ice cream with breakfast might be good," I said.

"I am here to make these sorts of sacrifices for my family," Dad said, jumping up. "Red Velvet, Chunky Monkey, and vanilla."

Mom swatted his butt as he got up to go on his mission. "Vanilla?" she asked, as if it were a surprise after all these years.

"I like my ice cream the way I like my women," Dad said. "Plain and simple."

"Then why the hell did you marry me?" Mom winked at him.

"Because for every rule, there is an exception. I'm off to the freezer. Monkey pancakes a la mode."

We watched him leave. "We're here for you, Grace," Mom said.

"I know."

She stood up as if to go, hesitated, and then sat back down.

"Indie knows about Kya. I told him. And he understands. He had a girlfriend once who was kind of messed up. She broke his heart. Over and over again." She pressed her lips tight and then sighed. "Her mom was a drug addict and she still had a lot of issues. He wanted to help her, but he finally had to let go."

"Shari?" I gasped, remembering the drama that had gone on in the house a few years back. Breakups. Reconciliations. Moody Indie and then she'd disappeared.

"Yup. It was hard for him. He really cared about her."

"Wow. I didn't know." I rubbed my nose and tugged my earring. "I always thought Indie messed that up. He hasn't been serious about anyone since."

"It hurt him. Some people cause a lot of pain without really meaning to." She reached over and patted my knee.

Tears sprung up in my eyes and the hurt inside throbbed. "I miss Kya."

She nodded. "I know. You'll have to allow yourself time to mourn, Grace. When you lose a best friend, well, it's like the death of a loved one or breaking up with a boyfriend. Hard."

"But it's the right thing?"

She leaned forward and, for the first time in a long time, hugged me close. I clung on for dear life. "In your heart, you already know," she whispered into the top of my head. "You know it was the right thing. For you."

"But what about James?" I tried to blink them back but tears spilled out of my eyes, racing each other down my cheeks.

Mom let go and wiped my tears away with her fingers. "No

crying on your birthday. Come on downstairs." She stood up, held out her hand, and waited for me to go down with her.

From the stairs, I saw Indie at the kitchen table, setting out the dishes. He glanced up. "Mom tell you Kya's not working at Splatterfest anymore?" he asked as I walked down the stairs.

Mom shushed him. "Lord, Indie, have you heard of tact?" she asked.

"What?" Indie said. "Grace needs to know." He waved a fork at me before placing it down at the proper place setting. "She called and gave Dad her notice this morning. She didn't show up for her shift last night."

I sighed and walked past the living room into the kitchen. It smelled like pancakes and brewing coffee. I pressed my lips tight and sighed.

"You okay?" Dad asked. "Ice cream is on the counter."

"I'll be all right." I glanced at him in front of the grill, wearing his bikini apron, pouring pancake batter into his monkey mold.

"What about James?" I asked softly.

"What about him?" Dad asked.

"Did he put in his notice too?" I asked.

"Why would I do that?" a familiar voice piped up.

I spun around. My heart tripped with happiness. James was watching us from the living room. He sat on the floor, in front of our TV playing Nintendo. I'd missed him when I walked by.

"James! You came!" I ran to the living room.

"Well, I couldn't exactly miss monkey pancakes and Nintendo on your birthday, could I?"

I plunked down on the carpet beside him. "James!" I shouted and then punched him on the arm. "Why didn't you come to my room?"

"Ouch." He frowned at me and rubbed his arm. "I think that's something I have to give up for a while."

"Are we still friends?" I asked, as if I were a little kid.

"Grace," he said, "you're my best friend. That's not going to change."

I wrapped my arms around him and squeezed as hard as I could.

"Awww," Mom yelled from the kitchen. "Hold that pose, I need to grab my camera."

We both groaned and he pushed me away and held out a controller.

"Prepare to have your ass kicked," he said. "I'm not holding back because it's your birthday."

I couldn't stop grinning at him but didn't take the controller.

"Stop staring at me." He rolled his eyes. "Nice socks."

"I got them from my best friend," I said.

He pointed to a gift bag sitting by his feet. "If you're not going to play the game, at least open your present."

I reached for it and pulled out a silver bracelet. A charm hung from it. Best Friends Forever.

"So what about this cute girl you've been bugging me about?" he asked. "Chantelle? You going to introduce me or just dangle the promise of her in my face?"

I hugged him close. "I am definitely introducing you. How about tonight?"

We'd work out a new normal.

After breakfast, I called Levi and asked him if I could bring a friend or two to dinner. And then I got my gear together for the game.

Kya would be there. That part I was dreading.

chapter twenty-eight

I smiled at the giant of a guy walking toward me. Lucas. He stopped and waited and then we fell in step with each other. Voices shouted and ballers wandered around us in various states of dress.

"You're getting better," I told him. "You made a couple of good hits." It was true. He'd been invited to play with Lola's new team. I watched his game, and he'd done okay.

"Thanks," he said. "What about you? I hear the Grinders are watching you."

I smiled. Not what I wanted to talk to him about. I stopped walking. He did too.

"Thanks. I mean, I never thanked you. For what you did. With Steve."

He shrugged and grinned. "I'm not just a redneck with shit for brains," he said, repeating me verbatim.

"Yeah, you kind of are," I said, but grinned. "I'm kidding. You're definitely not." I paused, searching for the right words and then went with the simplest. "I'm sorry it never worked out with Kya."

He shrugged. "I guess I wasn't her type. But how about you? You and Levi have a big date tonight, I hear?"

I smiled and nodded, remembering that Levi kicked him out of the house for the night. "He's a good guy." We walked toward the concession stand.

"He is," Lucas agreed. "Watch his temper. He had a thing with a guy at his old school. My mom said it was pretty bad. He won't talk about it much. But be careful."

"I already know about it," I said. Lucas didn't know the whole story but it wasn't my job to fill him in on the hows and whys.

"Did you tell him what happened with Steve?" I asked.

"I figure that's your call."

It was on my list of things to do. No more secrets.

Someone called his name and he glanced past me and waved at a buddy. "That's a teammate. I gotta go. See you inside, Grace."

• • •

Before my game, Lola pulled me aside and asked me to her office.

"Sit down, Grace." She sat on the other side of her desk, watching me, tapping a pencil on her clipboard.

"You're good, Grace. Reliable. I like you." Behind her, a clock ticked. She raised an eyebrow. "But I have to admit, Kya's asked for a second chance to prove herself. Her attitude seems better and her play is smoking hot. She really wants a chance with the Grinders next year."

I nodded but didn't say anything.

She narrowed her eyes. The clock kept ticking off seconds. Tick. Tick. Tick.

"So. It's down to you two." She sat forward and put her clipboard on her desk. "I have to give a report to Betty soon. She wants to know which of you should take the last spot with the Grinders. She likes you a lot, but Kya is stronger."

I let out a breath slowly. "I thought there were two spots next year."

"Chantelle is Betty's first pick," Lola said it without apology.

I bit my lip. Damn.

Tick. Tick. Tick.

"I want you to tell me why I should recommend you over Kya." Lola sat back in her chair, her hands behind her head. Waiting.

I bit my lip tighter and stared at a spot on the floor. I didn't say anything and neither did she.

"Show me you want this." She leaned forward. "Why are you a better choice?" she prompted.

I opened my mouth. Shut it. I'd looked out for Kya for so long, it was hard to let go. I knew how much a spot on the team would mean for her future. She would do well at that college. It would mean getting away from her family, away from the guilt and shame of her past. It could change her life.

"You giving up that easily?" Lola asked. "Come on, Grace. I want you to fight for a spot. Fight for yourself. Show me you want it."

I pressed my lips tighter. Playing for the Grinders could change my life too. But if I got what I wanted, Kya wouldn't.

With a sour expression, Lola stood, shook her head, and pushed away from her desk. "I don't have time to waste," she said. "I want to recommend the right person. The one who wants it more."

"I want this," I shouted. "I'm more of a team player," I said quieter without looking up. "I add value. I communicate well. I think on my feet. My grades are better and I'm responsible. I won't screw this up."

Lola sat slowly down in her chair. I looked her in the eye. She smiled. "That's my girl."

• • •

I walked out of Lola's office ready for a game. My heart pounded in my ears. Kya strutted toward me in full gear, her equipment bag over her shoulder, her gun in her hand. Her jersey was new. I squinted. So was her gun.

Kya stared at me. I stared back, daring her to see that she'd hurt me but that I would survive. I wouldn't feel guilty about sticking up for myself. No one else had my back. I had to have my own.

The ache of losing her would fade along with the feelings of betrayal. I knew she'd be in my heart forever. One way or another.

We nodded at each other.

"Grace," a deep voice said from behind her. I ignored the pops of paintball fire from the arena and narrowed my eyes. Steve Blender trailed behind her. He wore a matching jersey. He stepped around her and glared at me. "Kya's going to mow you down out there. And the Grinders want her. Not you. I bought her some top of the line stuff."

"Shut up, Steve," Kya said without looking at him. "I don't need your money or your toys to kick her ass."

I laughed out loud as Kya walked away from us.

"What the hell are you laughing at?" Steve asked.

"Papers," I said, grinning at him.

He glared at me. "What are you talking about?"

I laughed again. "She's going to give you your papers. As in walking papers. Soon. Trust me, I know the signs. You're done." He hid his worry behind a scowl. "You can pretend you're a big tough guy and you don't give a crap, but you've never had a girl like Kya. You must have known it wouldn't last."

"You don't know shit," he said.

My gear bag weighed me down and I switched it to my other arm. "I know Kya."

Kya stormed back then and walked straight at me. My heart raced. My palms got sweaty.

"Give me a minute, would you?" she said to Steve.

He narrowed his eyes at me but glanced at Kya and then nodded and left, his tail between his legs.

"Man, you really are good at that," I said, shaking my head with wonder. Despite everything, the girl knew how to make guys act like puppets.

She reached into the backpack she was carrying and pulled something out. "Happy birthday." She threw a box at me. I caught it midair. Nerds.

"I got those for you," she said, and inhaled deeply. "You're still my best friend."

A couple of paintball guys jogged past and shouted our names. Neither of us looked. I thought about what she said. I could forgive her. I could start the cycle all over again. Or I could let go.

I held up my wrist. I'd gone to the tattoo parlor. Kya had made an appointment for two, but I went alone. It was me who sat down in the burgundy leather chair. I'd watched the ink-filled needles pierce my skin. Two fingers entwined. Underneath it the initials. BBS. Buds before studs. Permanently under my skin. Like Kya. It still hurt. The pain would fade. But the mark would be there.

She held her breath. "That's so cool."

"I'll always love you, Kya," I said quietly. "But I can't do it anymore. You hurt me too much."

She took a deep breath and stepped back. She nodded. "Okay," she said. "I get it." The sad look on her face almost made me relent. Almost.

"Good luck," she said. And then she straightened her back. "I decided to go for the Grinders after all." There wasn't malice in her voice but it didn't make my fresh wounds sting any less. "I'm going to be working with Lola. She's awesome."

She headed off toward Steve and his friends. I grinned. No one said I didn't like competition.

Someone punched my arm and I turned. "There you are." Chantelle bounced up and down beside me. "I've been searching for you. We're up soon. We have to talk strategy."

"Sure." I smiled and threw the box of Nerds at her and she automatically lifted her hand to catch them. "What're these?" she asked, a puzzled look on her face.

"Candies. You want 'em?"

"Sure." She smiled and popped open the box and poured some into her mouth.

"You busy later tonight?" I asked. "After the game?"

"No. Why?"

"It's my birthday. My boyfriend invited me for dinner." I giggled when I said boyfriend and then swallowed and continued, "I called to see if I could bring a couple of friends. I invited my other best friend, James. You want to come too?"

Her eyes lit up and she smiled. "That would be cool!"

I smiled back. Chantelle put her arm around me and we took off to play as a team in the arena.

• • •

Heading out of the locker room after the game, I glanced over and saw Kya standing with Steve.

I didn't want to be angry or bitter but traces of both lingered. I supposed someday it really would hurt less.

I climbed inside my car. Chattering happily and asking questions about James, Chantelle got in the passenger seat beside me. We were on our way to pick him up and then off to Levi's for dinner. I had a great feeling about her and James.

I lifted my hand and waved at Kya.

Good-bye.

An aching loss swooped through me.

And then I drove on.

acknowledgments

The writing of a book is in many ways a solo and private journey, but when you're lucky enough to be published, it truly becomes a shared experience. I am so thankful to Leah Hultenschmidt, my sparkling editor at Sourcebooks, for her input in this story. She truly helped me find my way into the lives of these two girls and their male best friend. Leah is an amazing person all round and a pleasure to work with.

How I Lost You stemmed from a simple phrase that made us both laugh. Buds before studs. The bond of girlfriends and then the heartache that accompanies a best friend breakup. I've talked to many, many women or girls who remember the sting and hurt of fighting with a best friend. There's a deep, deep love for best friends, especially in our teens. Memories of those teen friendships transcend time. (And often outshine time spent with boyfriends. Yes. Really.)

Next I really want to thank the readers who are picking up my books and reading them!!! It is such a privilege to have people respond to what I've written. I love hearing from you and I love that my books make you feel things and relate to my characters. Thanks to the passionate community of Book Bloggers for doing what you do and helping foster that love of books among the YA community.

As usual, I had help along the way as I drafted *How I Lost You*. I would like to thank the insight of my trusted writing friends Linda Duddridge, Jennifer Jahbley, Laura Bjorkman, and Denise Jaden.

I also want to thank and express my appreciation to the wonderful people at Sourcebooks. I really am proud and honored to be an author for the "Sourcebooks family." Dominique Raccah has created such a wonderful company and a real pride in the people who work for her. Todd Stocke leads the editing helm with enthusiasm and grace. Thanks to Aubrey Poole, Kimberly Manley, and Jillian Bergsma for their attention to detail, and to Derry Wilkens who does an amazing job promoting the Sourcebooks authors (and wears the best sneakers). Also thanks to the Sourcebooks sales teams who get out and promote books to bookstores and libraries. Coming from a background in sales, I love me some sales people. And anyone else at Sourcebooks who I haven't named, know that your contribution to this book is appreciated!

Thanks to Jill Corcoran, my lovely agent, who is always in my corner and isn't afraid to tell me when my hair needs to be fixed. How awesome are you? Answer = very.

Also thanks to my sister, Tracey MacLeod, and my mom, Heather MacLeod, for looking after my son so I could finish this book. And as always, thanks to my two favorite guys in the world, my favorite husband, Larry, and my favorite child, Max. Without you two, none of this writing books stuff would be possible.

Lastly, this book is for you. You and your best friend. Whatever your story. Cherish the good times.

about the author

Rita Award-nominated author Janet Gurtler has collected a few best friends in her travels, but only one best friend ever broke her heart. Though it was almost thirty years ago, she still remembers the pain like it was yesterday. Janet lives in Calgary, Alberta, Canada, with her husband and son. She's a member of SCWBI and RWA and a Board Member of the Writer's Guild of Alberta. You can find Janet on Twitter and Facebook, or visit her website at www.janetgurtler.com.